The Other
P·a·r·i·s

G K H a l l · F I C T I O N

The Other
P · a · r · i · s

Mavis Gallant

G.K.HALL&CO.
Boston, Massachusetts
1986

The following stories appeared originally in *The New Yorker:*
"The Other Paris," "The Picnic," "Wing's Chips," "One
Morning in June," "Señor Pinedo," "A Day Like Any Other,"
"The Legacy," "Going Ashore," and "Autumn Day"; in
Charm: "The Deceptions of Marie-Blanche," and "About
Geneva"; and in *Harper's Bazaar:* "Poor Franzi."

This G. K. Hall paperback edition is reprinted by arrangement
with the author.

First G. K. Hall printing, 1986.

Library of Congress Cataloging-in-Publication Data

Gallant, Mavis.
  The other Paris.

  I. Title.
[PR9199.3.G26O8   1986]   813′.54   85-24910
ISBN 0-8398-2895-0 (pbk.)

Contents

The Other
P·a·r·i·s

The Other Paris

By the time they decided what Carol would wear for her wedding (white with white flowers), it was the end of the afternoon. Madame Germaine removed the sketchbooks, the scraps of net and satin, the stacks of *Vogue*; she had, already, a professional look of anxiety, as if it could not possibly come out well. One foresaw seams ripped open, extra fittings, even Carol's tears.

Odile, Carol's friend, seemed disappointed. "White isn't *original*," she said. "If it were me, I would certainly not be married in all that rubbish of lace, like a First Communion." She picked threads from her skirt fastidiously, as if to remove herself completely from Carol and her unoriginal plans.

I wonder if anyone has ever asked Odile to marry him, Carol thought, placidly looking out the window. As her wedding approached, she had more and more the engaged girl's air of dissociation: nothing mattered until the wedding, and she could not see clearly beyond it. She was sorry for all the single girls of the world, particularly those who were, like Odile, past thirty. Odile looked sallow and pathetic, huddled into a sweater and coat, turning over samples of lace with a disapproving air. She seemed all of a piece with the day's weather and the chilly air of the dressmaker's flat. Outside, the street was still damp from a rain earlier in the day. There were no trees in sight, no flowers, no comforting glimpse of park. No one in this part of Paris would have known it was spring.

"Even *blue*," said Odile. But there was evidently no conversation to be had with Carol, who had begun to hum, so she said to the dressmaker, "Just imagine! Miss Frazier came to Paris to work last autumn, and fell in love with the head of her department."

"*Non!*" Madame Germaine recoiled, as if no other client had ever brought off such an extraordinary thing.

"Fell in love with Mr. Mitchell," said Odile, nodding. "At first sight, *le coup de foudre*."

"At first sight?" said the dressmaker. She looked fondly at Carol.

"Something no one would have expected," said Odile. "Although Mr. Mitchell is charming. *Charming*."

"I think we ought to go," said Carol.

Odile looked regretfully, as if she had more to say. Carol made an appointment for the following day, and the two left the flat together, Odile's sturdy heels making a clatter as they went down the staircase.

"Why were you so funny just then?" Odile said. "I didn't say anything that wasn't true, and you know how women like that love to hear about weddings and love and everything. And it's such a wonderful story about you and Mr. Mitchell. I tell it to everyone."

This, Carol thought, could not be true, for Odile was rarely interested in anyone but herself, and had never shown the least curiosity about Carol's plans, other than offering to find a dressmaker.

"It was terribly romantic," Odile said, "whether you admit it or not. You and Mr. Mitchell. Our Mr. Mitchell."

It penetrated at last that Odile was making fun of her.

People had assured Carol so often that her engagement was romantic, and she had become so accustomed to the word, that Odile's slight irony was perplexing. If anyone had asked Carol at what precise moment she fell in love, or where Howard Mitchell proposed to her, she would have imagined, quite sincerely, a scene that involved all at once the Seine, moonlight, barrows of violets, acacias in flower, and a confused, misty background of the Eiffel Tower and little crooked streets. This was what everyone expected, and she had nearly come to believe it herself.

Actually, he had proposed at lunch, over a tuna-fish salad. He and Carol had known each other less than three weeks, and their conversation, until then had been limited to their office — an American government agency — and the people in it. Carol was twenty-two; no one had proposed to her before, except an unsuitable medical student with no money and eight years' training still to go. She was under the illusion that in a short time she would be so old no one would ask her again. She accepted at once, and Howard celebrated by ordering an extra bottle of wine. Both would have liked champagne, as a more emphatic symbol of the unusual, but each was too diffident to suggest it.

The fact that Carol was not in love with Howard Mitchell did not dismay her in the least. From a series of helpful college lectures on marriage she had learned that a common interest, such as a liking for Irish setters, was the true basis for happiness, and that the illusion of love was a blight imposed by the film industry, and almost entirely responsible for the high rate of divorce. Similar economic backgrounds, financial security, belonging to the same church — these were the pillars of the married union. By an astonishing coincidence, the fathers of Carol and Howard were both attorneys and both had been defeated in their one attempt to get elected a judge. Carol and Howard were both vaguely Protestant, although a serious discussion of religious beliefs would have gravely embarrassed them. And Howard, best of all, was sober, old enough to know his own mind, and absolutely reliable. He was an economist who had had sense enough to attach himself to a corporation that continued to pay his salary during his loan to the government. There was no reason for the engagement or the marriage to fail.

Carol, with great efficiency, nearly at once set about the business of falling in love. Love required only the right conditions, like a geranium. It would wither exposed to bad weather or in dismal surroundings; indeed, Carol rated the chances of love in a cottage or a furnished room at zero. Given a good climate, enough money, and a pair of good-natured, *intelligent* (her college lectures had stressed this) people, one had only to sit back and watch it grow. All winter, then, she looked for these right conditions in Paris. When, at first, nothing happened, she blamed it on the weather. She was often convinced she would fall deeply in love with Howard if only it would stop raining. Undaunted, she waited for better times.

Howard had no notion of any of this. His sudden proposal to Carol had been quite out of character — he was uncommonly cautious — and he alternated between a state of numbness and a state of self-congratulation. Before his engagement he had sometimes been lonely, a malaise he put down to overwork, and he was discontented with his bachelor households, for he did not enjoy collecting old pottery or making little casserole dishes. Unless he stumbled on a competent housemaid, nothing ever got done. This in itself would not have spurred him into marriage had he not been seriously unsettled by the visit of one of his sisters, who advised him to marry some nice girl before it was too late. "Soon," she told him, "you'll just be a person who fills in at dinner."

Howard saw the picture at once, and was deeply moved by it. Retreating by inches, he said he knew of no one who would do.

Nonense, his sister said. There were plenty of nice girls everywhere. She then warned him not to marry a French girl, who might cause trouble once he got her home to Chicago, or a Catholic, because of the children, and to avoid anyone fast, nervous, divorced, or over twenty-four. Howard knew a number of girls in Paris, most of whom worked in his office or similar agencies. They struck him as cheerful and eager, but aggressive — not at all what he fancied around the house. Just as he was becoming seriously baffled by this gap in his life, Carol Frazier arrived.

He was touched by her shy good manners, her earnest college French. His friends liked her, and, more important, so did the wives of his friends. He had been seriously in love on earlier occasions, and did not consider it a reliable emotion. He and Carol got on well, which seemed to him a satisfactory beginning. His friends, however, told him that she was obviously in love with him and that it was pretty to see. This he expected, not because he was vain but because one took it for granted that love, like a harmless familiar, always attended young women in friendships of this nature. Certainly he was fond of Carol and concerned for her comfort. Had she complained of a toothache, he would have seen to it that she got to a dentist. Carol was moved to another department, but they met every day for lunch and dinner, and talked without discord of any kind. They talked about the job Howard was returning to in Chicago; about their wedding, which was to take place in the spring; and about the movies they saw together. They often went to parties, and then they talked about everyone who had been there, even though they would see most of them next day, at work.

It was a busy life, yet Carol could not help feeling that something had been missed. The weather continued unimproved. She shared an apartment in Passy with two American girls, a temporary ménage that might have existed anywhere. When she rode the Métro, people pushed and were just as rude as in New York. Restaurant food was dull, and the cafés were full of Coca-Cola signs. No wonder she was not in love, she would think. Where was the Paris she had read about? Where were the elegant and expensive-looking women? Where, above all, were the men, those men with their gay good looks and snatches of merry song, the delight of English lady novelists? Traveling through Paris to and from work, she saw only shabby girls bundled into raincoats, hurrying along in the rain, or men who needed a haircut. In the famous parks, under the drizzly trees, children whined peevishly and were slapped. She sometimes thought that perhaps if she and Howard had French friends . . . She suggested it to him.

"You have a French friend," said Howard. "How about Odile?"

But that was not what Carol meant. Odile Pontmoret was Howard's secretary, a thin, dark woman who was (people said) the niece of a count who had gone broke. She seldom smiled and, because her English was at once precise and inaccurate, often sounded sarcastic. All winter she wore the same dark skirt and purple pullover to work. It never occurred to anyone to include her in parties made up of office people, and it was not certain that she would have come anyway. Odile and Carol were friendly in an impersonal way. Sometimes, if Howard was busy, they lunched together. Carol was always careful not to complain about Paris, having been warned that the foreign policy of her country hinged on chance remarks. But her restraint met with no answering delicacy in Odile, whose chief memory of her single trip to New York, before the war, was that her father had been charged twenty-four dollars for a taxi fare that, they later reasoned, must have been two dollars and forty cents. Repeating this, Odile would look indignantly at Carol, as if Carol had been driving the taxi. "And there was no service in the hotel, no service at all," Odile would say. "You could drop your nightgown on the floor and they would sweep around it. And still expect a tip."

These, her sole observations of America, she repeated until Carol's good nature was strained to the limit. Odile never spoke of her life outside the office, which Carol longed to hear about, and she touched on the present only to complain in terms of the past. "Before the war, we traveled, we went everywhere," she would say. "Now, with our poor little franc, everything is finished. I work to help my family. My brother publicizes wines — *Spanish* wines. We work and work so that our parents won't feel the change and so that Martine, our sister, can study music."

Saying this, she would look bewildered and angry, and Carol would have the feeling that Odile was somehow blaming her. They usually ate in a restaurant of Odile's choice — Carol was tactful about this, for Odile earned less than she did — where the food was lumpy and inadequate and the fluorescent lighting made everyone look ill. Carol would glance around at the neighboring tables, at which sat glum and noisy Parisian office workers and shop clerks, and observe that everyone's coat was too long or too short, that the furs were tacky.

There must be more to it than this, she would think. Was it possible that these badly groomed girls liked living in Paris? Surely the sentimental songs about the city had no meaning for them. Were many of them in love, or — still less likely — could any man be in love with any of them?

Every evening, leaving the building in which she and Howard worked, she would pause on the stair landing between the first and second floors to look through the window at the dark winter twilight, thinking that an evening, a special kind of evening, was forming all over the city, and that she had no part in it. At the same hour, people streamed out of an old house across the street that was now a museum, and Carol would watch them hurrying off under their umbrellas. She wondered where they were going and where they lived and what they were having for dinner. Her interest in them was not specific; she had no urge to run into the street and introduce herself. It was simply that she believed they knew a secret, and if she spoke to the right person, or opened the right door, or turned down an unexpected street, the city would reveal itself and she would fall in love. After this pause at the landing, she would forget all her disappointments (the Parma violets she had bought that were fraudulently cut and bound, so that they died in a minute) and run the rest of the way down the stairs, meaning to tell Howard and see if he shared her brief optimism.

On one of these evenings, soon after the start of the cold weather, she noticed a young man sitting on one of the chairs put out in an inhospitable row in the lobby of the building, for job seekers. He looked pale and ill, and the sleeves of his coat were short, as if he were still grow-ing. He stared at her with the expression of a clever child, at once bold and withdrawn. She had the impression that he had seen her stop at the window on the landing and that he was, for some reason, amused. He did not look at all as if he belonged there. She mentioned him to Howard.

"That must have been Felix," Howard said. "Odile's friend." He put so much weight on the word "friend" that Carol felt there was more, a great deal more, and that, although he liked gossip as well as anyone else, he did not find Odile's affairs interesting enough to discuss. "He used to wait for her outside every night. Now I guess he comes in out of the rain."

"But she's never mentioned him," Carol protested. "And he must be younger than she is, and so pale and funny-looking! Where does he come from?"

Howard didn't know. Felix was Austrian, he thought, or Czech. There was something odd about him, for although he obviously hadn't enough to eat, he always had plenty of American cigarettes. That was a bad sign. "Why are you so interested?" he said. But Carol was not interested at all.

After that, Carol saw Felix every evening. He was always polite and sometimes murmured a perfunctory greeting as she passed his chair. He continued to look tired and ill, and Carol wondered if it was true that he hadn't enough to eat. She mentioned him to Odile, who was surprisingly willing to discuss her friend. He was twenty-one, she said, and without relatives. They had all been killed at the end of the war, in the final bombings. He was in Paris illegally, without a proper passport or working papers. The police were taking a long time to straighten it out, and meanwhile, not permitted to work, Felix "did other things." Odile did not say what the other things were, and Carol was rather shocked.

That night, before going to sleep, she thought about Felix, and about how he was only twenty-one. She and Felix, then, were closer in age than he was to Odile or she herself was to Howard. When I was in school, he was in school, she thought. When the war stopped, we were fourteen and fifteen . . . But here she lost track, for where Carol had had a holiday, Felix's parents had been killed. Their closeness in age gave her unexpected comfort, as if someone in this disappointing city had some tie with her. In the morning she was ashamed of her disloyal thoughts — her closest tie in Paris was, after all, with Howard — and decided to ignore Felix when she saw him again. That night, when she passed his chair, he said "Good evening," and she was suddenly acutely conscious of every bit of her clothing: the press of the belt at her waist, the pinch of her earrings, the weight of her dress, even her gloves, which felt as scratchy as sacking. It was a disturbing feeling; she was not sure that she liked it.

"I don't see why Felix should just sit in that hall all the time," she complained to Howard. "Can't he wait for Odile somewhere else?"

Howard was too busy to worry about Felix. It occurred to him that Carol was being tiresome, and that this whining over who sat in the hall was only one instance of her new manner. She had taken to complaining about their friends, and saying she wanted to meet new people and see more of Paris. Sometimes she looked at him helplessly and eagerly, as if there were something he ought to be saying or doing. He was genuinely perplexed; it seemed to him they got along well and were reasonably happy together. But Carol was changing. She hunted up odd, cheap restaurants. She made him walk in the rain. She said that they ought to see the sun come up from the steps of the Sacré-Coeur, and actually succeeded in dragging him there, nearly dead of cold. And, as he might have foreseen, the expedition came to nothing, for it was a rainy dawn and a suspicious gendarme sent them both home.

At Christmas, Carol begged him to take her to the carol singing in the Place Vendôme. Here, she imagined, with the gentle fall of snow and the small, rosy choirboys singing between lighted Christmas trees, she would find something — a warm memory that would, later, bring her closer to Howard, a glimpse of the Paris other people liked. But, of course, there was no snow. Howard and Carol stood under her umbrella as a fine, misty rain fell on the choristers, who sang over and over the opening bars of "Il est né, le Divin Enfant," testing voice levels for a broadcast. Newspaper photographers drifted on the rim of the crowd, and the flares that lit the scene for a newsreel camera blew acrid smoke in their faces. Howard began to cough. Around the square, the tenants of the Place emerged on their small balconies. Some of them had champagne glasses in their hands, as if they had interrupted an agreeable party to step outside for a moment. Carol looked up at the lighted open doorways, through which she could see a painted ceiling, a lighted chandelier. But nothing happened. None of the people seemed beautiful or extraordinary. No one said, "Who *is* that charming girl down there? Let's ask her up!"

Howard blew his nose and said that his feet were cold; they drifted over the square to a couturier's window, where the Infant Jesus wore a rhinestone pin, and a worshiping plaster angel extended a famous brand of perfume. "It just looks like New York or something," Carol said, plaintive with disappointment. As she stopped to close her umbrella, the wind carried to her feet a piece of mistletoe and, glancing up, she saw that cheap tinsel icicles and bunches of mistletoe had been tied on the street lamps of the square. It looked pretty, and rather poor, and she thought of the giant tree in Rockefeller Center. She suddenly felt sorry for Paris, just as she had felt sorry for Felix because he looked hungry and was only twenty-one. Her throat went warm, like the prelude to a rush of tears. Stooping, she picked up the sprig of mistletoe and put it in her pocket.

"Is this all?" Howard said. "Was this what you wanted to see?" He was cold and uncomfortable, but because it was Christmas, he said nothing impatient, and tried to remember, instead, that she was only twenty-one.

"I suppose so."

They found a taxi and went on to finish the evening with some friends from their office. Howard made an amusing story of their adventure in the Place Vendôme. She realized for the first time that something could be perfectly accurate but untruthful — they had not found any part of that evening funny — and that this might cover more areas of experience than the occasional amusing story. She looked at Howard thoughtfully, as if she had learned something of value.

The day after Christmas, Howard came down with a bad cold, the result of standing in the rain. He did not shake it off for the rest of the winter, and Carol, feeling guiltily that it was her fault, suggested no more excursions. Temporarily, she put the question of falling in love to one side. Paris was not the place, she thought; perhaps it had been, fifty years ago, or whenever it was that people wrote all the songs. It did not occur to her to break her engagement.

She wore out the winter working, nursing Howard's cold, toying with office gossip, and, now and again, lunching with Odile, who was just as unsatisfactory as ever. It was nearly spring when Odile, stopping by Carol's desk, said that Martine was making a concert début the following Sunday. It was a private gathering, a subscription concert. Odile sounded vague. She dropped two tickets on Carol's desk and said, walking away, "If you want to come."

"If I *want* to!"

Carol flew away to tell Howard at once. "It's a sort of private musical thing," she said. "There should be important musicians there, since it's a début, and all Odile's family. The old count — everyone." She half expected Odile's impoverished uncle to turn up in eighteenth-century costume, his hands clasped on the head of a cane.

Howard said it was all right with him, provided they needn't stand out in the rain.

"Of course not! It's a *concert*." She looked at the tickets; they were handwritten slips bearing mimeographed numbers. "It's probably in someone's house," she said. "In one of those lovely old drawing rooms. Or in a little painted theatre. There are supposed to be little theatres all over Paris that belong to families and that foreigners never see."

She was beside herself with excitement. What if Paris had taken all winter to come to life? Some foreigners lived there forever and never broke in at all. She spent nearly all of one week's salary on a white feather hat, and practiced a few graceful phrases in French. "*Oui, elle est charmante,*" she said to her mirror. "*La petite Martine est tout à fait ravissante. Je connais très bien Odile. Une coupe de champagne? Mais oui, merci bien. Ah, voici mon fiancé! Monsieur Mitchell, le Baron de . . .*" and so forth.

She felt close to Odile, as if they had been great friends

for a long time. When, two days before the concert, Odile remarked, yawning, that Martine was crying night and day because she hadn't a suitable dress, Carol said, "Would you let me lend her a dress?"

Odile suddenly stopped yawning and turned back the cuffs of her pullover as if it were a task that required all her attention. "That would be very kind of you," she said, at last.

"I mean," said Carol, feeling gauche, "would it be all right? I have a lovely pale green tulle that I brought from New York. I've only worn it twice."

"It sounds very nice," said Odile.

Carol shook the dress out of its tissue paper and brought it to work the next day. Odile thanked her without fervor, but Carol knew by now that that was simply her manner.

"We're going to a private musical début," she wrote to her mother and father. "The youngest niece of the Count de Quelquechose . . . I've lent her my green tulle." She said no more than that, so that it would sound properly casual. So far, her letters had not contained much of interest.

The address Odile had given Carol turned out to be an ordinary, shabby theatre in the Second Arrondissement. It was on an obscure street, and the taxi driver had to stop and consult his street guide so often that they were half an hour late. Music came out to meet them in the empty lobby, where a poster said only "J. S. Bach." An usher tiptoed them into place with ill grace and asked Carol please to have some thought for the people behind her and remove her hat. Carol did so while Howard groped for change for the usher's tip. She peered around: the theatre was less than half filled, and the music coming from the small orchestra on the stage had a thin, echoing quality, as if it were traveling around an empty vault. Odile was nowhere in sight. After a moment, Carol saw Felix sitting alone a few rows away. He smiled — much too familiarly, Carol thought. He looked paler than usual, and almost deliberately untidy. He might at least have taken pains for the concert. She felt a spasm of annoyance, and at the same time her heart began to beat so quickly that she felt its movement must surely be visible.

What ever is the matter with me, she thought. If one could believe all the arch stories on the subject, this was traditional for brides-to-be. Perhaps, at this unpromising moment, she had begun to fall in love. She turned in her seat and stared at Howard; he looked much as always. She settled back and began furnishing in her mind the apartment they would have in Chicago. Sometimes the theatre lights went on, startling her out of some problem involving draperies and Venetian blinds; once Howard went out to smoke. Carol had just finished papering a bedroom green and white when Martine walked onstage, with her violin. At the same moment, a piece of plaster bearing the painted plump foot of a nymph detached itself from the ceiling and crashed into the aisle, just missing Howard's head. Everyone stood up to look, and Martine and the conductor stared at Howard and Carol furiously, as if it were their fault. The commotion was horrifying. Carol slid down in her seat, her hands over her eyes. She retained, in all her distress, an impression of Martine, who wore an ill-fitting blue dress with a little jacket. She had not worn

Carol's pretty tulle; probably she had never intended to.

Carol wondered, miserably, why they had come. For the first time, she noticed that all the people around them were odd and shabby. The smell of stale winter coats filled the unaired theatre; her head began to ache, and Martine's violin shrilled on her ear like a penny whistle. At last the music stopped and the lights went on. The concert was over. There was some applause, but people were busy pulling on coats and screaming at one another from aisle to aisle. Martine shook hands with the conductor and, after looking vaguely around the hall, wandered away.

"Is this all?" said Howard. He stood up and stretched. Carol did not reply. She had just seen Felix and Odile together. Odile was speaking rapidly and looked unhappy. She wore the same skirt and pullover Carol had seen all winter, and she was carrying her coat.

"Odile!" Carol called. But Odile waved and threaded her way through the row of seats to the other side of the theatre, where she joined some elderly people and a young man. They went off together backstage.

Her family, Carol thought, sickening under the snub. And she didn't introduce me, or even come over and speak. She was positive now that Odile had invited her only to help fill the hall, or because she had a pair of tickets she didn't know what to do with.

"Let's go," Howard said. Their seats were near the front. By the time they reached the lobby, it was nearly empty. Under the indifferent eyes of the usher, Howard guided Carol into her coat. "They sure didn't put on much of a show for Martine," he said.

"No, they didn't."

"No flowers," he said. "It didn't even have her name on the program. No one would have known."

It had grown dark, and rain poured from the edge of the roof in an unbroken sheet. "You stay here," said Howard. "I'll get a taxi."

"No," said Carol. "Stay with me. This won't last." She could not bring herself to tell him how hurt and humiliated she was, what a ruin the afternoon had been. Howard led her behind the shelter of a billboard.

"That dress," he went on. "I thought you'd lent her something."

"I had. She didn't wear it. I don't know why."

"Ask Odile."

"I don't care. I'd rather let it drop."

He agreed. He felt that Carol had almost knowingly exposed herself to an indignity over the dress, and pride of that nature he understood. To distract her, he spoke of the job waiting for him in Chicago, of his friends, of his brother's sailboat.

Against a background of rain and Carol's disappointment, he sounded, without meaning to, faintly homesick. Carol picked up his mood. She looked at the white feather hat the usher had made her remove and said suddenly, "I wish I were home. I wish I were in my own country, with my own friends."

"You will be," he said, "in a couple of months." He hoped she would not begin to cry.

"I'm tired of the way everything is here — old and rotten and falling down."

"You mean that chunk of ceiling?"

She turned from him, exasperated at his persistently

missing the point, and saw Felix not far away. He was leaning against the ticket booth, looking resignedly at the rain. When he noticed Carol looking at him, he said, ignoring Howard, "Odile's backstage with her family." He made a face and went on, "No admission for us foreigners."

Odile's family did not accept Felix; Carol had barely absorbed this thought, which gave her an unexpected and indignant shock, when she realized what he had meant by "us foreigners." It was rude of Odile to let her family hurt her friend; at the same time, it was even less kind of them to include Carol in a single category of foreigners. Surely Odile could see the difference between Carol and this pale young man who "did other things." She felt that she and Felix had been linked together in a disagreeable way, and that she was floating away from everything familiar and safe. Without replying, she bent her head and turned away, politely but unmistakably.

"Funny kid," Howard remarked as Felix walked slowly out into the rain, his hands in his pockets.

"He's horrible," said Carol, so violently that he stared at her. "He's not funny. He's a parasite. He lives on Odile. He doesn't work or anything, he just hangs around and stares at people. Odile says he has no passport. Well, why doesn't he *get* one? Any man can work if he wants to. Why are there people like that? All the boys I ever knew at home were well brought up and manly. I never knew anyone like Felix."

She stopped, breathless, and Howard said, "Well, let Odile worry."

"Odile!" Carol cried. "Odile must be crazy. What is she thinking of? Her family ought to put a stop to it.

The whole thing is terrible. It's bad for the office. It ought
to be stopped. Why, he'll never marry her! Why should
he? He's only a boy, an orphan. He needs friends, and con-
nections, and somebody his own age. Why should he
marry Odile? What does he want with an old maid from
an old, broken-down family? He needs a good meal, and
— and help." She stopped, bewildered. She had been
about to say "and love."

Howard, now beyond surprise, felt only a growing wave
of annoyance. He did not like hysterical women. His
sisters never behaved like that.

"I want to go *home*," said Carol, nearly wailing.

He ran off to find a taxi, glad to get away. By "home"
he thought she meant the apartment she shared with the
two American girls in Passy.

For Carol, the concert was the end, the final *clou*. She
stopped caring about Paris, or Odile, or her feelings for
Howard. When Odile returned her green dress, nicely
pressed and folded in a cardboard box, she said only, "Just
leave it on my desk." Everyone seemed to think it normal
that now her only preoccupation should be the cut of her
wedding dress. People began giving parties for her. The
wash of attention soothed her fears. She was good-tempered, and did not ask Howard to take her to tiresome
places. Once again he felt he had made the right decision,
and put her temporary waywardness down to nerves. After
a while, Carol began lunching with Odile again, but she did
not mention the concert.

As for Felix, Carol now avoided him entirely. Sometimes
she waited until Odile had left the office before leaving
herself. Again, she braced herself and walked briskly past

him, ignoring his "Good evening." She no longer stopped
on the staircase to watch the twilight; her mood was different. She believed that something fortunate had happened to her spirit, and that she had become invulnerable.
Soon she was able to walk by Felix without a tremor, and
after a while she stopped noticing him at all.

"Have you noticed winter is over?" Odile said. She and
Carol had left the dressmaker's street and turned off on
a broad, oblique avenue. "It hasn't rained for hours. This
was the longest winter I remember, although I think one
says this every year."

"It was long for me, too," Carol said. It was true that
it was over. The spindly trees of the avenue were covered
with green, like a wrapping of tissue. A few people sat out
in front of shops, sunning themselves. It was, suddenly,
like coming out of a tunnel.

Odile turned to Carol and smiled, a rare expression for
her. "I'm sorry I was rude at Madame Germaine's just
now," she said. "I don't know what the matter is nowadays
— I am dreadful to everyone. But I shouldn't have been
to you."

"Never mind," said Carol. She flushed a little, for Howard had taught her to be embarrassed over anything as
direct as an apology. "I'd forgotten it. In fact, I didn't
even notice."

"Now you are being nice," said Odile unhappily. "Really,
there is something wrong with me. I worry all the time,
over money, over Martine, over Felix. I think it isn't
healthy." Carol murmured something comforting but in-

distinct. Glancing at her, Odile said, "Where are you off to now?"

"Nowhere. Home, I suppose. There's always something to do these days."

"Why don't you come along with me?" Odile stopped on the street and took her arm. "I'm going to see Felix. He lives near here. Oh, he would be so surprised!"

"*Felix?*" Automatically Carol glanced at her watch. Surely she had something to do, some appointment? But Odile was hurrying her along. Carol thought, Now, this is all wrong. But they had reached the Boulevard de Grenelle, where the Métro ran overhead, encased in a tube of red brick. Light fell in patterns underneath; the boulevard was lined with ugly shops and dark, buff-painted cafés. It was a far cry from the prim street a block or so away where the dressmaker's flat was. "Is it far?" said Carol nervously. She did not like the look of the neighborhood. Odile shook her head. They crossed the boulevard and a few crooked, narrow streets filled with curbside barrows and marketing crowds. It was a section of Paris Carol had not seen; although it was on the Left Bank, it was not pretty, not picturesque. There were no little restaurants, no students' hotels. It was simply down-and-out and dirty, and everyone looked ill-tempered. Arabs lounging in doorways looked at the two girls and called out, laughing.

"Look straight ahead," said Odile. "If you look at them, they come up and take your arm. It's worse when I come alone."

How dreadful of Felix to let Odile walk alone through streets like this, Carol thought.

"Here," said Odile. She stopped in front of a building

on which the painted word "Hôtel" was almost effaced. They climbed a musty-smelling staircase, Carol taking care not to let her skirt brush the walls. She wondered nervously what Howard would say when he heard she had visited Felix in his hotel room. On a stair landing, Odile knocked at one of the doors. Felix let them in. It took a few moments, for he had been asleep. He did not look at all surprised but with a slight bow invited them in, as if he frequently entertained in his room.

The room was so cluttered, the bed so untidy, that Carol stood bewildered, wondering where one could sit. Odile at once flung herself down on the bed, dropping her handbag on the floor, which was cement and gritty with dirt.

"I'm tired," she said. "We've been choosing Carol's wedding dress. White, and *very* pretty."

Felix's shirt was unbuttoned, his face without any color. He glanced sidelong at Carol, smiling. On a table stood an alcohol stove, some gaudy plastic bowls, and a paper container of sugar. In the tiny washbasin, over which hung a cold-water faucet, were a plate and a spoon, and, here and there on the perimeter, Felix's shaving things and a battered toothbrush.

"Do sit on that chair," he said to Carol, but he made no move to take away the shirt and sweater and raincoat that were bundled on it. Everything else he owned appeared to be on the floor. The room faced a court and was quite dark. "I'll heat up this coffee," Felix said, as if casting about for something to do as a host. "Miss Frazier, sit down." He put a match to the stove and a blue flame leaped along the wall. He stared into a saucepan of coffee, sniffed it, and added a quantity of cold water. "A new

PX has just been opened," he said to Odile. He put the saucepan over the flame, apparently satisfied. "I went around to see what was up," he said. "Nothing much. It is really sad. Everything is organized on such a big scale now that there is no room for little people like me. I waited outside and finally picked up some cigarettes — only two cartons — from a soldier."

He talked on, and Carol, who was not accustomed to his conversation, could not tell if he was joking or serious. She had finally decided to sit down on top of the raincoat. She frowned at her hands, wondering why Odile didn't teach him to make coffee properly and why he talked like a criminal. For Carol, the idea that one might not be permitted to work was preposterous. She harbored a rigid belief that anyone could work who sincerely wanted to. Picking apples, she thought vaguely, or down in a mine, where people were always needed.

Odile looked at Carol, as if she knew what she was thinking. "Poor Felix doesn't belong in this world," she said. "He should have been killed at the end of the war. Instead of that, every year he gets older. In a month, he will be twenty-two."

But Odile was over thirty. Carol found the gap between their ages distasteful, and thought it indelicate of Odile to stress it. Felix, who had been ineffectively rinsing the plastic bowls in cold water, now poured the coffee out. He pushed one of the bowls toward Odile; then he suddenly took her hand and, turning it over, kissed the palm. "Why should I have been killed?" he said.

Carol, breathless with embarrassment, looked at the brick wall of the court. She twisted her fingers together until they hurt. How can they act like this in front of me, she thought, and in such a dirty room? The thought that they might be in love entered her head for the first time, and it made her ill. Felix, smiling, gave her a bowl of coffee, and she took it without meeting his eyes. He sat down on the bed beside Odile and said happily, "I'm glad you came. You both look beautiful."

Carol glanced at Odile, thinking, Not beautiful, not by any stretch of good manners. "French girls are all attractive," she said politely.

"Most of them are frights," said Felix. No one disputed it, and no one but Carol appeared distressed by the abrupt termination of the conversation. She cast about for something to say, but Odile put her bowl on the floor, said again that she was tired, lay back, and seemed all at once to fall asleep.

Felix looked at her. "She really can shut out the world whenever she wants to," he said, suggesting to Carol's startled ears that he was quite accustomed to see her fall asleep. Of course, she might have guessed, but why should Felix make it so obvious? She felt ashamed of the way she had worried about Felix, and the way she had run after Odile, wanting to know her family. This was all it had come to, this dirty room. Howard was right, she thought. It doesn't pay.

At the same time, she was perplexed at the intimacy in which she and Felix now found themselves. She would have been more at ease alone in a room with him than with Odile beside him asleep on his bed.

"I must go," she said nervously.

"Oh, yes," said Felix, not stopping her.

"But I can't find my way back alone." She felt as if she might cry.

"There are taxis," he said vaguely. "But I can take you to the Métro, if you like." He buttoned his shirt and looked around for a jacket, making no move to waken Odile.

"Should we leave her here?" said Carol. "Shouldn't I say goodbye?"

He looked surprised. "I wouldn't think of disturbing her," he said. "If she's asleep, then she must be tired." And to this Carol could think of nothing to say.

He followed her down the staircase and into the street, dark now, with stripes of neon to mark the cafés. They said little, and because she was afraid of the dark and the Arabs, Carol walked close beside him. On the Boulevard de Grenelle, Felix stopped at the entrance to the Métro.

"Here," he said. "Up those steps. It takes you right over to Passy."

She looked at him, feeling this parting was not enough. She had criticized him to Howard and taught herself to ignore him, but here, in a neighborhood where she could not so much as find her way, she felt more than ever imprisoned in the walls of her shyness, unable to say, "Thank you," or "Thanks for the coffee," or anything perfunctory and reasonable. She had an inexplicable and uneasy feeling that something had ended for her, and that she would never see Felix, or even Odile, again.

Felix caught her look, or seemed to. He looked around, distressed, at the Bar des Sportifs, and the *sportifs* inside it, and said, "If you would lend me a little money, I could buy you a drink before you go."

His unabashed cadging restored her at once. "I haven't

time for a drink," she said, all briskness now, as if he had with a little click dropped into the right slot. "But if you'll promise to take Odile to dinner, I'll lend you two thousand francs."

"Fine," said Felix. He watched her take the money from her purse, accepted it without embarrassment, and put it in the pocket of his jacket.

"Take her for a nice dinner somewhere," Carol repeated.

"Of course."

"Oh!" He exasperated her. "Why don't you act like other people?" she cried. "You can't live like this all the time. You could go to America. Mr. Mitchell would help you. I know he would. He'd vouch for you, for a visa, if I asked him too."

"And Odile? Would Mr. Mitchell vouch for Odile too?"

She glanced at him, startled. When Felix was twenty-five, Odile would be nearly forty. Surely he had thought of this? "She could go, too," she said, and added, "I suppose."

"And what would we do in America?" He rocked back and forth on his heels, smiling.

"You could work," she said sharply. She could not help adding, like a scold, "For once in your life."

"As cook and butler," said Felix thoughtfully, and began to laugh. "No, don't be angry," he said, putting out his hand. "One has to wait so long for American papers. I know, I used to do it. To sit there all day and wait, or stand in the queue — how could Odile do it? She has her job to attend to. She has to help her family."

"In America," said Carol, "she would make more money, she could help them even more." But she could not see clearly the picture of Felix and Odile combining their salaries in a neat little apartment and faithfully remitting a portion to France. She could not imagine what on earth Felix would do for a living. Perhaps he and Odile would get married; something told her they would not. "I'm sorry," she said. "It's really your own business. I shouldn't have said anything at all." She moved away, but Felix took her hand and held it.

"You mean so well," he said. "Odile is right, you know. I ought to have been killed, or at least disappeared. No one knows what to do with me or where I fit. As for Odile, her whole family is overdue. But we're not — how does it go in American papers, under the photographs? — 'Happy Europeans find new life away from old cares.' We're not that, either."

"I suppose not. I don't know." She realized all at once how absurd they must look, standing under the Métro tracks, holding hands. Passersby looked at them, sympathetic.

"You shouldn't go this way, looking so hurt and serious," he said. "You're so nice. You mean so well. Odile loves you."

Her heart leaped as if he, Felix, had said he loved her. But no, she corrected herself. Not Felix but some other man, some wonderful person who did not exist.

Odile loved her. Her hand in his, she remembered how he had kissed Odile's palm, and she felt on her own palm the pressure of a kiss; but not from Felix. Perhaps, she thought, what she felt was the weight of his love for Odile, from which she was excluded, and to which Felix now politely and kindly wished to draw her, as if his and Odile's ability to love was their only hospitality, their only way of paying debts. For a moment, standing under the noisy trains on the dark, dusty boulevard, she felt that she had at last opened the right door, turned down the right street, glimpsed the vision toward which she had struggled on winter evenings when, standing on the staircase, she had wanted to be enchanted with Paris and to be in love with Howard.

But that such a vision could come from Felix and Odile was impossible. For a moment she had been close to tears, like the Christmas evening when she fould the mistletoe. But she remembered in time what Felix was — a hopeless parasite. And Odile was silly and immoral and old enough to know better. And they were not married and never would be, and they spent heaven only knew how many hours in that terrible room in a slummy quarter of Paris.

No, she thought. What she and Howard had was better. No one could point to them, or criticize them, or humiliate them by offering to help.

She withdrew her hand and said with cold shyness, "Thank you for the coffee, Felix."

"Oh that." He watched her go up the steps to the Métro, and then he walked away.

Upstairs, she passed a flower seller and stopped to buy a bunch of violets, even though they would be dead before she reached home. She wanted something pretty in her hand to take away the memory of the room and the Arabs and the dreary cafés and the messy affairs of Felix and Odile. She paid for the violets and noticed as she did so that the little scene — accepting the flowers, paying for them — had the gentle, nostalgic air of something past.

Soon, she sensed, the comforting vision of Paris as she had once imagined it would overlap the reality. To have met and married Howard there would sound romantic and interesting, more and more so as time passed. She would forget the rain and her unshared confusion and loneliness, and remember instead the Paris of films, the street lamps with their tinsel icicles, the funny concert hall where the ceiling collapsed, and there would be, at last, a coherent picture, accurate but untrue. The memory of Felix and Odile and all their distasteful strangeness would slip away; for "love" she would think, once more, "Paris," and, after a while, happily married, mercifully removed in time, she would remember it and describe it and finally believe it as it had never been at all.

Autumn Day

I WAS eighteen when I married Walt and nineteen when I followed him to Salzburg, where he was posted with the Army of Occupation. We'd been married eleven months, but separated for so much of it that my marriage really began that autumn day, when I got down from the train at Salzburg station. Walt was waiting, of course. I could see him in the crowd of soldiers, tall and anxious-looking, already a little bald even though he was only twenty-nine. The first thought that came into my head wasn't a very nice one: I thought what a pity it was he didn't look more like my brother-in-law. Walt and my brother-in-law were first cousins; that was how we happened to meet. I had always liked my brother-in-law and felt my sister was lucky to have him, and I suppose that was really why I wanted Walt. I thought it would be the same kind of marriage.

I waved at Walt, smiling, the way girls do in illustrations. I could almost see myself, fresh and pretty, waving to someone in uniform. This was eight years ago, soon after the war; the whole idea of arriving to meet a soldier somewhere seemed touching and brave and romantic. When Walt took me in his arms, right in front of everyone, I was so engulfed by the *idea* of the picture it made that I thought I would cry. But then I remembered my luggage and turned away so that I could keep an eye on it. I had matching blue plaid suitcases, given me by my married sister as a going-away present, and I didn't want to lose them right at the start of my married life.

"Oh, Walt," I said, nearly in tears, "I don't see the hatbox."

Those were the first words I'd spoken, except for hello or something like that.

Walt laughed and said something just as silly. He said, "You look around ten years old."

Immediately, I felt defensive. I looked down at my camel's-hair coat and my scuffed, familiar moccasins, and I thought, What's wrong with looking young? Walt didn't know, of course, that my married sister had already scolded me for dressing like a little girl instead of a grownup.

"You're not getting ready to go back to school, Cissy," she'd said. "You're married. You're going over there to be with your husband. You'll be mixing with grown-up married couples. And for goodness' sake stop sucking your pearls. Of all the baby habits!"

"Well," I told her, "you brought me up, practically. Whose fault is it if I'm a baby now?"

My pearls were always pink with lipstick, because I had a trick of putting them in my mouth when I was pretending to be stubborn or puzzled about something. Up till now, my sister had always thought it cute. I had always been the baby of the family, the motherless child; even my wedding had seemed a kind of game, like dressing up for a party. Now they were pushing me out, buying luggage, criticizing my clothes, sending me off to live thousands of miles away with a strange man. I couldn't understand the change. It turned all my poses into real feelings: I became truly stubborn, and honestly perplexed. I took the trousseau check my father had given me and bought exactly the sort of clothes I'd always worn, the skirts and sweaters, the blouses with Peter Pan collars. There wasn't one grown-up dress, not even a pair of high-heeled shoes. I wanted to make my sister sorry, to make her see that I was too young to be going away. Then, too, I couldn't imagine another way of dressing. I felt safer in my girlhood uniforms, the way you feel in a familiar house.

I remembered all that as I walked along the station platform with Walt, awkwardly holding hands, and I thought, I suppose now I'll have to change. But not too soon, not too fast.

That was how I began my married life.

In those days, Salzburg was still coming out of the war. All the people you saw on the streets looked angry and in a hurry. There were so many trucks and jeeps clogging the roads, so many soldiers, so much scaffolding over the narrow sidewalks that you could hardly get around. We couldn't find a place to live. The Army had taken over whole blocks of apartments, but even with the rebuilding and the requisitioning, Walt and I had to wait three months before there was anything ready for us. During those months — October, November, December — we lived in a farmhouse not far out of town. It was a real farm, not a hotel. The owner of the place, Herr Enrich, was a polite man and spoke English. When he first saw me, he said right away that he had taken in boarders before the war, but quite a different type — artists and opera singers, people who had come for the Salzburg Festival. "Now," he said politely, "one cannot choose." I wondered if that was meant for us. I looked at Walt, but he didn't seem to care. Later, Walt told me not to listen to Herr Enrich. He told me not to talk about the war, not to mix with the other people on the farm, to make friends with Army wives. Go for walks. Years later, I came across this a little girl learning a lesson. I wrote it all down on a slip of paper: Don't talk war. Avoid people on farm. Meet Army wives. Go for walks. Years later, I came across this list and I showed it to Walt, but he didn't remember what it was about. When I told him this was a line of conduct he had laid down for me, he didn't believe it. He hardly remembers our life on the farm. Yet those three months stand out in my memory like a special little lifetime, neither girlhood nor marriage. It was a time when I didn't like what I was, but didn't know what I wanted to be. In a way, I tried to do the right things. I followed Walt's instructions.

I didn't talk about the war; there was no one to talk to. I didn't mix with the people on the farm. They didn't want to mix with me. There were six boarders besides us: a Hungarian couple named de Kende — dark and fat with gold teeth; and a family from Vienna with two children. The family from Vienna looked like rabbits. They had moist noses and pink eyes. All four wore the Salzburg costume, and they looked like rabbits dressed up. Sometimes I smiled at the two children, but they never smiled back. I wondered if they had been told not to, and if they had a list of instructions like mine: Don't mix with Americans. Don't talk to Army wives . . . We ate at a long table in the dining room, all of us together. There was a tiled stove in a corner, and the room was often so hot that the windows steamed and ran as if it were raining inside. Most of the time Walt ate with the Army. He was always away for lunch, and then I would be alone with these people — the Enrichs, the de Kendes from Hungary, and the rabbity family from Vienna. Only Mr. de Kende and his wife ever tried to speak to me in English. Mr. de Kende had a terrible accent, but I once understood him to say that he had been a wealthy man in his own country and had owned four factories. Now he traveled around Austria in an old car selling dental supplies. "What do you think of that for Yalta justice?" he said, pointing his fork at me over the table. The others all suddenly stared at me, alert and silent, waiting for my reply. But I didn't understand. All I could think of then was that my brother-in-law was a dentist, and I remembered how he'd taken me into his home when my mother died, and how kind he had been, and I had to hold my breath to keep from crying in front of them all. At last, I said, "Well, goodness, it's quite a coincidence, because my sister happens to be married to a dental surgeon." Mr. de Kende just grunted, and they all went back to their food.

I told Walt about it, but all he said was, "Don't bother with them. Why don't you get to know some Army wives?"

He didn't understand how hard it was. We lived out of town, and I didn't know how to go about meeting anyone on my own. I thought it was up to Walt to take me around and introduce me to people, but he had only one friend in Salzburg and seemed to think that was enough. Walt's friend's name was Marvin McColl. He and Walt came from the same town and had gone to the same school. He seemed to have more in common with Marv than with me, but they were the same age, so it seemed only natural. Walt wanted me to be friends with Marv's wife, Laura.

He said we were going to be together a lot and it would help if we girls were friends. Laura was twenty-six. She had long hair and big eyes and always looked as if someone had just hurt her feelings. She had no girl friends in Salzburg, other than me. She hated foreigners and couldn't stand Army wives. Three times a week, or more, Walt and I went out with the McColls. We went to the movies or drank beer in their apartment. Marv hardly spoke to me, except when he'd been drinking. Then he would get tears in his eyes and tell me I was the first and only girl Walt had ever taken seriously, and how they'd never thought Walt would ever marry. He said I was lucky to get Walt, and he hoped I'd make him happy.

"Dry your tears, Marv," Laura would say, rather sarcastically. She would leave Walt and Marv together and take me to another part of the room, so that we could talk. Our conversations were always the same. I would talk about home, and Laura would tell me how much she hated Salzburg and how Marv didn't understand her and her problems. Meanwhile, Marv and Walt drank beer and talked about people I didn't know and places I'd never been. On the way home, Walt would always ask me if I'd had a good time, and before I could answer he'd tell me again that Marv was his best friend and what a lot of fun the four of us were going to have together in Salzburg. I didn't mind the evenings so much, but I didn't care one bit for the afternoons I had to spend alone with Laura, because then she would curl up with a drink, girls together, and tell me the most awful things about her private life with Marv — the sort of thing my married sister would never have said. As for me, they could have cut my tongue out before I'd have talked about Walt. Naturally, I never repeated any of this to Walt. The truth was that he and I never talked much about anything. I didn't know him well enough, and I kept feeling that our real married life hadn't started, that there was nothing to say and wouldn't be for years.

I don't know if I was unhappy or happy in those days. It wasn't what I'd expected, none of it, being married, or being an Army wife, or living in Europe. Everything — even conversation — seemed so much in the future that I couldn't get my feet on the ground and start living. It seemed to me it had been that way all my life, and that being married hadn't settled anything at all. My mother died when I was little, and my father married again, and then I went to live with my married sister. Whenever I seemed low or moody, my sister would say, "Wait till you grow up. Wait till you have a home. Everything will seem different." Now I was married, and I still didn't have a home, and there was Walt saying, "We'll have our own place soon. You'll be all right then." I never told him I was unhappy — I wasn't sure myself if that was exactly the trouble — but often I could see that he was trying to think of the right thing to say to me, hesitating as if he was baffled or just didn't know me well enough to speak out. I was lonely in the daytimes, and terribly shy and unhappy at night. Walt was silent a lot, and often I simply burst into tears for no reason at all. Tears didn't seem to bother him. He expected girls to be nervous and difficult at times; he didn't like it, but he thought it was part of married life. I think he and Marv talked it over, and Marv told him how it was with Laura. Maybe Laura had been worse before they'd got the apartment. I know they had waited seven months, living in one room. Laura wouldn't be easy in one room. Anyway, I don't know where the notion came from, but Walt truly believed, if I was silent, or pale, or forlorn, that an apartment would make everything right.

I never thought about the apartment, except when Walt mentioned it. I wanted to be away from the farm, but I didn't know where I wanted to be. Our room at the farm was small, cold, and coldly clean. We slept in twin beds. At night, after Walt left me and went back to his own bed and went straight off to sleep, I lay close to the wall, trying to imagine it was a wall somewhere else — but where? At my married sister's, I had slept on a couch in the dining room. I didn't want to be there again. The daytime was worse, in a way, because I had to be up and around, and didn't know what to do with myself. I did a lot of laundering; I washed my sweaters until the wool matted. I'd always been clean, but now, being married, I felt I couldn't get things clean enough any more. Walt had told me to go for walks. Once every day, at least, I set out for a walk, a scarf over my hair, my head bent into the wind. I never went far — I was afraid of getting lost — and I felt that I looked like a miserable cat as I skirted the muddy tracks on the road outside the farm. I had never lived in the country before, and it seemed crazy to just walk around with nothing special to look at. The sky was always gray and low, as if you could touch it. It seemed made of felt. The sky at home was never like that; at least, it didn't press down on you. Herr Enrich said this was the Salzburg autumn sky, and that the clouds were low because they were holding snow. It was frightening, in a way, to think that behind all that felt there were tireless whirlpools of snow, moving and silent.

One afternoon when I was tramping aimlessly around the yard, I heard somebody singing. I couldn't tell if the singer was a man or a woman, and I couldn't make out the words of the song. But the voice was the nicest I had ever heard. I stood still with my hands pulled up into my sleeves, because of the cold, and I looked up to the top of the house, where the voice was coming from. I wondered if it was the radio in someone's room, but then the singer stopped and sang the same phrase four or five times. The kitchenmaids were sitting on a bench in the yard, plucking chickens for supper in front of an open brazier. They stopped talking and listened, too, very still, and the yard was like one of those fairy tales where everyone is suddenly frozen for a thousand years. But then the voice stopped completely, and we became ourselves again, the girls working and giggling, and me trudging about on my eternal walks.

That night, Herr Enrich mentioned the singer. It was an American, a woman. Her name was Dorothy West. She had finished a concert tour in three countries and was here to rest. She was tired and didn't want to meet people and was having all her meals in her room.

"She used to come to us before the war," Herr Enrich

said, looking conceited. "We are so pleased that she has remembered us and come back."

I said, timidly, "I'm American, too. Maybe she'd like to just meet me."

Herr Enrich said, "No, no one," like a dragon, so, of course, I didn't say more.

Every day, then, I heard Miss West. Her voice, deep and sure, filled the sky, and I heard her even in the woods far behind the house, where I dragged my feet on my dull walks. The people at the table told me she sang in French and Italian as well as English and German, but I didn't recognize a thing. Having her there had made them somewhat friendlier with me; also, I was beginning to understand a little German. It made a nicer atmosphere, but not one you would call home. Some days, Miss West's accompanist came out from Salzburg, where he stayed in a hotel. He was a small man in a shabby raincoat; it was a surprise to me that she should have anyone so poor. When he came, everyone was locked out of the dining room (the only really warm room of the house, because it contained the stove), and they worked together at a piano there. The accompanist had written a new song for her; that is, he had set a poem to music. The Enrichs stood out in the hall, where they could listen. Afterward, Herr Enrich told me it was a famous poem called "Herbsttag," which meant "Autumn Day," and he translated it for me. The translation was slow and clumsy, and didn't rhyme the way a real poem should. But when he came to the part about it being autumn and not having a house to live in, I suddenly felt that this poem had something to do with me. It was autumn here, and Walt and I hadn't a house, either. It

was the first time I had ever had this feeling about a poem
— that it had something to do with me. I got Herr Enrich
to write it down in German, and I memorized the line,
"*Wer jetzt kein Haus hat, baut sich keines mehr.*" The
rest was all about writing letters and going for lonely walks
— exactly the life I was leading. I wished more than ever
that I might meet Miss West and tell her how much I liked
her singing, and even how much this poet had understood
me. I wanted to know someone outside my marriage. I
felt that I would never get to know Walt, partly because
he was ten years older, but more simply because he was
a man. It seemed to me that a girl friend was the only real
friend you could have. I don't know why I attached so
much to the idea of Miss West: I thought that because I
had liked her voice this gave me some sort of claim on her.
I realize now what a crazy idea this was, but I was only
nineteen and in a foreign country.

Soon after this, the first snow fell. It snowed in the
night. In the morning, the ground in the yard outside was
covered with a lacy pattern, the imprints of the feet of
birds. There were hundreds of tiny birds, yellow and
brown, in the woods behind the farm. They came from
Finland and were going to Italy and had got lost. Herr
Enrich found one frozen and brought it in while we were
at breakfast. It lay on the palm of his hand. Its feet stuck
foolishly in the air, like matchsticks. Its eyes were glazed.

Herr Enrich stroked the yellow feathers in its brown
wings. "This is the smallest bird in Europe," he said.

Walt never talked to anyone much, but this time he
spoke up and said it was true: he had read it in the Salzburg paper. He got up and fished out the local paper from

a pile on a bench by the stove and pointed to the headline. Herr Enrich read it aloud: "SMALLEST BIRD IN EUROPE VISITS SALZBURG." I just sat and stared at Walt. I didn't know until that minute that he read German or that he ever bothered to read the local paper. It wasn't important after all, you don't say to your wife, "Hey, I read German." But I felt more than ever that I needed a friend, someone simple enough for me to understand and simple enough to understand me. The rest of the people at the table went on talking about the bird, and when they had finished discussing it and had all touched its frozen wings, Herr Enrich opened the door of the tiled stove and threw the bird inside. I looked again at Walt, but he didn't seem to notice how horrible this was.

Mrs. de Kende, the Hungarian woman, smiled her toothy gold smile at me over the table, as if she sympathized. I had never liked her until then. We sat on after the others had left, and she leaned forward and whispered, "Come up to my room. We can talk." I was glad, although she was too old to be a friend for me, and I really disliked her looks. Her hair was black and dry, and rolled in an untidy bun. There were always ends trailing on her neck. Her room was next to ours, but I had never been in it before. It was stuffy and rather dark. She had an electric plate and a little coffeepot. "I creep up here to make coffee," she said, shutting the door. "I can't drink the stuff Frau Enrich makes. Don't ever tell her I've invited you here."

"Why not?"

"She might be jealous. She might take it as a slander against her coffee. She might think I was trying to get something from you; American coffee. She might make trouble. Much trouble." She spread out her fat fingers to show how big the trouble would be. "You don't know how people are," she said. "You don't know what the world is."

I sat straight in my chair, like a little girl on a visit. I drank the coffee she poured for me. It tasted like tap water.

"Good?" she asked me.

"Oh, yes."

I began to take in the room. It was littered with clothing. The bed wasn't made; just the covers pulled over the pillows. From the back of a chair, a dirty cotton brassière hung by a strap. The word "marriage" came into my head. It reminded me of something — a glimpse of my married sister's bedroom on a Sunday morning, untidy and inexplicably frightening.

"What a funny little girl you are," Mrs. de Kende said. "You remind me of the little bird Herr Enrich brought in." She put down her cup and took my face in her hands. Her fingers were cold. I tried to smile. "One longs to speak to you," she said. "I long so for a friend." She let me go and looked around the room. "I have a terrible secret," she said. "The burden of a secret is too much for one person. Some things *must* be shared. Do you understand?"

"Yes," I said. "I do understand."

Mrs. de Kende looked at me for a long time in a rather dramatic way. I began to feel silly, and didn't know what to do with my empty cup. I hoped she wouldn't touch me again. Suddenly she said, "My husband is a Jew."

"Well," I said. I was still fretting about the cup, and finally put it on the floor.

"Never tell," Mrs. de Kende said. "Swear."

"I won't tell." There was no one I could tell. I still

hadn't a friend. Walt wouldn't have found it interesting, and Laura McColl thought all foreigners were crazy.

Mrs. de Kende seemed disappointed, as if I should have had some reaction. But I didn't know what she wanted. She said, "Do you realize what would happen if it were known? We wouldn't be welcome in this house. It would be terrible," she said, clasping and unclasping her hands. "My husband would lose his clients. None of the dentists would buy from him. De Kende isn't our real name. How could it be? The Kendes were aristocrats. Oh, what a foolish woman I am," she said. "Look at my life, at the way I am forced to live. I am the daughter of an Army officer. God is punishing me for having married a Jew. Forgive me, Holy Mother of Jesus," she said, closing her eyes.

I sat with my hands in my lap and wished myself away. At last, because she didn't seem to notice me any more, I got up quietly and went to my room. It was the first visit I'd had with anyone in Salzburg, except for the McColls.

That afternoon, I had to see Laura. Walt wanted us to be friends, so whenever she asked me over for tea, I took the bus in to Salzburg and listened to her complaints about Marv. Tea really meant having drinks. Laura would make sweet drinks for me, putting in lots of fruit and sugar so that I wouldn't taste the liquor, but I always had a headache coming home on the bus later on. Laura had a lot of time every day to think about her troubles. She had a maid, and a nurse for the baby, and the long autumn afternoons got on her nerves. She met me at the door, wearing velvet slacks and a pullover with a lot of jewelry. We settled down, and she started in right away about Marv. Although it was early, all the lights were on. They lived in a furnished apartment full of glass and china shelves, which seemed to take up all the air and light. It was the maid's day off, so the nurse brought in our drinks. She was young and thin and wore rouge. Laura watched her in silence as she carefully lowered a tray with bottles and glasses and a bowl of ice to a table near us. Suddenly Laura said, "Look at that bitch." I must have seemed stupid, because she said, "I mean *her*," and pointed with her foot to the nurse. "This bitch that Marv's brought in," she said. "Wouldn't you think he'd have more respect for his own baby? That's what it is now," she said. "He's not satisfied having them outside. Now he has to have them in the house." I looked at the nurse, but she didn't seem to understand. "Oh, Cissy," Laura cried, "he's got her in the house, to be around me, to look after my baby," and she sent the bowl of ice flying across the room. I heard glass shatter and closed my eyes, as if I were still with Mrs. de Kende, hearing that awful praying. When I opened them, Laura was crying softly, and the nurse was on her knees cleaning up the mess. There was more color than ever in her cheeks. She was young, but she looked hard. Laura was hard, too, but in a different way. I suddenly felt sorry for Marv, caught between these two women — although, of course, he didn't deserve pity.

Usually, I never talked to Walt about Marv and Laura. When he asked about my afternoons in town, I would say that Laura and I had drinks and told each other's fortune with Laura's Tarot cards. He seemed to think that was a good way of spending time. But that night, I thought I had better tell him something. It had been such a terrible day for me, with the scene in the morning, and Laura in the afternoon, it seemed to me that he might listen and be sympathetic. When we were alone, after dinner, I started to tell him about Laura and the nurse. He cut me off at once. He said that Marv was his best friend, and that Laura had a lot of imagination and not enough to do. All right, I thought, you big pig, see if I ever tell you anything again. I sulked a bit, but he didn't notice. So then I remembered my headache from the drinks, and complained about it, which made him nice. I decided to remember that: If I'm sick, he'll be nice.

After that, the days went on as before. I walked and washed and heard the singer and saw the trays going up to her room. I never saw her. I never seemed to be around at the right time. She went to Vienna for a week, and the house was so empty I could have cried. Then she came back, and there was a great hustle on the staircase, maids running up and down carrying things to be pressed. Herr Enrich said that she was going home to America soon.

"Couldn't I just meet her before she goes?" I asked him. "Would you even just take her a note from me? Just a note?"

He explained all over again, as if I were a dim-witted child, that Miss West came to the farm in order to rest, and had given strict orders about intruders. "If I begin carrying messages," he said, "she will never come again."

"Maybe I could just leave a note in her door," I said. "Then it wouldn't be your fault."

"I cannot prevent you," Herr Enrich said.

I went up to my room and began writing notes. The final note said:

Dear Miss West, I am an American girl, the wife of an Occupation Forces sergeant. We live one floor down from you. I would like to tell you how much I have loved your singing and how much I have specially enjoyed "Herbsttag," the most beautiful song I have ever heard in my life, with sincere best wishes, Cecilia Rowe, Mrs. Walter T. Rowe.

I copied it out on the monogrammed paper my married sister had given me, and I went quietly up the stairs and pushed the note under Miss West's door. I waited around all day, but nothing happened. Walt came home, and then we went out to the movies with Laura and Marv. Laura told me in detail how to make a custard with brown-sugar sauce, even though she knew I never did any cooking at the farm. Marv and Laura seemed normal together — at least, they weren't fighting — and later on, when we were back at the farm, Walt reminded me of the story I'd tried to tell him about the nurse. "Laura's talk doesn't mean a thing," he said. "Girls always talk about their husbands."

"I don't," I said.

"Not yet," said Walt. He meant it for a joke, but I was hurt. When he came over to my bed that night, I pretended to be asleep. I felt wicked and deceitful. At the same time, I couldn't help being surprised at how easily it worked, and I was annoyed that he didn't try harder to wake me up. I was so confused about how I felt that I didn't know how to behave any more. In the morning, I sulked and didn't speak, but Walt didn't even notice. As soon as he had gone off to Salzburg, there was a telephone call from Laura. She asked me to come over right away. She said that she and Marv had had a terrible fight after the movies, and that she had tried to kill herself twice. I went in at once, and found her looking about the same as always. She had been drinking, and seemed restless and depressed. I stayed with her all day, and by midafternoon she had talked herself out and seemed calmer. She sat in a chair with her feet tucked up and sipped a glass of brandy. She had done talking about herself, and suddenly seemed ready to start in on me. She looked at me over the glass and said, "You don't look too well either, Cissy. Anything wrong?"

"No." I didn't want to tell her about Walt and the deceitful thing I had done. Besides, the whole story behind it — our marriage and Salzburg and my wanting a friend — was too complicated to explain.

But Laura kept on looking, and she laughed and said, "I'll bet you've started a baby."

I cried, "Oh, no, no, no! Don't say that."

Laura said, "Well, you will someday, you know. If you haven't already. You needn't be so upset."

"Oh," I cried, "I never will! Don't say that. I don't *want* to."

"Christ, you don't have to want it," Laura said. "Look at me. And look at the mess I'm in. If I hadn't had the baby, we wouldn't have needed a nurse. If we hadn't needed a nurse, Marv wouldn't have dared . . ."

She was off again, and, for once, I was glad, because it kept her from talking about me. A baby! My heart beat as if I had been running. How could I take care of a tiny baby when I wasn't ready to take care of myself, when I couldn't even wear high heels and dress like a grownup? All the way home, late that afternoon, I thought about it, and I realized what Walt's visits to my bed might mean. I don't know why I hadn't thought about it before. I'd taken it for granted that I was too young and unready, and that my real married life hadn't started, and that nothing would happen on that account. I knew better, of course. It was just that I hadn't given it much thought.

It was late November, and the days were short. When I arrived at the farm, it was already quite dark. I stood in the doorway, wiping my shoes on the mat, and looked through the hall into the dining room. There was Miss West's piano. There were the rabbity people and Mrs. de Kende, sitting by the stove. The lights were on. The clocks ticked. I could smell the *Sauerbraten* cooking for supper. It was the atmosphere of late evening, and I felt as if here, in this part of the world, one night ran into the next with no day in between. As I shut the door, Herr Enrich came toward me, smiling, holding out a pale blue envelope. I knew at once that it was from Miss West. I snatched it, and my hands shook so much that I tore into the note as well. It was a nice note, inviting me to have lunch with her the next day in her room. I folded the torn note carefully and put it back. I felt happy and curiously delivered. I thought: Here is someone whose room won't be dirty, who doesn't drink all day, who won't frighten me, *who hasn't got a husband.* The note had been friendly. I thought, I have a friend.

Herr Enrich stood there, waiting, curious. "I'm having lunch with Miss West," I told him. "Tomorrow, in her room." I wanted him to realize I had been right all along, that she had wanted to meet me.

"Tomorrow?" he said in his polite, smiling way. "That scarcely seems possible. Miss West has gone."

"Gone where?"

"To America," he said. "She took the afternoon train to Zurich. She flies from there."

"But she left me this note," I said. I can still see myself, somehow, as if I had been a spectator all along, standing in the hall with my camel's-hair coat and my cold bare legs and my childish bobby socks, looking at Herr Enrich, holding on to the pale blue note.

"The tomorrow was today," Herr Enrich said, as if the triumph were his after all. "She left the note for you yesterday. But you went out in the evening, and then again this morning." He spread his hands in mock despair, as if to say that I was always out.

I muttered stupidly, "But I never go out — " and then flew past him, up the stairs, up to her room. I flung open the door without knocking and turned on the light. A strong current from the window slammed the door behind me. The bed was stripped, the room was being aired. I opened the heavy wardrobe: a few hangers swayed on the crossbar. She had left nothing in the wardrobe, nothing in the chest of drawers. I went slowly down to my room and, in the darkened hall, saw Mrs. de Kende. She had come up from the dining room and was sitting quietly on a chair. Still sitting, she grabbed my arm and squeezed it.

"You told," she said.

"What?"

"About my husband. About his being — you know."

"I didn't," I said. "Leave me alone." I pulled away.

"He has just come in," she said in a low voice. "He has lost two clients in Salzburg, both the same day. There could only be one reason. They found out. You told."

"I didn't," I said again. "Leave me alone."

She didn't get hysterical but said quietly, "It is my fault. I wanted to trust someone. God is punishing me." She got up and went into her room.

I could feel my heart in my breast, as hard and cool as a pebble. I sat down where she had been, in the dark, until

I heard Walt come in. He spoke to Herr Enrich and then came up the stairs. "Walt," I said. He stopped, looking around, and I flung myself at him and cried, "She's gone, the singer has gone home, it's all over and I'll never meet her, I'll never have a friend!"

Faces appeared on the stairs — white, astonished faces. I had always been so quiet. Walt said to them, "It's all right," and he led me into our room. "Who's gone?" he said, shutting the door.

"The singer," I said. I leaned against him and wept and wept. "I wanted to meet her. I wanted terribly much to meet her. I'm sick of this house. I'm sick of the woman next door. I'm sick of Laura. I don't want a baby."

"Are you having a baby?" said Walt.

"I don't know." I pulled away and went over to the chest of drawers to find a handkerchief. I dried my eyes and blew my nose. Walt stood by the door, watching me. His arms hung at his sides. He looked helpless.

"Are you having a baby?" he said again.

"I told you, I don't know. I don't think so. It was just something Laura said."

"It might be a good thing for you," said Walt.

"You mean a good thing like having an apartment?" I combed my hair, tugging at it. I think I hated him at that moment. Then I caught sight of him in the mirror; he looked helpless, and unhappy, and I remembered what Marv had said — that I was the first girl Walt had taken seriously, and how his friends had never thought he'd get married. I wondered if he was sorry he'd got married, and, for the first time, I wondered if being married was as hard for him as for me.

In the next room, Mrs. de Kende was muttering — praying, I supposed. I felt guilty about her, in a vague way, as if I had let her down; as if I were really the one who had told about her husband. But that was just a momentary feeling. Mrs. de Kende was old and crazy, not a young girl like me. I began to dress to go out. Walt and I were having supper with Marv and Laura, and then we were going to the movies. I didn't want to spend my evening that way, but I felt there was no stopping things now, that I was married and had better take things as they came. The singer had gone. I'd have to manage without help, without a friend more important than Walt. I wondered if all of this — my crying, Walt being bewildered — was married life, not just the preliminary.

Walt moved away from the door and sat down on his bed. "What about this singer?" he said. "Was she going to give you lessons, or something?"

"It was just crazy," I said.

"You'll be all right, Cissy," he said. "Living out here has got you down."

"I know," I said. "When we get our own place." We looked briefly, almost timidly, at each other in the mirror, and I knew we were thinking the same thing: the apartment will make the difference; something's got to.

Your girlhood doesn't vanish overnight. I know, now, what a lot of wavering goes on, how you step forward and back again. The frontier is invisible; sometimes you're over without knowing it. I do know that some change began then, at that moment, and I felt an almost unbearable nostalgia for the figure I was leaving behind, the shell of the girl who had got down from the train in September, the pretty girl with all the blue plaid luggage. I could never be that girl again, not entirely. Too much had happened in between.

"We'll be all right," I echoed to Walt, and I repeated it to myself, over and over, "I'll be all right; we'll be all right."

But we're not safe yet, I thought, looking at my husband — this stranger, mute, helpless, fumbling, enclosed. Oh, we're not safe. Not by a long shot. But we'll be all right. Take my word for it. We'll be all right.

Poor Franzi

So HERE you are," said Franzi Ebendorf's grandmother.
She held out her sunburned hand to Elizabeth Dunn, but
her eyes were on her grandson. They settled down to the
table she had saved on the crowded hotel terrace, its floating white cover anchored in the wind by a jar of flowers.
She might have been waiting some time: bees swooped
familiarly at the jam, pollen had shaken down to the empty
plates. She had eaten nothing. The bread overlapped in its
basket, brown on white, and the cake was wrapped in linen,
like a well-made bed. She glanced at the table, and then
clapped her hands for the coffee.

The sound of it gave the people at the next table an excuse to turn. Their name was Wright, they were from Balti-
more, and they had been limp with curiosity ever since
Franzi's ramshackle roadster had turned off the winding
mountain road. Stranded in the Austrian mountains by the
hay fever of one of their party, they were spending a hot and
empty fortnight, with little to say. Spinning out the event
of their afternoon coffee, they had watched Baronin Eben-

dorf climbing up from the valley on foot, her rings blinking
in the sun a quarter mile to the hotel terrace.

"Well, look at that," young Coralie Wright had said to
her mother. "And we send *them* money!" This was not a
serious remark; it was intended only to tease and annoy an
English Miss Mewling to whom Coralie's brother, Charlie,
had unaccountably attached himself, and who now shared
their table and much of their day. Miss Mewling, wearing
the local costume worked in cross-stitch, sat up straighter
and remarked:

"It is possible that none of your country's money reaches
the Baronin. She is a very poor old lady who lives in a farmhouse in the valley. She lost everything in the war, and all
but two of her family. One of them lives in Salzburg, a
grandson, a thoroughly useless person. She waits for him
here every Sunday and he never comes."

"Maybe he doesn't have the bus fare," said Coralie.

"He is engaged to an American," said Miss Mewling, in
the treble tones of a member of the Royal Family delivering
an address over the air. "His young friend, although I can't
say that I know her, must be very foolish."

"It's easy for young girls to be carried away," said Mrs.
Wright, whose main difficulties on the journey had been
with Coralie and her sister Joan.

"And young men," said Coralie, looking hard at Charlie.
It had been Coralie's and her sister's wish to spend the summer alone in Europe, and it was no fault of theirs that the
party included their mother, a brother, and an elderly
cousin who had to lie down every day. "Miss Mewling
should be careful, too."

"I traveled with my father until his death," said Miss

Mewling, placid. "He was an excellent judge of character."

"I'm sure he was," said Mrs. Wright, now interested only in Baronin Ebendorf, who had placed herself at the next table, her cane resting on the bench beside her. "Just the same, I tell the girls, you have to be careful. Nowadays, they all want to marry Americans, just to get into the country. It's worse than the old fortune hunters. Someone in Paris even asked Coralie to have a *mariage blanc*, and promised to pay afterward for the divorce."

"She thought it meant being married in a church," Charlie said.

"I see," said Miss Mewling, who was not listening but frowning into the sun behind him. "That's him, the grandson," she said. "That's his car, the old thing that looks held together with string. That must be the girl with him."

"Are you sure?" Coralie said. "He's terribly good-looking. He looks sort of Danish. The girl looks like nothing." She sounded wistful and her mother glanced at her sharply.

"Most certainly not Danish," said Miss Mewling. "They all have a little Czech, although they deny it. And he has no manners." Pressed by Coralie, she admitted that although she and Franzi had been twice introduced, he never spoke. "He wouldn't behave that way if one cared, or took pains," said Miss Mewling. "But nowadays, who can afford that kind of nonsense?"

In a moment they were able to turn and stare at Elizabeth Dunn, who, evidently, could. Elizabeth was studying Franzi's grandmother and wondering what it would be like to take her to America and send her to live with her own parents up in Brewster. She tried to imagine the sunburned old creature with her ringed stubby hands reclining in a

garden chair while her mother talked about the rose cut-
tings. She smiled quickly at Franzi, as if they were sharing
the joke, but he had rolled a ladybug on its back and was
passively watching its struggles. She looked at the two,
Franzi and his grandmother, searching for physical likeness
and finding only the same measure of blandness and good
manners and something evasive that might be panic. She
often did this, weighing her marriage as if she had shopped
out of season for a costly and perishable fruit.

She had not chosen to fall in love any more than one
would choose the measles over a simple cold; but, as she
had written her worried parents, there it was. Happy, she
glanced around the sunny terrace, although her shortsighted
gaze could carry her no more than a few feet. Mistaking
for hostility the intent stare of myopia, the Wrights and
Miss Mewling, turned all at once like a coy chorus, were
swept back to their coffee cups, indignant.

"She's twenty-eight, at least," said Coralie. "At least
that." For some reason this pleased the table, and Miss
Mewling confided that to her certain knowledge, Franzi
was no more than twenty-three.

"I am very happy today," the Baronin was saying. "I am
so glad you like your ring. I gave it to Franzi for you, but I
was afraid you would find it old-fashioned."

"I love it," said Elizabeth. "I didn't know it was yours.
Franzi didn't say."

"I forgot," said Franzi, and smiled the smile, bemused
and distant, that caused people to call him at once by his
Christian name, and a diminutive at that. Elizabeth said
nothing: she had already decided that his motives were
none of her affair, that they must not at any cost embark

on an agglutinative relationship of sharing every thought. She could not complain about Franzi. He showed no desire to share her thoughts.

They finished their coffee and Franzi made the first move to go. While his grandmother paid, fishing for coins in a deep linen handbag, he released the ladybug and sent it through space, clinging to a leaf. Elizabeth frowned and pressed his feet under the table, meaning that perhaps he ought to pay. Misunderstanding the pressure, and the look, he stared across at her, taking notice for the first time. Sometimes she seemed to swim deliberately into the focus of his attention and he would look, eyes wide, as if perplexed at their being together. Elizabeth, who had read a great deal about love but was ignorant of its processes, found the look adorable. As they left the terrace she slipped her hand into his, which was observed by everyone but Coralie, who, when it was told to her, accidentally bit her tongue.

The three drove away in Franzi's rattling car and dropped the Baronin at the farmhouse where she boarded. "How nice it is," said Elizabeth, looking at the white-painted house with its broad carved balcony and flowering vines. "It must be quite old."

"Yes, old," said the Baronin, mistaking this for insult. Being old, the house was damp; the leaded vine-encumbered windows admitted chinks of greenish light. Winters, in the rainy season, the old woman remained in bed for days on end.

"We'll come again, whenever you like," Elizabeth promised. "And you must come into town, too, and let us take you to dinner." She kissed the Baronin, who, alarmed at the familiarity, glanced helplessly at Franzi. He bent down, permitting his grandmother to kiss him on the forehead, and then waited until she was indoors before driving away.

"She's wonderful," Elizabeth said into his ear, over the sound of the motor. "We should visit her often."

"She doesn't expect it," Franzi said.

It was one week after this, on a hot July evening, that Franzi learned of his grandmother's death. It had been painless, and nearly quick. She had died on Sunday morning, of a cerebral hemorrhage, at the hour when Franzi and Elizabeth were driving to St. Gilgen to swim. Her death was a mercy, the doctor said, for she might have lingered for years, blurred in speech and totally paralyzed. Franzi drove out to the farmhouse on Monday evening, after his grandmother had been removed, and sorted over her few belongings. There was a little money, and the deed to an old property near Mistelbach, in the Russian zone. He had already decided that in order to survive he must not encumber himself, and he kindled a small fire in the stove that stood against the wall and committed the paper to it.

There was little else to salvage: the good pieces of jewelry had been sold, and there were only useless stones left, in old-fashioned settings. He gathered them into a handkerchief and put the handkerchief in his pocket. There were photographs of his grandparents, of his father, of his sister Adelaide and himself as children in the garden at Landeck, before the house that had received a direct bomb hit while his father and mother sat in the dining room, with nothing to eat. His sister had married and gone to Australia, and she had not written to anyone for three years. Her husband farmed, her children were called Ian and Doreen, and she

would have left them all in a minute had there been anywhere else to go.

After he had burned the pictures, and a package of letters
he did not trouble to read, he found a photograph in a silver
frame of his grandmother's sister as a girl. She sat in a
high-backed chair, dressed in a striped taffeta frock that
stopped short of her buttoned boots. Her hair was held
back by a ribbon as big as her head, and she clasped her
hands palm upward, as if she expected something to fall
into them. He struggled with the picture for a while, but
it was held fast, and he finally carried it away as it was.

He was on his way out when the farmer's wife, Frau
Stangl, with whom his grandmother had lived, stopped him
and mentioned the funeral. It was to be on Wednesday;
she and her husband had made all the arrangements, even
to remembering that the Baronin was Protestant, and she
hoped he was pleased with what they had done. Franzi
assured her that whatever she had planned was quite all
right. Frau Stangl twisted her apron in her hands like a
child and whispered that there had been expenses. Considering, Franzi selected from the handkerchief a garnet
brooch and a pair of earrings and said he expected that
would cover everything. At this Frau Stangl began to cry.

"I'll keep them," she said. "I couldn't sell them. It
wouldn't be right."

"As you like," said Franzi, and hurried away.

He drove straight to Elizabeth, who expressed concern,
sympathy, and even cried a little when he gave her a ring
and a locket and the picture of his great-aunt. She looked
at the picture and said: "You have no one now in the world
but me." She asked about the funeral and then, to spare
him, said no more.

The two spent their working hours on opposite sides of Salzburg. Elizabeth, who had a temporary job with the American occupation forces, sat under a tiring light in one of the gray buildings ringing the Mozartplatz. Franzi was connected in the loosest imaginable manner with a firm that sold electrical comforts in the bombed vicinity of the railway station. The firm was in chronic difficulties, what with Austrian factories producing too little, and American things costing too much, and no one in Austria being able to afford thirty-part vacuum cleaners or caring much for jump-up toasters.

"It's different for you," Franzi's partner, Herr Rattner, often said, mournful. "By Christmas you'll be in America." Fortunately, that week someone was coming in to see about electric heaters for a hospital and Franzi's name, usually of no more utility than Schneider or Schmidt, might be helpful. "You talk to them," Herr Rattner said. "I am ill." He went into his office and arranged himself tenderly on a couch. He admired American business practices and copied behavior he had seen in films: he would have liked a switchboard and a girl like Betty Grable in *Rosies Skandalchronik*, but there was only Franzi.

Elizabeth chose that moment to ring up. She seldom did this from her office, for her alliance was not approved of, and more than one person of authority had taken her to lunch and counseled second thoughts.

"I've arranged for time off this afternoon," she said to Franzi. "I'd like to go to the funeral with you, if I may."

He was about to ask, "What funeral?" but then he remembered and said, "It's terrible, but I can't go."

"Is anything wrong?"

"No." With his free hand he worked open a package of

American cigarettes and pulled one out. "No. I just can't get away."

"I've never heard of such a thing. Did you explain to Mr. Rattner?"

"Yes. Are you laughing at something?"

"No," said Elizabeth, shocked. "Although I was thinking . . . it's a joke, in English I mean, about going to one's grandmother's funeral."

"I see," said Franzi. Not seeing, he nonetheless smiled politely.

"I can't understand Mr. Rattner," Elizabeth said. Out of the misty workings of the firm, she had somehow identified their relationship as employer and employee. "Look, where is the funeral?"

"Just a moment," Franzi said. "Someone came in." He put down the telephone and crossed to the office where Herr Rattner was lying down. He leaned into the room. "Where is my grandmother's funeral?"

"Your what?" They regarded each other soberly.

"She lived near Elsbethen," Franzi said.

"Then she'll be buried there. You're not leaving me today, are you?"

"No." He closed the door quietly and picked up the telephone. "Elsbethen," he said. "It's a little old church. We've passed it in the car."

"Yes. I think I know." Embarrassed, she paused, and said, "If you can't go, perhaps I ought to. I mean, I'd like to."

"That would be nice of you."

"Unless you'd rather I didn't." It had occurred to her that he might not want strangers about: all morning she had thought about the world that separated them and how his family, all of them, had moved into an increasingly desolate landscape, saying that things were changing, until there was only Franzi left to know that now things had changed. "My poor Franzi," she said.

He had been looking for a match and now found one in a desk drawer. "It would be nice if you could go," he repeated. He was suddenly conscious that the day was hot, and that he had had no lunch: counting his money that morning, he had been able to put together only enough to take Elizabeth to dinner. He was about to add that she might enjoy the funeral, for he often committed these absurdities in conversation, following only the rhythm of the sentences and thinking all the while of something else. He was at that moment looking at a sample electric heater that stood on his desk, and thinking, to no purpose, that the rate of exchange between the dollar and the schilling was thirty-three at the hotel down the street, and that the Jews before the bombed-out church gave only thirty.

"Well," said Elizabeth, still hesitating, not wishing to be tactless, "I'll call you again when I get back. Are you sure you don't mind? It's just that I think that someone, that one of us . . ." Feeling foolish, she at last said goodbye.

Up at the hotel, the Wrights and Miss Mewling had decided to attend the funeral of Baronin Ebendorf. Their visit nearly at an end, they were badly on each other's nerves and it seemed a neutral enough excursion. They were not exactly strangers to the Ebendorfs for, as Miss Mewling once more pointed out, she and Franzi had been twice introduced.

The hotel was full of gossip about Franzi, how his grand-

mother had lain speechless and unmoving for two days,
looking at the door through which he might, but did not,
appear: how he had stolen her jewelry and burned her will.
Conscience-stricken, he had given the Stangls, who had
cared for the old lady until her death, a trinket of no value.
One could only guess what the vanished testament had
willed to them.

All of this had been passed up the mountain to the
chambermaids and on to the Wrights. "Can you imagine?"
they asked one another. "He hasn't done one solitary thing
about the funeral, hasn't sent flowers, just left everything to
those poor peasants!" They wondered how he would behave, and Coralie, in fancy, exchanged with him a long
look of understanding over the open grave. "It's a good
thing we're going," Coralie said. "The hotelier said he was
glad we were going because they have no family here."
Starting down the mountain, each of them saw the abandoned churchyard and the minister at his lonely task, reading prayers with no one to hear.

This thought, and this curiosity, drew together in the
cemetery more than a dozen persons, among them Elizabeth. Her arrival caused a disturbed murmur, for the
Stangls, who were providing the funeral, stood a little forward of the rest, replacing next of kin. They wondered if
they should move away for Elizabeth: they had paid for the
funeral out of helplessness and decency, and they felt, momentarily, cheated of their small acquittance. Nervous,
they faced the coffin that lay on the path before the church,
the flames of the candles at its four corners stretching and
diminishing in the wind. Elizabeth unwittingly settled the
matter by stepping behind them in order to remove herself

from the Wrights, whose milky looks of kindness displeased
and confused her. Frau Stangl, vindicated, smoothed her
black cotton gloves.

A Protestant, the Baronin could not be buried from the
church: her coffin lay on the ground covered with a lacy
shawl, marked with the wax of other candles and other
deaths. The Lutheran minister, who had been fetched
from another town, droned unfamiliar words in German.
"*Du, Augusta Adelaide,*" he said coldly, looking over his
prayer book to the coffin. Frau Stangl stared around the
churchyard, at the decorated wrought-iron crosses, and began to cry.

So that was her name, Elizabeth thought. Ever since
Franzi had given her the picture of his great-aunt, without
troubling to identify it, she had struggled to connect the
clear-eyed girl in the taffeta dress with Baronin Ebendorf
pouring coffee, her rings crammed together as if she dared
leave nothing in her room. What had happened between,
thickened the eyelids, thinned the mouth, she could not
have said: age, of course, and trouble, and fear. Of these
Franzi had had his share, all but the age. She thought of
the sister who never wrote, and the solitariness that had
separated him even from his grandmother; nothing else
must ever happen to him, now that he has me, she told
herself. On the wall of the church, beside which they stood,
evergreen wreaths hung on pegs, stirring in the wind. They
looked like Christmas garlands, inwoven with berries; she
guessed that the local people had made them and she
wondered which of them Franzi had sent.

The row of mourners stirred. Coralie tied the streamers
of her lacy black hat and prodded Joanie, who wore dark

glasses, as if she had been crying hard. They looked at Elizabeth who had not seen the four pall bearers pick up the coffin and, as the little procession circled once around the churchyard, found herself crowded into the Stangls. The procession was trailed by fair-haired school children, pious frauds, who had passed the cemetery on an errand and seen something of interest going on. They ringed the grave, and Elizabeth, peering blindly, decided that the Baronin had had strange friends: peasants and school children and well-dressed Americans.

The coffin was lowered. One by one the mourners shook earth on it from a shovel, shuddering at the noise it made. Coralie Wright wiped her eyes: they were going to Italy in two days and then home, and she had had no fun at all. "We might as well be dead," she said to her sister.

Miss Mewling, who had disapproved of the proceedings from start to end looked coldly at Coralie and said aloud, "She was the end of a good line. We have buried a way of life."

"Oh, Miss Mewling," said Mrs. Wright, distressed. She had seen in the funeral a morbid foretaste of her own. Only Charlie, who had stopped speaking to his family because of Miss Mewling, had nothing to say. They filed by the Stangls, who shook everyone's hand, as if they were guests leaving a party. Elizabeth said soberly, "You have been very kind." She felt nearly as if she ought to make some excuse for Franzi. Frau Stangl, wearing the garnet brooch, brimmed over and sobbed. "Such a sweet little churchyard! She would have loved it!"

"I know, I know," said Elizabeth, not understanding. They must have loved her very much, she thought.

She could not wait the twenty minutes that separated her from Salzburg to speak to Franzi, and she called him from the inn that was also a bus stop. The telephone rang a long time and then it was answered by Herr Rattner. "Moment," he said. As a door was opened and shut she heard a burst of laughter: Herr Rattner's cinematic business methods were in full flower and glasses clinked and the man who had come to see about electric heaters was telling them a funny story.

"Franzi!" Elizabeth cried. It surprised her a little that he sounded so cheerful.

"I can't hear you," he said. "You sound queer."

She had wanted to say: I'm sorry that your grandmother did not inherit the earth, as had been arranged, but was buried instead by a few peasants and some tourists. But an American sergeant stood shuffling behind her, waiting to use the telephone, and she said instead, "I'm not going back to work. Meet me at the terminal by the railway station and we'll go somewhere and talk. It's right near your office."

"But I can't leave today," he said. "I told you, remember?"

"I wish you could meet me for a few minutes," she said. "The funeral upset me a little. About you, I mean."

"About me?" Then he said, "Oh, the funeral! So you went! Well, my little conscience."

"I wanted to go," she said. Her voice rose.

"You mustn't be upset," he said. There were voices behind him, and she finally said quickly:

"It's all right. I'll see you when you're free."

After she had put up the telephone she walked out to the highway to wait for her bus. The Wrights sat together at a

round painted table, drinking apple juice. They were waiting for a taxi: although it would be expensive, they were
unable to find their way about on foot, even with Miss
Mewling to guide them. "Blind as a bat," said Coralie, as
Elizabeth walked straight past them.

She was frowning. It had not been her intention to be
the little conscience of anyone, and only her pity for Franzi
excused her from being angry or even hurt. Did he not
want me to go? she wondered. Far down the road she heard
the rattle of the ancient bus and she looked around the
country, at the hazy summer mountains, as if she had been
told she was never to see them again. Behind the solid
peaks were softer shapes, shifting and elusive: she could not
have said if they were clouds or mountains. But then, she
thought, no one can, unless they have better eyes than
mine, and know the country very well. She settled into the
bus and closed her eyes. What will happen to me if I marry
him? she wondered; and what would become of Franzi if
she were to leave him? Now, as she had fifty times in her
own room at Salzburg, she eliminated one by one a parade
of hazards and arrived, restored, to the place where he
would not be waiting.

"You should have heard the way she talked to him on the
phone." said Coralie. "I was right near, trying to get cigarettes. She was practically ordering him, on the day of his
grandmother's funeral. Poor Franzi."

"Poor both of them," said Mrs. Wright, and she looked
at the dust where Elizabeth had vanished, at the sheltering
haze, and the landscape that none of them knew.

Going Ashore

At Tangier it was surprisingly cold, even for December. The sea was lead, the sky cloudy and low. Most of the passengers going ashore for the day came to breakfast wrapped in scarves and sweaters. They were, most of them, thin-skinned, elderly people, less concerned with the prospect of travel than with getting through another winter in relative comfort; on bad days, during the long crossing from the West Indies, they had lain in deck chairs, muffled as mummies, looking stricken and deceived. When Emma Ellenger came into the breakfast lounge barelegged, in sandals, wearing a light summer frock, there was a low flurry of protest. Really, Emma's mother should take more care! The child would catch her death.

Feeling the disapproval almost as an emanation, like the salt one breathed in the air, Emma looked around for someone who liked her — Mr. Cowan, or the Munns. There were the Munns, sitting in a corner, frowning over their toast, coffee, and guidebooks. She waved, although they had not yet seen her, threaded her way between the closely spaced tables, and, without waiting to be asked, sat down.

Miss and Mrs. Munn looked up with a single movement. They were daughter and mother, but so identically frizzy, tweedy, and elderly that they might have been twins. Mrs. Munn, the kindly twin, gazed at Emma with benevolent, rather popping brown eyes, and said, "Child, you'll freeze in that little dress. Do tell your mother — now, don't forget to tell her — that the North African winter can be treacherous, very treacherous indeed." She tapped one of the brown paper-covered guidebooks that lay beside her coffee tray. The Munns always went ashore provided with books, maps, and folders telling them what to expect at every port of call. They differed in every imaginable manner from Emma and her mother, who seldom fully understood where they were and who were often daunted and upset (particularly Mrs. Ellenger) if the people they encountered ashore were the wrong color or spoke an unfamiliar language.

"You should wear a thick scarf," Mrs. Munn went on, "and warm stockings." Thinking of the Ellengers' usual wardrobe, she paused, discouraged. "The most important parts of the — " But she stopped again, unable to say "body" before a girl of twelve. "One should keep the throat and the ankles warm," she said, lowering her gaze to her book.

"We can't," Emma said respectfully. "We didn't bring anything for the cruise except summer dresses. My mother thought it would be warm all the time."

"She should have inquired," Miss Munn said. Miss Munn was crisper, taut; often the roles seemed reversed, and it appeared that she, of the two, should have been the mother.

"I guess she didn't think," Emma said, cast down by all the things her mother failed to do. Emma loved the Munns. It was distressing when, as now, they failed to approve of her. They were totally unlike the people she was accustomed to, with their tweeds, their pearls, their strings of fur that bore the claws and muzzles of some small, flattened beast. She had fallen in love with them the first night aboard, during the first dinner out. The Munns and the Ellengers had been seated together, the dining-room steward having thought it a good plan to group, at a table for four, two solitary women and their solitary daughters.

The Munns had been so kind, so interested, asking any number of friendly questions. They wondered how old Emma was, and where Mr. Ellenger might be ("In Heaven," said Emma, casual), and where the Ellengers lived in New York.

"We live all over the place." Emma spoke up proudly. It was evident to her that her mother wasn't planning to say a word. *Somebody* had to be polite. "Most of the time we live in hotels. But last summer we didn't. We lived in an apartment. A big apartment. It wasn't our place. It belongs to this friend of my mother's, Mr. Jimmy Salter, but he was going to be away, and the rent was paid anyway, and we were living there already, so he said — he said — " She saw her mother's face and stopped, bewildered.

"That was nice," said Mrs. Munn, coloring. Her daughter looked down, smiling mysteriously.

Emma's mother said nothing. She lit a cigarette and blew the smoke over the table. She wore a ring, a wedding band, a Mexican necklace, and a number of clashing bracelets. Her hair, which was long and lighter even than Emma's, had been carefully arranged, drawn into a tight chignon and circled with flowers. Clearly it was not for Miss or Mrs. Munn that she had taken such pains; she had expected a different table arrangement, one that included a man. Infinitely obliging, Mrs. Munn wished that one of them were a man. She bit her lip, trying to find a way out of this unexpected social thicket. Turning to Emma, she said, a little wildly, "Do you like school? I mean I see you are not in school. Have you been ill?"

Emma ill? The idea was so outrageous, so clearly a criticism of Mrs. Ellenger's care, that she was forced, at last, to take notice of this pair of frumps. "There's nothing the matter with my daughter's health," she said a little too loudly. "Emma's never been sick a day. From the time she was born, she's had the best of everything — the best food, the best clothes, the best that money can buy. Emma, isn't that right?"

Emma said yes, hanging her head and wishing her mother would stop.

"Emma was born during the war," Mrs. Ellenger said, dropping her voice. The Munns looked instantly sympathetic. They waited to hear the rest of the story, some romantic misadventure doomed by death or the fevered nature of the epoch itself. Mrs. Munn puckered her forehead, as if already she were prepared to cry. But evidently that part of the story had ceased to be of interest to Emma's mother. "I had a nervous breakdown when she was born," Mrs. Ellenger said. "I had plenty of troubles. My God, troubles!" Brooding, she suddenly dropped her cigarette into the dregs of her coffee cup. At the sound it made, the two ladies winced. Their glances crossed. Noticing, Emma wondered what her mother had done now. "I never took my troubles out on Emma," Mrs. Ellenger said. "No, Emma had the best, always the best. I brought her up like a little lady. I kept her all in white — white shoes, white blankets, white bunny coats, white hand-knitted angora bonnets. When she started to walk, she had little white rubbers for the rain. I got her a white buggy with white rubber tires. During the *war*, this was. Emma, isn't it true? Didn't you see your pictures, all in white?"

Emma moved her lips.

"It was the very best butter," Miss Munn murmured.

"She shows your care," Mrs. Munn said gently. "She's a lovely girl."

Emma wanted to die. She looked imploringly at her mother, but Mrs. Ellenger rushed on. It was important, deeply important, that everyone understand what a good mother she had been. "Nobody has to worry about Emma's school, either," she said. "I teach her, so nobody has to worry at all. Emma loves to study. She reads all the time. Just before dinner tonight, she was reading. She was reading Shakespeare. Emma, weren't you reading Shakespeare?"

"I had this book," Emma said, so low that her answer was lost. The Munns began to speak about something else, and Emma's mother relaxed, triumphant.

In truth, Emma had been reading Shakespeare. While they were still unpacking and settling in, she had discovered among their things a battered high school edition of *The Merchant of Venice*. Neither she nor her mother had ever seen it before. It was in the suitcase that contained Mrs. Ellenger's silver evening slippers and Emma's emergency supply of comic books. Emma opened the book and read, "You may do so; but let it be so hasted that supper be ready at the farthest by five of the clock." She closed the book and dropped it. "It must have come from Uncle Jimmy Salter's place," she said. "The maid must have put it in when she helped us pack." "I didn't know he could read," Mrs. Ellenger said. She and Mr. Salter had stopped being friends. "We'll mail it back sometime. It'll be a nice surprise."

Of course, they had never mailed the book. Now, at Tangier, it was still with them, wedged between the comic books and the silver slippers. It had never occurred to Emma's mother to give the book to a steward, or the purser, still less take it ashore during an excursion; the mechanics of wrapping and posting a parcel from a strange port were quite beyond her. The cruise, as far as she was concerned, had become a series of hazards; attempting to dispatch a volume of Shakespeare would have been the last straw. She was happy, or at least not always *un*happy, in a limited area of the ship — the bar, the beauty salon, and her own cabin. As long as she kept to this familiar, hotel-like circuit, there was almost no reason to panic. She had never before been at sea, and although she was not sickened by the motion of the ship, the idea of space, of endless leagues of water, perplexed, then frightened, then, finally, made her ill. It had come to her, during the first, dismal dinner out, that her life as a pretty young woman was finished. There were no men on board — none, at least, that would do — and even if there had been, it was not at all certain that any of them would have desired her. She saw herself flung into an existence that included the Munns, censorious, respectable, prying into one's affairs. At that moment, she had realized what the cruise would mean: She was at sea. She was adrift on an ocean whose immenseness she could not begin to grasp. She was alone, she had no real idea of their route, and it was too late to turn back. Embarking on the cruise had been a gesture, directed against the person Emma called Uncle Jimmy Salter. Like any such gesture, it had to be carried through, particularly since it had been received with total indifference, even relief.

Often, even now, with twenty-four days of the cruise behind and only twenty more to be lived through, the fears she had experienced the first evening would recur: She was at sea, alone. There was no one around to tip stewards, order drinks, plan the nights, make love to her, pay the bills, tell her where she was and what it was all about. How had this happened? However had she mismanaged her life to such a degree? She was still young. She looked at herself in the glass and, covering the dry, darkening skin below her eyes, decided she was still pretty. Perplexed, she went to the beauty salon and had her hair washed by a sympathetic girl, a good listener. Then, drugged with heat, sated with shared confidences, she wandered out to the first-class bar and sat at her own special stool. Here the sympathetic girl was replaced by Eddy, the Eurasian bartender from Hong Kong. Picking up the thread of her life, Mrs. Ellenger talked to Eddy, describing her childhood and her step-mother. She told him about Emma's father, and about the time she and Emma went to California. Talking, she tried to pretend she was in New York and that the environment of the ship was perfectly normal and real. She played with her drink, smiling anxiously at herself in the mirror behind the bar.

Eddy wasn't much of an audience, because he had other things to do, but after a time Mrs. Ellenger became so engrossed in her own recital, repeating and recounting the errors that had brought her to this impasse, that she scarcely noticed at all.

"I was a mere child, Eddy," she said. "A child. What did I know about life?"

"You can learn a lot about life in a job like mine," Eddy said. Because he was half Chinese, Eddy's customers expected him to deliver remarks tinged with Oriental wisdom. As a result, he had got into the habit of saying anything at all as if it were important.

"Well, I got Emma out of it all." Mrs. Ellenger never seemed to hear Eddy's remarks. "I've got my Emma. That's something. She's a big girl, isn't she, Eddy? Would you take her for only twelve? Some people take her for fourteen. They take us for sisters."

"The Dolly Sisters," Eddy said, esconced on a reputation that had him not only a sage but a scream.

"Well, I never try to pass Emma off as my sister," Mrs. Ellenger went on. "Oh, it's not that I couldn't. I mean enough people have told me. And I was a mere child myself when she was born. But I don't care if they know she's my daughter. I'm *proud* of my Emma. She was born during the war. I kept her all in white . . ."

Her glass slid away, reminding her that she was not in New York but at sea. It was no use. She thought of the sea, of travel, of being alone; the idea grew so enormous and frightening that, at last, there was nothing to do but go straight to her cabin and get into bed, even if it was the middle of the day. Her head ached and so did her wrists. She took off her heavy jewelry and unpinned her hair. The cabin was gray, chintzed, consolingly neutral; it resembled all or any of the hotel rooms she and Emma had shared in the past. She was surrounded by her own disorder, her own scent. There were yesterday's clothes on a chair, trailing, smelling faintly of cigarette smoke. There, on the dressing table, was an abandoned glass of brandy, an unstoppered bottle of cologne.

She rang the service bell and sent someone to look for Emma.

"Oh, Emma, darling," she said when Emma, troubled and apprehensive, came in. "Emma, why did we come on this crazy cruise? I'm so unhappy, Emma."

"I don't know," Emma said. "I don't know why we came at all." Sitting on her own bed, she picked up her doll and played with its hair or its little black shoes. She had outgrown dolls as toys years before, but this doll, which had no name, had moved about with her as long as she could remember. She knew that her mother expected something from this winter voyage, some miracle, but the nature of the miracle was beyond her. They had shopped for the cruise all summer — Emma remembered that — but when she thought of those summer weeks, with Uncle Jimmy Salter away, and her mother sulking and upset, she had an impression of heat and vacancy, as if no one had been contained in the summer season but Mrs. Ellenger and herself. Left to themselves, she and her mother had shopped; they had bought dresses and scarves and blouses and bathing suits and shoes of every possible color. They bought hats to match the dresses and bags to match the shoes. The boxes the new clothes had come in piled up in the living room, spilling tissue.

"Is he coming back?" Emma had asked once.

"I'm not waiting for *him* to make up *his* mind," her mother had said, which was, to Emma, scarcely an answer at all. "I've got my life, too. I mean," she amended, "we have, Emma. We've got a life, too. We'll go away. We'll go on a cruise or something."

"Maybe he'd like that," Emma had said, with such innocent accuracy that her mother, presented with the thought, stared at her, alarmed. "Then he could have the place all to himself."

In November, they joined the cruise. They had come aboard wearing summer dresses, confident in the climate promised by travel posters — the beaches, the blue-painted seas, the painted-yellow suns. Their cabin was full of luggage and flowers. Everything was new — their white bags, the clothes inside them, neatly folded, smelling of shops.

"It's a new life, Emma," said Mrs. Ellenger.

Emma had caught some of the feeling, for at last they were doing something together, alone, with no man, no Uncle Anyone, to interfere. She felt intensely allied to her mother, then and for several days after. But then, when it became certain that the miracle, the new life, had still to emerge, the feeling disappeared. Sometimes she felt it again just before they reached land — some strange and unexplored bit of coast, where anything might happen. The new life was always there, just before them, like a note indefinitely suspended or a wave about to break. It was there, but nothing happened.

All this, Emma sensed without finding words, even in her mind, to give the idea form. When her mother, helpless and lost, asked why they had come, she could only sit on her bed, playing with her doll's shoe, and, embarrassed by the spectacle of such open unhappiness, murmur, "I don't know. I don't know why we came at all."

Answers and explanations belonged to another language, one she had still to acquire. Even now, in Tangier, longing to explain to the Munns about the summer dresses, she knew she had better not begin. She knew that there must be a simple way of putting these things in words, but when Mrs. Munn spoke of going ashore, of the importance of keeping the throat and ankles warm, it was not in Emma's grasp to explain how it had come about that although she and her mother had shopped all summer and had brought with them much more luggage than they needed, it now developed that they had nothing to wear.

"Perhaps we shall see you in Tangier, later today," said Mrs. Munn. "You must warn your mother about Tangier. Tell her to watch her purse."

Emma nodded vigorously. "I'll tell her."

"And tell her to be careful about the food if you lunch ashore," Mrs. Munn said, beginning to gather together her guidebooks. "No salads. No fruit. Only bottled water. Above all, no native restaurants."

"I'll tell her," Emma said again.

After the Munns had departed, she sat for a moment, puzzled. Certainly they would be lunching in Tangier. For the first time, now she remembered something. The day before (or had it been the day before that?) Emma had invited Eddy, the bartender, to meet them in Tangier for lunch. She had extended the invitation with no sense of what it involved, and no real concept of place and time. North Africa was an imaginary place, half desert, half jungle. Then, this morning, she had looked through the porthole above her bed. There was Tangier, humped and yellowish, speckled with houses, under a wintry sky. It was not a jungle but a city, real. Now the two images met and blended. Tangier was a real place, and somewhere in those piled-up city blocks was Eddy, waiting to meet them for lunch.

She got up at once and hurried back to the cabin. The lounge was clearing; the launch, carrying passengers ashore across the short distance that separated them from the harbor, had been shuttling back and forth since nine o'clock.

Emma's mother was up, and — miracle — nearly dressed. She sat at the dressing table, pinning an artificial camellia into her hair. She did not turn around when Emma came in but frowned at herself in the glass, concentrating. Her dress was open at the back. She had been waiting for Emma to come and do it up. Emma sat down on her own bed. In honor of the excursion ashore, she was wearing gloves, a hat, and carrying a purse. Waiting, she sorted over the contents of her purse (a five-dollar bill, a St. Christopher medal, a wad of Kleenex, a comb in a plastic case), pulled on her small round hat, smoothed her gloves, sighed.

Her mother looked small and helpless, struggling with the awkward camellia. Emma never pitied her when she suffered — it was too disgraceful, too alarming — but she sometimes felt sorry for some detail of her person; now she was touched by the thin veined hands fumbling with flower and pins, and the thin shoulder blades that moved like wings. Her pity took the form of exasperation; it made her want to get up and do something crazy and rude — slam a door, say all the forbidden words she could think of. At last, Mrs. Ellenger stood up, nearly ready. But, no, something had gone wrong.

"Emma, I can't go ashore like this," her mother said. She sat down again. "My dress is wrong. My shoes are wrong. Look at my eyes. I look old. Look at my figure. Before I had you, my figure was wonderful. Never have a baby, Emma. Promise me."

"O.K.," Emma said. She seized the moment of pensive distraction — her mother had a dreamy look, which meant she was thinking of her pretty, fêted youth — and fastened her mother's dress. "You look lovely," Emma said rapidly. "You look just beautiful. The Munns said to tell you to dress warm, but it isn't cold. Please, let's go. Please, let's hurry. All the other people have gone. Listen, we're in *Africa*."

"That's what so crazy," Mrs. Ellenger said, as if at last she had discovered the source of all her grievances. "What am I doing in Africa?"

"Bring a scarf for your head," said Emma. "Please, let's go."

They got the last two places in the launch. Mrs. Ellenger bent and shuddered and covered her eyes; the boat was a terrible ordeal, windy and smelling of oil. She felt chilled and vomitous. "Oh, Emma," she moaned.

Emma put an arm about her, reassuring. "It's only a minute," she said. "We're nearly there now. Please look up. Why don't you look? The sun's come out."

"I'm going to be sick," Mrs. Ellenger said.

"No, you're not."

At last they were helped ashore, and stood, brushing their wrinkled skirts, on the edge of Tangier. Emma decided she had better mention Eddy right away.

"Wouldn't it be nice if we sort of ran into Eddy?" she

said. "He knows all about Tangier. He's been here before. He could take us around."

"Run into *who*?" Mrs. Ellenger took off the scarf she had worn in the launch, shook it, folded it, and put it in her purse. Just then, a light wind sprang up from the bay. With a little moan, Mrs. Ellenger opened her bag and took out the scarf. She seemed not to know what to do with it, and finally clutched it to her throat. "I'm so cold," she said. "Emma, I've never been so cold in my whole life. Can't we get away from here? Isn't there a taxi or something?"

Some of their fellow passengers were standing a short distance away in a sheeplike huddle, waiting for a guide from a travel bureau to come and fetch them. They were warmly dressed. They carried books, cameras, and maps. Emma suddenly thought of how funny she and her mother must look, alone and baffled, dressed for a summer excursion. Mrs. Ellenger tottered uncertainly on high white heels.

"I think if we just walk up to that big street," Emma said, pointing. "I even see taxis. Don't worry. It'll be all right." Mrs. Ellenger looked back, almost wistfully, to the cruise ship; it was, at least, familiar. "Don't look *that* way," said Emma. "Look where we're going. Look at Africa."

Obediently, Mrs. Ellenger looked at Africa. She saw hotels, an avenue, a row of stubby palms. As Emma had said, there were taxis, one of which, at their signals, rolled out of a rank and drew up before them. Emma urged her mother into the cab and got in after her.

"We might run into Eddy," she said again.

Mrs. Ellenger saw no reason why, on this particular day, she should be forced to think about Eddy. She started to

say so, but Emma was giving the driver directions, telling
him to take them to the center of town. "But what if we
did see Eddy?" Emma asked.

"Will you stop that?" Mrs. Ellenger cried. "Will you
stop that about Eddy? If we see him, we see him. I guess
he's got the same rights ashore as anyone else!"

Emma found this concession faintly reassuring. It did
not presage an outright refusal to be with Eddy. She
searched her mind for some sympathetic reference to him
— the fact, for instance, that he had two children named
Wilma and George — but, glancing sidelong at her mother,
decided to say nothing more. Mrs. Ellenger had admitted
Eddy's rights, a point that could be resurrected later, in
case of trouble. They were driving uphill, between houses
that looked, Emma thought, neither interesting nor African. It was certainly not the Africa she had imaged the day
she invited Eddy — a vista of sand dunes surrounded by
jungle, full of camels, lions, trailing vines. It was hard now
to remember just why she had asked him, or if, indeed, she
really had. It had been morning. The setting was easy to
reconstruct. She had been the only person at the bar; she
was drinking an elaborate mixture of syrup and fruit con-
cocted by Eddy. Eddy was wiping glasses. He wore a white
coat, from the pocket of which emerged the corner of a
colored handkerchief. The handkerchief was one of a dozen
given him by a kind American lady met on a former cruise;
it bore his name, embroidered in a dashing hand. Emma
had been sitting, admiring the handkerchief, thinking about
the hapless donor ("She found me attractive, et cetera, et
cetera," Eddy had once told her, looking resigned) when
suddenly Eddy said something about Tangier, the next port,

and Emma had imagined the three of them together —
herself, her mother, and Eddy.

"My mother wants you to go ashore with us in Africa,"
she had said, already convinced this was so.

"What do you mean, ashore?" Eddy said. "Take you
around, meet you for lunch?" There was nothing unusual
in the invitation, as such; Eddy was a great favorite with
many of his clients. "It's funny she never mentioned it."

"She forgot," Emma said. "We don't know anyone in
Africa, and my mother always likes company."

"I know *that*," Eddy said softly, smiling to himself. With
a little shovel, he scooped almonds into glass dishes. "What
I mean is your mother actually said" — and here he imi-
tated Mrs. Ellenger, his voice going plaintive and high —
" 'I'd just adore having dear Eddy as our guest for lunch.'
She actually said that?"

"Oh, Eddy!" Emma had to laugh so hard at the very idea
that she doubled up over her drink. Eddy could be so witty
when he wanted to be, sending clockwork spiders down the
bar, serving drinks in trick glasses that unexpectedly
dripped on people's clothes! Sometimes, watching him
being funny with favorite customers, she would laugh until her stomach ached.

"I'll tell you what," Eddy said, having weighed the invitation. "I'll meet you *in* Tangier. I can't go ashore with
you, I mean — not in the same launch; I have to go with
the crew. But I'll meet you there."

"Where'll you meet us?" Emma said. "Should we pick
a place?"

"Oh, I'll find you," Eddy said. He set his plates of almonds at spaced intervals along the bar. "Around the

center of town. I know where you'll go." He smiled again his secret, superior smile.

They had left it at that. Had Eddy really said the center of town, Emma wondered now, or had she thought that up herself? Had the whole scene, for that matter, taken place, or had she thought that up, too? No, it was real, for, their taxi having deposited them at the Plaza de Francia, Eddy at once detached himself from the crowd on the street and came toward them.

Eddy was dapper. He wore a light suit and a square-shouldered topcoat. He closed their taxi door and smiled at Emma's mother, who was paying the driver.

"Look," Emma said. "Look who's here!"

Emma's mother moved over to a shopwindow and became absorbed in a display of nylon stockings; presented with a *fait accompli*, she withdrew from the scene — turned her back, put on a pair of sunglasses, narrowed her interest to a single stocking draped on a chrome rack. Eddy seemed unaware of tension. He carried several small parcels, his purchases. Jauntily he joined Mrs. Ellenger at the window.

"This is a good place to buy nylons," he said. "In fact, you should stock up on everything you need, because it's tax free. Anything you buy here, you can sell in Spain."

"My daughter and I have everything we require," Mrs. Ellenger said. She walked off and then quickened her step, so that he wouldn't appear to be walking with them.

Emma smiled at Eddy and fell back very slightly, striking a balance between the two. "What did you buy?" she said softly. "Something for Wilma and George?"

"Lots of stuff," said Eddy. "Now, this café right here," he called after Mrs. Ellenger, "would be a good place to sit down. Right here, in the Plaza de Francia, you can see everyone important. They all come here, the high society of two continents."

"Of two continents," Emma said, wishing her mother would pay more attention. She stared at all the people behind the glass café fronts — the office workers drinking coffee before hurrying back to their desks, the tourists from cruise ships like their own.

Mrs. Ellenger stopped. She extended her hand to Emma and said, "My daughter and I have a lot of sightseeing to do, Eddy. I'm sure there are things you want to do, too." She was smiling. The surface of her sunglasses, mirrored, gave back a small, distorted public square, a tiny Eddy, and Emma, anguished, in gloves and hat.

"Oh, Eddy!" Emma cried. She wanted to say something else, to explain that her mother didn't understand, but he vanished, just like that, and moments later she picked out his neat little figure bobbing along in the crowd going downhill, away from the Plaza. "Eddy sort of expected to stay with us," she said.

"So I noticed," said Mrs. Ellenger. They sat down in a café — not the one Eddy had suggested, but a similar café nearby. "One Coca-Cola," she told the waiter, "and one brandy-and-water." She sighed with relief, as if they had been walking for hours.

Their drinks came. Emma saw, by the clock in the middle of the square, that it was half past eleven. It was warm in the sun, as warm as May. Perhaps, after all, they had been right about the summer dresses. Forgetting Eddy, she looked around. This was Tangier, and she, Emma Ellenger, was sitting with the high society of two continents. Out-

side was a public square, with low buildings, a café across
the street, a clock, and, walking past in striped woollen
cloaks, Arabs. The Arabs were real; if the glass of the window had not been there, she could have touched them.

"There's sawdust or something in my drink," Mrs. Ellenger said. "It must have come off the ice." Nevertheless,
she drank it to the end and ordered another.

"We'll go out soon, won't we?" Emma said, faintly
alarmed.

"In a minute."

The waiter brought them a pile of magazines, including a
six-month-old *Vogue*. Mrs. Ellenger removed her glasses,
looking pleased.

"We'll go soon?" Emma repeated.

There was no reply.

The square swelled with a midday crowd. Sun covered
their table until Mrs. Ellenger's glasses became warm to
the touch.

"Aren't we going out?" Emma said. "Aren't we going to
have anything for lunch?" Her legs ached from sitting still.

"You could have something here," Mrs. Ellenger said,
vague.

The waiter brought Emma a sandwich and a glass of
milk. Mrs. Ellenger continued to look at *Vogue*. Sometimes passengers from their ship went by. They waved
gaily, as if Tangier were the last place they had ever expected to see a familiar face. The Munns passed, walking
in step. Emma thumped on the window, but neither of the
ladies turned. Something about their solidarity, their sure-
ness of purpose, made her feel lonely and left behind. Soon
they would have seen Tangier, while she and her mother

might very well sit here until it was time to go back to the ship. She remembered Eddy and wondered what he was doing.

Mrs. Ellenger had come to the end of her reading material. She seemed suddenly to find her drink distasteful. She leaned on her hand, fretful and depressed, as she often was at that hour of the day. She was sorry she had come on the cruise and said so again. The warm ports were cold. She wasn't getting the right things to eat. She was getting so old and ugly that the bartender, having nothing better in view, and thinking she would be glad of anything, had tried to pick her up. What was she doing here, anyway? Her life . . .

"I wish we could have gone with Eddy," Emma said, with a sigh.

"Why, Emma," Mrs. Ellenger said. Her emotions jolted from a familiar track, it took her a moment or so to decide how she felt about this interruption. She thought it over, and became annoyed. "You mean you'd have more fun with that Chink than with me? Is that what you're trying to tell me?"

"It isn't that exactly. I only meant, we *could* have gone with him. He's been here before. Or the Munns, or this other friend of mine, Mr. Cowan. Only, he didn't come ashore today, Mr. Cowan. You shouldn't say 'Chink.' You should say 'Chinese person,' Mr. Cowan told me. Otherwise it offends. You should never offend. You should never say 'Irishman.' You should say 'Irish person.' You should never say 'Jew.' You should say — "

"Some cruise!" said Mrs. Ellenger, who had been listening to this with an expression of astounded shock, as if

Emma had been repeating blasphemy. "All I can say is
some cruise. Some selected passengers! What else did he
tell you? What does he want with a little girl like you, anyway? Did he ever ask you into his stateroom — anything
like that?"

"Oh, goodness, no!" Emma said impatiently; so many of
her mother's remarks were beside the point. She knew all
about not going anywhere with men, not accepting presents,
all that kind of thing. "His stateroom's too small even for
him. It isn't the one he paid for. He tells the purser all the
time, but it doesn't make any difference. That's why he
stays in the bar all day."

Indeed, for most of the cruise, Emma's friend had sat in
the bar writing a long journal, which he sent home, in in-
stallments, for the edification of his analyst. His analyst,
Mr. Cowan had told Emma, was to blame for the fact that
he had taken the cruise. In revenge, he passed his days
writing down all the things at fault with the passengers and
the service, hoping to make the analyst sad and guilty.
Emma began to explain her own version of this to Mrs.
Ellenger, but her mother was no longer listening. She
stared straight before her in the brooding, injured way
Emma dreaded. Her gaze seemed turned inward, rather
than to the street, as if she were concentrating on some
terrible grievance and struggling to bring it to words.

"You think I'm not a good mother," she said, still not
looking at Emma, or, really, at anything. "That's why you
hang around these other people. It's not fair. I'm good to
you. Well, am I?"

"Yes," said Emma. She glanced about nervously, wondering if anyone could hear.

"Do you ever need anything?" her mother persisted. "Do you know what happens to a lot of kids like you? They get left in schools, that's what happens. Did I ever do that to you?"

"No."

"I always kept you with me, no matter what anyone said. You mean more to me than anybody, any man. You know that. I'd give up anyone for you. I've even done it."

"I know," Emma said. There was a queer pain in her throat. She had to swallow to make it go away. She felt hot and uncomfortable and had to do something distracting; she took off her hat, rolled her gloves into a ball and put them in her purse.

Mrs. Ellenger sighed. "Well," she said in a different voice, "if we're going to see anything of this town, we'd better move." She paid for their drinks, leaving a large tip on the messy table, littered with ashes and magazines. They left the café and, arm in arm, like Miss and Mrs. Munn, they circled the block, looking into the dreary windows of luggage and furniture stores. Some of the windows had been decorated for Christmas with strings of colored lights. Emma was startled; she had forgotten all about Christmas. It seemed unnatural that there should be signs of it in a place like Tangier. "Do Arabs have Christmas?" she said.

"Everyone does," Mrs. Ellenger said. "Except——" She could not remember the exceptions.

It was growing cool, and her shoes were not right for walking. She looked up and down the street, hoping a taxi would appear, and then, with one of her abrupt, emotional changes, she darted into a souvenir shop that had taken her eye. Emma followed, blinking in the dark. The shop was tiny. There were colored bracelets in a glass case, leather slippers, and piles of silky material. From separate corners of the shop, a man and a woman converged on them.

"I'd like a bracelet for my little girl," Mrs. Ellenger said.

"For Christmas?" said the woman.

"Sort of. Although she gets plenty of presents, all the time. It doesn't have to be anything special."

"What a fortunate girl," the woman said absently, unlocking the case.

Emma was not interested in the bracelet. She turned her back on the case and found herself facing a shelf on which were pottery figures of lions, camels, and tigers. They were fastened to bases marked "*Souvenir de Tanger,*" or "*Recuerdo.*"

"Those are nice," Emma said, to the man. He wore a fez, and leaned against the counter, staring idly at Mrs. Ellenger. Emma pointed to the tigers. "Do they cost a lot?"

He said something in a language she could not understand. Then, lapsing into a creamy sort of English, "They are special African tigers." He grinned, showing his gums, as if the expression "African tigers" were a joke they shared. "They come from a little village in the mountains. There are interesting old myths connected with them." Emma looked at him blankly. "They are magic," he said.

"There's no such thing," Emma said. Embarrassed for him, she looked away, coloring deeply.

"This one," the man said, picking up a tiger. It was glazed in stripes of orange and black. The seam of the factory mold ran in a faint ridge down its back; the glaze had already begun to crack. "This is a special African tiger," he said. "It is good for ten wishes. Any ten."

"There's no such thing," Emma said again, but she took the tiger from him and held it in her hand, where it seemed to grow warm of its own accord. "Does it cost a lot?"

The man looked over at the case of bracelets and exchanged a swift, silent signal with his partner. Mrs. Ellenger, still talking, was hesitating between two enamelled bracelets.

"Genuine Sahara work," the woman said of the more expensive piece. When Mrs. Ellenger appeared certain to choose it, the woman nodded, and the man said to Emma, "The tiger is a gift. It costs you nothing."

"A present?" She glanced toward her mother, busy counting change. "I'm not allowed to take anything from strange men" rose to her lips. She checked it.

"For Christmas," the man said, still looking amused. "Think of me on Christmas Day, and make a wish."

"Oh, I will," Emma said, suddenly making up her mind. "Thanks. Thanks a lot." She put the tiger in her purse.

"Here, baby, try this on," Mrs. Ellenger said from across the shop. She clasped the bracelet around Emma's wrist. It was too small, and pinched, but everyone exclaimed at how pretty it looked.

"Thank you," Emma said. Clutching her purse, feeling the lump the tiger made, she said, looking toward the man, "Thanks, I love it."

"Be sure to tell your friends," he cried, as if the point of the gift would otherwise be lost.

"Are you happy?" Mrs. Ellenger asked kissing Emma. "Do you really love it? Would you still rather be with Eddy and these other people?" Her arm around Emma, they left the shop. Outside, Mrs. Ellenger walked a few steps, looking piteously at the cars going by. "Oh, Gōd, let there be a taxi," she said. They found one and hailed it, and she collapsed inside, closing her eyes. She had seen as much of Tangier as she wanted. They rushed downhill. Emma, her face pressed against the window, had a blurred impression of houses. Their day, all at once, spun out in reverse; there was the launch, waiting. They embarked and, in a moment, the city, the continent, receded.

Emma thought, confused, Is that all? Is that all of Africa?

But there was no time to protest. Mrs. Ellenger, who had lost her sunglasses, had to be consoled and helped with her scarf. "Oh, thank God!" she said fervently, as she was helped from the launch. "Oh, my God, what a day!" She tottered off to bed, to sleep until dinner.

The ship was nearly empty. Emma lingered on deck, looking back at Tangier. She made a detour, peering into the bar; it was empty and still. A wire screen had been propped against the shelves of bottles. Reluctantly, she made her way to the cabin. Her mother had already gone to sleep. Emma pulled the curtain over the porthole, dimming the light, and picked up her mother's scattered clothes. The new bracelet pinched terribly; when she unclasped it, it left an ugly greenish mark, like a bruise. She rubbed at the mark with soap and then cologne and finally most of it came away. Moving softly, so as not to waken her mother, she put the bracelet in the suitcase that contained her comic books and Uncle Jimmy Salter's *Merchant of Venice*. Remembering the tiger, she took it out of her purse and slipped it under her pillow.

The bar, suddenly, was full of noise. Most of it was coming from a newly installed loudspeaker. "Oh, little town of Bethlehem," Emma heard, even before she opened the heavy glass doors. Under the music, but equally amplified, were the voices of people arguing, the people who, somewhere on the ship, were trying out the carol recordings. Eddy hadn't yet returned. Crew members, in working clothes, were hanging Christmas decorations. There was a small silver tree over the bar and a larger one, real, being lashed to a pillar. At one of the low tables in front of the bar Mr. Cowan sat reading a travel folder.

"Have a good time?" he asked, looking up. He had to bellow because "Oh, Little Town of Bethlehem" was coming through so loudly. "I've just figured something out," he said, as Emma sat down. "If I take a plane from Madrid, I can be home in sixteen hours."

"Are you going to take it?"

"I don't know," he said, looking disconsolately at the folder. "Madrid isn't a port. I'd have to get off at Gibraltar or Malaga and take a train. And then, what about all my stuff? I'd have to get my trunk shipped. On the other hand," he said, looking earnestly at Emma, talking to her in the grown-up, if mystifying, way she liked, "why should I finish this ghastly cruise just for spite? They brought the mail on today. There was a letter from my wife. She says I'd better forget it and come home for Christmas."

Emma accepted without question the new fact that Mr. Cowan had a wife. Eddy had Wilma and George, the Munns had each other. Everyone she knew had a life, complete, that all but excluded Emma. "Will you go?" she repeated, unsettled by the idea that someone she liked was going away.

"Yes," he said. "I think so. We'll be in Gibraltar tomor-

row. I'll get off there. How was Tangier? Anyone try to
sell you a black-market Coke?"

"No," Emma said. "My mother bought a bracelet. A
man gave me an African tiger."

"What kind of tiger?"

"A toy," said Emma. "A little one."

"Oh. Damn bar's been closed all day," he said, getting
up. "Want to walk? Want to go down to the other bar?"

"No, thanks. I have to wait here for somebody," Emma
said, and her eyes sought the service door behind the bar
through which, at any moment, Eddy might appear. After
Mr. Cowan had left, she sat, patient, looking at the folder
he had forgotten.

Outside, the December evening drew in. The bar began
to fill; passengers drifted in, compared souvenirs, talked in
high, excited voices about the journey ashore. It didn't
sound as if they'd been in Tangier at all, Emma thought. It
sounded like some strange, imagined city, full of hazard and
adventure.

". . . so this little Arab boy comes up to me," a man was
saying, "and with my wife standing right there, right there
beside me, he says — "

"Hush," his wife said, indicating Emma. "Not so loud."

Eddy and Mrs. Ellenger arrived almost simultaneously,
coming, of course, through separate doors. Eddy had his
white coat on, a fresh colored handkerchief in the pocket.
He turned on the lights, took down the wire screen. Mrs.
Ellenger had changed her clothes and brushed her hair. She
wore a flowered dress, and looked cheerful and composed.
"All alone, baby?" she said. "You haven't even changed, or
washed your face. Never mind, there's no time now."

Emma looked at the bar, trying in vain to catch Eddy's eye. "Aren't you going to have a drink before dinner?"

"No. I'm hungry. Emma, you look a mess." Still talking, Mrs. Ellenger ushered Emma out to the dining room. Passing the bar, Emma called, "Hey, Eddy, hello," but, except to throw her a puzzling look, he did not respond.

They ate in near silence. Mrs. Ellenger felt rested and hungry, and, in any case, had at no time anything to communicate to the Munns. Miss Munn, between courses, read a book about Spain. She had read aloud the references to Gibraltar, and now turned to the section on Malaga, where they would be in two days. "From the summit of the Gibralfaro," she said, "one has an excellent view of the city and harbor. Two asterisks. At the state-controlled restaurant, refreshments . . ." She looked up and said, to Mrs. Munn, who was listening hard, eyes shut, "That's where we'll have lunch. We can hire a horse and *calesa.* It will kill the morning and part of the afternoon."

Already, they knew all about killing time in Malaga. They had never been there, but it would hold no surprise; they would make no mistakes. It was no use, Emma thought. She and her mother would never be like the Munns. Her mother, she could see, was becoming disturbed by this talk of Gibraltar and Malaga, by the threat of other ventures ashore. Had she not been so concerned with Eddy, she would have tried, helpfully, to lead the talk to something else. However, her apology to Eddy was infinitely more urgent. As soon as she could, she pushed back her chair and hurried out to the bar. Her mother dawdled behind her, fishing in her bag for a cigarette.

Emma sat up on one of the high stools and said, "Eddy,

where did you go? What did you do? I'm sorry about the lunch."

At that, he gave her another look, but still said nothing. Mrs. Ellenger arrived and sat down next to Emma. She looked from Emma to Eddy, eyebrows raised.

Don't let her be rude, Emma silently implored an undefined source of assistance. Don't let her be rude to Eddy, and I'll never bother you again. Then, suddenly, she remembered the tiger under her pillow.

There was no reason to worry. Eddy and her mother seemed to understand each other very well. "Get a good lunch, Eddy?" her mother asked.

"Yes. Thanks."

He moved away from them, down the bar, where he was busy entertaining new people, two men and a woman, who had come aboard that day from Tangier. The woman wore harlequin glasses studded with flashing stones. She laughed in a sort of bray at Eddy's antics and his funny remarks. "You can't get mad at him," Emma heard her say to one of the men. "He's like a monkey, if a monkey could talk."

"Eddy, our drinks," Mrs. Ellenger said.

Blank, polite, he poured brandy for Mrs. Ellenger and placed before Emma a bottle of Coca-Cola and a glass. Around the curve of the bar, Emma stared at the noisy woman, Eddy's new favorite, and the two fat old men with her. Mrs. Ellenger sipped her brandy, glancing obliquely in the same direction. She listened to their conversation. Two were husband and wife, the third a friend. They had picked up the cruise because they were fed up with North Africa. They had been traveling for several months. They were tired, and each of them had had a touch of colic.

Emma was sleepy. It was too much, trying to understand Eddy, and the day ashore. She drooped over her drink. Suddenly, beside her, Mrs. Ellenger spoke. "You really shouldn't encourage Eddy like that. He's an awful show-off. He'll dance around like that all night if you laugh enough." She said it with her nicest smile. The new people stared, taking her in. They looked at her dress, her hair, her rings. Something else was said. When Emma took notice once more, one of the two men had shifted stools, so he sat halfway between his friends and Emma's mother. Emma heard the introductions: Mr. and Mrs. Frank Timmins. Mr. Boyd Oliver. Mrs. Ellenger. Little Emma Ellenger, my daughter.

"Now, don't tell me that young lady's your daughter," Mr. Boyd Oliver said, turning his back on his friends. He smiled at Emma, and, just because of the smile, she suddenly remembered Uncle Harry Todd, who had given her the complete set of Sue Barton books, and another uncle, whose name she had forgotten, who had taken her to the circus when she was six.

Mr. Oliver leaned toward Mrs. Ellenger. It was difficult to talk; the bar was filling up. She picked up her bag and gloves from the stool next to her own, and Mr. Oliver moved once again. Polite and formal, they agreed that that made talking much easier.

Mr. Oliver said that he was certainly glad to meet them. The Timminses were wonderful friends, but sometimes, traveling like this, he felt like the extra wheel. Did Mrs. Ellenger know what he meant to say?

They were all talking: Mr. Oliver, Eddy, Emma's mother, Mr. and Mrs. Timmins, the rest of the people who had drifted in. The mood, collectively, was a good one. It had been a wonderful day. They all agreed to that, even Mrs. Ellenger. The carols had started again, the same record. Someone sang with the music: "Yet in thy dark streets shineth the everlasting light . . ."

"I'd take you more for *sisters*," Mr. Oliver said.

"Really?" Mrs. Ellenger said. "Do you really think so? Well, I suppose we are, in a way. I was practically a child myself when she came into the world. But I wouldn't try to pass Emma off as my sister. I'm proud to say she's my daughter. She was born during the war. We only have each other."

"Well," Mr. Oliver said, after thinking this declaration over for a moment or so, "that's the way it should be. You're a brave little person."

Mrs. Ellenger accepted this. He signaled for Eddy, and she turned to Emma. "I think you could go to bed now. It's been a big day for you."

The noise and laughter stopped as Emma said her good nights. She remembered all the names. "Good night, Eddy," she said, at the end, but he was rinsing glasses and seemed not to hear.

Emma could still hear the carols faintly as she undressed. She knelt on her bed for a last look at Tangier; it seemed different again, exotic and remote, with the ring of lights around the shore, the city night sounds drifting over the harbor. She thought, Today I was in Africa . . . But Africa had become unreal. The café, the clock in the square, the shop where they had bought the bracelet, had nothing to do with the Tangier she had imagined or this present view from the ship. Still, the tiger was real: it was under her pillow, proof that she had been to Africa, that she had touched shore. She dropped the curtain, put out the light. To the sound of Christmas music, she went to sleep.

It was late when Mrs. Ellenger came into the cabin. Emma had been asleep for hours, her doll beside her, the tiger under her head. She came out of a confused and troubled dream about a house she had once lived in, somewhere. There were new tenants in the house; when she tried to get in, they sent her away. She smelled her mother's perfume and heard her mother's voice before opening her eyes. Mrs. Ellenger had turned on the light at the dressing table and dropped into the chair before it. She was talking to herself, and sounded fretful. "Where's my cold cream?" she said. "Where'd I put it? Who took it?" She put her hand on the service bell and Emma prayed: It's late. Don't let her ring . . . The entreaty was instantly answered, for Mrs. Ellenger changed her mind and pulled off her earrings. Her hair was all over the place, Emma noticed. She looked all askew, oddly put together. Emma closed her eyes. She could identify, without seeing them, by the sounds, the eau de cologne, the make-up remover, and the lemon cream her mother used at night. Mrs. Ellenger undressed and pulled on the nightgown that had been laid out for her. She went into the bathroom, put on the light, and cleaned her teeth. Then she came back into the cabin and got into bed with Emma. She was crying. She lay so close that Emma's face was wet with her mother's tears and sticky with lemon cream.

"Are you awake?" her mother whispered. "I'm sorry, Emma. I'm so sorry."

"What for?"

"Nothing," Mrs. Ellenger said. "Do you love your mother?"

"Yes." Emma stirred, turning her face away. She slipped a hand up and under the pillow. The tiger was still there.

"I can't help it, Emma," her mother whispered. "I can't live like we've been living on this cruise. I'm not made for it. I don't like being alone. I need friends." Emma said nothing. Her mother waited, then said, "He'll go ashore with us tomorrow. It'll be someone to take us around. Wouldn't you like that?"

"Who's going with us?" Emma said. "The fat old man?"

Her mother had stopped crying. Her voice changed. She said, loud and matter-of-fact, "He's got a wife someplace. He only told me now, a minute ago. Why? Why not right at the beginning, in the bar? I'm not like that. I want something different, a *friend*." The pillow between their faces was wet. Mrs. Ellenger rubbed her cheek on the cold damp patch. "Don't ever get married, Emma," she said. "Don't have anything to do with men. Your father was no good. Jimmy Salter was no good. This one's no better. He's got a wife and look at how — Promise me you'll never get married. We should always stick together, you and I. Promise me we'll always stay together."

"All right," Emma said.

"We'll have fun," Mrs. Ellenger said, pleading. "Didn't we have fun today, when we were ashore, when I got you the nice bracelet? Next year, we'll go someplace else. We'll go anywhere you want."

"I don't want to go anywhere," Emma said.

But her mother wasn't listening. Sobbing quietly, she went to sleep. Her arm across Emma grew heavy and slack.

Emma lay still; then she saw that the bathroom light had been left on. Carefully, carrying the tiger, she crawled out over the foot of the bed. Before turning out the light, she looked at the tiger. Already, his coat had begun to flake away. The ears were chipped. Turning it over, inspecting the damage, she saw, stamped in blue: "Made in Japan." The man in the shop had been mistaken, then. It was not an African tiger, good for ten wishes, but something quite ordinary.

She put the light out and, in the dim stateroom turning gray with dawn, she got into her mother's empty bed. Still holding the tiger, she lay, hearing her mother's low breathing and the unhappy words she muttered out of her sleep.

Mr. Oliver, Emma thought, trying to sort things over, one at a time. Mr. Oliver would be with them for the rest of the cruise. Tomorrow, they would go ashore together. "I think you might call Mr. Oliver Uncle Boyd," her mother might say.

Emma's grasp on the tiger relaxed. There was no magic about it; it did not matter, really, where it had come from. There was nothing to be gained by keeping it hidden under a pillow. Still, she had loved it for an afternoon, she would not throw it away or inter it, like the bracelet, in a suitcase. She put it on the table by the bed and said softly, trying out the sound, "I'm too old to call you Uncle Boyd. I'm thirteen next year. I'll call you Boyd or Mr. Oliver, whatever you choose. I'd rather choose Mr. Oliver." What her mother might say then Emma could not imagine. At the moment, she seemed very helpless, very sad, and Emma turned over with her face to the wall. Imagining probable behavior was a terrible strain; this was as far as she could go.

Tomorrow, she thought, Europe began. When she got up, they would be docked in a new harbor, facing the outline of a new, mysterious place. "Gibraltar," she said aloud. Africa was over, this was something else. The cabin grew steadily lighter. Across the cabin, the hinge of the porthole creaked, the curtain blew in. Lying still, she heard another sound, the rusty cri-cri-cri of sea gulls. That meant they were getting close. She got up, crossed the cabin, and, carefully avoiding the hump of her mother's feet under the blanket, knelt on the end of her bed. She pushed the curtain away. Yes, they were nearly there. She could see the gulls swooping and soaring, and something on the horizon —a shape, a rock, a whole continent untouched and unexplored. A tide of newness came in with the salty air: she thought of new land, new dresses, clean, untouched, unworn. A new life. She knelt, patient, holding the curtain, waiting to see the approach to shore.

The Picnic

T HE THREE Marshall children were dressed and ready for the picnic before their father was awake. Their mother had been up since dawn, for the coming day of pleasure weighed heavily on her mind. She had laid out the children's clothes, so that they could dress without asking questions — clean blue denims for John and dresses sprigged with flowers for the girls. Their shoes, chalky with whitening, stood in a row on the bathroom window sill.

John, stubbornly, dressed himself, but the girls helped each other, standing and preening before the long looking glass. Margaret fastened the chain of Ellen's heart-shaped locket while Ellen held up her hair with both hands. Margaret never wore her own locket. Old Madame Pégurin, in whose house in France the Marshalls were living, had given her something she liked better — a brooch containing a miniature portrait of a poodle called Youckie, who had died of influenza shortly before the war. The brooch was edged with seed pearls, and Margaret had worn it all summer, pinned to her navy blue shorts.

"How very pretty it is!" the children's mother had said

when the brooch was shown to her. "How nice of Madame Pégurin to think of a little girl. It will look much nicer later on, when you're a little older." She had been trained in the school of indirect suggestion, and so skillful had she become that her children sometimes had no idea what she was driving at.

"I guess so," Margaret had replied on this occasion, firmly fastening the brooch to her shorts.

She now attached it to the front of the picnic frock, where, too heavy for the thin material, it hung like a stone. "It looks lovely," Ellen said with serious admiration. She peered through their bedroom window across the garden, and over the tiled roofs of the small town of Virolun, to the blooming summer fields that rose and fell toward Grenoble and the Alps. Across the town, partly hidden by somebody's orchard, were the neat rows of gray-painted barracks that housed American troops. Into this tidy settlement their father disappeared each day, driven in a jeep. On a morning as clear as this, the girls could see the first shining peaks of the mountains and the thin blue smoke from the neighboring village, some miles away. They were too young to care about the view, but their mother appreciated it for them, often reminding them that nothing in her own childhood had been half as agreeable. "You youngsters are very lucky," she would say. "Your father might just as easily as not have been stationed in the middle of Arkansas." The children would listen without comment, although it depressed them inordinately to be told of their good fortune. If they liked this house better than any other they had lived in, it was because it contained Madame Pégurin, her cat, Olivette, and her cook, Louise.

Olivette now entered the girls' bedroom soundlessly,

pushing the door with one paw. "Look at her. She's price-less," Margaret said, trying out the word.

Ellen nodded. "I wish one of us could go to the picnic with *her*," she said. Margaret knew that she meant not the cat but Madame Pégurin, who was driving to the picnic grounds with General Wirtworth, commander of the post.

"One of us might," Margaret said. "Sitting on the General's lap."

Ellen's shriek at the thought woke their father, Major Marshall, who, remembering that this was the day of the picnic, said, "Oh, God!"

The picnic, which had somehow become an Army re-sponsibility, had been suggested by an American magazine of such grandeur that the Major was staggered to learn that Madame Pégurin had never heard of it. Two research workers, vestal maidens in dirndl skirts, had spent weeks combing France to find the most typically French town. They had found no more than half a dozen; and since it was essential to the story that the town be near an American Army post, they had finally, like a pair of exhausted doves, fluttered to rest in Virolun. The picnic, they had explained to General Wirtworth, would be a symbol of unity between two nations — between the troops at the post and the resi-dents of the town. The General had repeated this to Colonel Baring, who had passed it on to Major Marshall, who had brought it to rest with his wife. "Oh, really?" Paula Marshall had said, and if there was any reserve — any bitterness — in her voice, the Major had failed to notice. The mammoth job of organizing the picnic had fallen just where he knew it would — on his own shoulders.

The Major was the post's recreation officer, and he was

beset by many difficulties. His status was not clear; sometimes he had to act as public relations officer — there being none, through an extraordinary oversight on the part of the General. The Major's staff was inadequate. It was composed of but two men: a lieutenant, who had developed measles a week before the picnic, and a glowering young sergeant who, the Major feared, would someday write a novel depicting him in an unfavorable manner. The Major had sent Colonel Baring a long memo on the subject of his status, and the Colonel had replied in person, saying, with a comic, rueful smile, "Just see us through the picnic, old man!"

The Major had said he would try. But it was far from easy. The research workers from the American magazine had been joined by a photographer who wore openwork sandals and had so far not emerged from the Hotel Bristol. Messages in his languid handwriting had been carried to Major Marshall's office by the research workers, and answers returned by the Major's sergeant. The messages were grossly interfering and never helpful. Only yesterday, the day before the picnic, the sergeant had placed before the Major a note on Hotel Bristol stationery: "Suggest folk dances as further symbol of unity. French wives teaching American wives, and so on. Object: Color shot." Annoyed, the Major had sent a message pointing out that baseball had already been agreed on as an easily recognized symbol, and the afternoon brought a reply: "Feel that French should make contribution. Anything colorful or indigenous will do."

"Baseball is as far as I'll go," the Major had said in his reply to this.

On their straggling promenade to breakfast, the children halted outside Madame Pégurin's door. Sometimes from behind the white-and-gold painted panels came the sound of breakfast — china on china, glass against silver. Then Louise would emerge with the tray, and Madame Pégurin, seeing the children, would tell them to come in. She would be sitting up, propped with a pillow and bolster. Her hair, which changed color after every visit to Paris, would be wrapped in a scarf and Madame herself enveloped in a trailing dressing gown streaked with the ash of her cigarette. When the children came in, she would feed them sugared almonds and pistachio creams and sponge cakes soaked in rum, which she kept in a tin box by her bedside, and as they stood lined up rather comically, she would tell them about little dead Youckie, and about her own children, all of whom had married worthless, ordinary, social-climbing men and women. "In the end," she would say, sighing, "there is nothing to replace the love one can bear a cat or a poodle."

The children's mother did not approve of these morning visits, and the children were frequently told not to bother poor Madame Pégurin, who needed her rest. This morning, they could hear the rustle of paper as Madame Pégurin turned the pages of *Le Figaro*, which came to Virolun every day from Paris. Madame Pégurin looked at only one section of it, the *Carnet du Jour* — the daily account of marriages, births and deaths — even though, as she told the children, one found in it nowadays names that no one had heard of, families who sounded foreign or commonplace. The children admired this single-minded reading, and they thought it "commonplace" of their mother to read books.

"Should we knock?" Margaret said. They debated this until their mother's low, reproachful "Children!" fetched them out of the upstairs hall and down a shallow staircase, the wall of which was papered with the repeated person of a shepherdess. Where a railing should have been were jars of trailing ivy they had been warned not to touch. The wall was stained at the level of their hands; once a week Louise went over the marks with a piece of white bread. But nothing could efface the fact that there were boarders, American Army tenants, in old Madame Pégurin's house.

During the winter, before the arrival of the Marshalls, the damage had been more pronounced; the tenants had been a Sergeant and Mrs. Gould, whose children, little Henry and Joey, had tracked mud up and down the stairs and shot at each other with water pistols all over the drawing room. The Goulds had departed on bad terms with Madame Pégurin, and it often worried Major Marshall that his wife permitted the Gould children to visit the Marshall children and play in the garden. Madame Pégurin never mentioned Henry's and Joey's presence; she simply closed her bedroom shutters at the sound of their voices, which, it seemed to the Major, was suggestion enough.

The Gould and Marshall children were to attend the picnic together; it was perhaps for this reason that Madame Pégurin rattled the pages of *Le Figaro* behind her closed door. She disliked foreigners; she had told the Marshall children so. But they, fortunately, did not consider themselves foreign, and had pictured instead dark men with curling beards. Madame Pégurin had tried, as well as she could, to ignore the presence of the Americans in Virolun, just as, long ago, when she traveled, she had overlooked the natives of whichever country she happened to be in. She had ignored the Italians in Italy and the Swiss in Switzerland, and she had explained this to Margaret and Ellen, who, agreeing it was the only way to live, feared that their mother would never achieve this restraint. For she *would* speak French, and she carried with her, even to market, a book of useful phrases.

Madame Pégurin had had many troubles with the Americans; she had even had troubles with the General. It had fallen to her, as the highest-ranking resident of Virolun, to entertain the highest-ranking American officer. She had asked General Wirtworth to tea, and he had finished off a bottle of whiskey she had been saving for eleven years. He had then been moved to kiss her hand, but this could not make up for her sense of loss. There had been other difficulties — the tenancy of the Goulds, and a row with Colonel Baring, whose idea it had been to board the Goulds and their hoodlum children with Madame Pégurin. Madame Pégurin had, indeed, talked of legal action, but nothing had come of it. Because of all this, no one believed she would attend the picnic, and it was considered a triumph for Major Marshall that she had consented to go, and to drive with the General, and to be photographed.

"I hope they take her picture eating a hot dog," Paula Marshall said when she heard of it.

"It was essential," the Major said reprovingly. "I made her see that. She's a symbol of something in this town. We couldn't do the thing properly without her."

"Maybe she just likes to have her picture taken, like anyone else," Paula said. This was, for her, an uncommonly catty remark.

The Major said nothing. He had convinced Madame Pégurin that she was a symbol only after a prolonged tea-time wordplay that bordered on flirtation. This was second nature to Madame Pégurin, but the Major had bogged down quickly. He kept coming around to the point, and Madame Pégurin found the point uninteresting. She wanted to talk about little Youckie, and the difference between French and American officers, and how well Major Marshall looked in his uniform, and what a good idea it was for Mrs. Marshall not to bother about her appearance, running as she did all day after the children. But the Major talked about the picnic and by the weight of blind obduracy won.

The little Marshalls, thinking of the sugared almonds and pistachio creams in Madame Pégurin's room, slid into their places at the breakfast table and sulked over their prunes. Before each plate was a motto, in their mother's up-and-down hand: "I will be good at the picnic," said John's. This was read aloud to him, to circumvent the happy excuse that he could not yet read writing. "I will not simper. I will help Mother and be an example. I will not ask the photographer to take my picture," said Ellen's. Margaret's said, "I will mind my own business and not bother Madame Pégurin."

"What's simper?" Ellen asked.

"It's what you do all day," said her sister. To their mother she remarked, "Madame is reading the *Figaro* in her bed." There was, in her voice, a reproach that Paula

Marshall did not spend her mornings in so elegant a manner, but Paula, her mind on the picnic, the eggs to be
hard-boiled, scarcely took it in.

"You might, just this once, have come straight to breakfast," she said, "when you know I have this picnic to think
of, and it means so much to your father to have it go well."
She looked, as if for sympathy, at the portrait of Madame
Pégurin's dead husband, who each day surveyed with a
melancholy face these strangers around his table.

"It means a lot to Madame, too," Margaret said. "Riding
there with the General! Perhaps one of us might go in the
same car?"

There was no reply.

Undisturbed, Margaret said, "She told me what she is
wearing. A lovely gray thing, and a big lovely hat, and
diamonds." She looked thoughtfully at her mother, who,
in her sensible cotton dress, seemed this morning more
than ever composed of starch and soap and Apple Blossom
cologne. She wore only the rings that marked her engagement and her wedding. At her throat, holding her collar,
was the fraternity pin Major Marshall had given her fifteen
years before. "Diamonds," Margaret repeated, as if their
mother might take the hint.

"Ellen, *dear*," said Paula Marshall. "There is, really, a
way to eat prunes. Do you children see *me* spitting?" The
children loudly applauded this witticism, and Paula went
on, "Do be careful of the table. Try to remember it isn't
ours." But this the Army children had heard so often it
scarcely had a meaning. "It isn't ours," they were told. "It
doesn't belong to us." They had lived so much in hotels
and sublet apartments and all-alike semi-detached houses

that Madame Pégurin's table, at which minor nobility had once been entertained, meant no more to them than the cross-legged picnic tables at that moment being erected in Virolun community soccer field.

"You're so fond of poor Madame," said Paula, "and all her little diamonds and trinkets. I should think you would have more respect for her furniture. Jewels are only a commodity, like tins of soup. Remember that. They're bought to be sold." She wondered why Madame Pégurin did not sell them — why she kept her little trinkets but had to rent three bedrooms and a drawing room to a strange American family.

"Baseball is as far as I'll go," said the Major to himself as he was dressing, and he noted with satisfaction that it was a fine day. Outside in the garden sat the children's friends Henry and Joey Gould. The sight of these fair-haired little boys, waiting patiently on a pair of swings, caused a cloud to drift across the Major's day, obscuring the garden, the picnic, the morning's fine beginning, for the Gould children, all unwittingly, were the cause of a prolonged disagreement between the Major and his wife.

"It's not that I'm a snob," the Major had explained. "God knows, no one could call me that!" But was it the fault of the Major that the Goulds had parted with Madame Pégurin on bad terms? Could the Major be blamed for the fact that the father of Henry and Joey was a sergeant? The Major personally thought that Sergeant Gould was a fine fellow, but the children of officers and the children of sergeants were not often invited to the same parties, and the children might, painfully, discover this for themselves. To the Major, it was clear and indisputable that the friendship should be stopped, or at least tapered. But Paula, unwisely, encouraged the children to play together. She had even asked Mrs. Gould to lunch on the lawn, which was considered by the other officers' wives in Virolun an act of great indelicacy.

Having the Gould children underfoot in the garden was particularly trying for Madame Pégurin, whose window overlooked their antics in her lily pond. She had borne with much; from her own lips the Major had heard about the final quarrel of the previous winter. It had been over a head of cauliflower — only slightly bad, said Madame Pégurin — that Mrs. Gould had dropped, unwrapped, into the garbage can. It had been retrieved by Louise, Madame Pégurin's cook, who had suggested to Mrs. Gould that it be used in soup. "I don't give my children rotten food," Mrs. Gould had replied, on which Louise, greatly distressed, had carried the slimy cauliflower in a clean towel up to Madame Pégurin's bedroom. Madame Pégurin, considering both sides, had then composed a message to be read aloud, in English, by Louise: "Is Mrs. Gould aware that many people in France have not enough to eat? Does she know that wasted food is saved for the poor by the garbage collector? Will she please in future wrap the things she wastes so that they will not spoil?" The message seemed to Madame Pégurin so fair, so unanswerable, that she could not understand why Mrs. Gould, after a moment of horrified silence, burst into tears and quite irrationally called Louise a Communist. This political quarrel had reached the ears of the General, who, insisting he could not have that sort of thing, asked Colonel Baring to straighten the difficulty out, since it was the Colonel's fault the Goulds had been sent there in the first place.

All this had given Virolun a winter of gossip, much of which was still repeated. One of the research workers had, quite recently, asked Major Marshall whether it was true that when young Mrs. Gould asked Madame Pégurin if she had a vacuum cleaner, she had been told, "No, I have a servant." Was this attitude widespread, the research worker had wanted to know. Or was the Army helping break down the feudal social barriers of the little town. Oh, yes, the Major had replied. Oh, yes, indeed.

Passing Louise on the staircase with Madame Pégurin's breakfast tray, the Major smiled, thinking of Madame Pégurin and of how fond she was of his children. Often, on his way to breakfast, he saw the children through the half-open door, watching her as she skimmed from her coffee a web of warm milk; Madame Pégurin's levees, his wife called them. Paula said that Madame Pégurin was so feminine it made her teeth ache, and that her influence on the children was deplorable. But the Major could not take this remark seriously. He admired Madame Pégurin, confusing her, because she was old and French and had once been rich, with courts and courtesans and the eighteenth century. In her presence, his mind took a literary turn, and he thought of vanished glories, something fine that would never return, gallant fluttering banners, and the rest of it.

He found his wife in the dining room, staring moodily at the disorder left by the children. "They've vanished," she said at once. "I sent them to wait in the garden with Joey and Henry, but they're not out there now. They must have crept in again by the front door. I think they were simply waiting for you to come down so that they could go up to *her* room." She was flushed with annoyance and the unexpected heat of the morning. "These red walls," she said, looking around the room. "They've made me so uncomfortable all summer I haven't enjoyed a single meal." She longed to furnish a house of her own once more, full of chintz and robin's-egg blue, and pictures of the children in frames.

In the red dining room, Madame Pégurin had hung yellow curtains. On a side table was a vase of yellow late summer flowers. The Major looked around the room, but with an almost guilty enjoyment, for, just as the Methodist child is seduced by the Roman service, the Major had succumbed in Madame Pégurin's house to something warm and rich, composed of red and yellow, and branching candelabra.

"If they would only stay in the garden," Paula said. "I hate it, always having to call them and fetch them. The girls, at least, could help with the sandwiches." She began to pile the plates one on another, drawing the crumbs on the tablecloth toward her with a knife. "And they're probably eating things. Glacéed pineapple. Cherries in something — something *alcoholic*. Really, it's too much. And you don't help."

She seemed close to tears, and the Major, looking down at his cornflakes, wondered exactly how to compose his face so that it would be most comforting. Paula was suspicious of extravagant tastes or pleasures. She enjoyed the nursery fare she gave the children, sharing without question their peas and lamb chops, their bland and innocent desserts.

Once, long ago, she had broken off an engagement only because she had detected in the young man's eyes a look of sensuous bliss as he ate strawberries and cream. And now her own children came to the table full of rum-soaked sponge cake and looked with condescension at their lemon jello.

"You exaggerate," the Major said, kindly. "Madame Pégurin takes a lot of trouble with the children. She's giving them a taste of life they might never have had."

"I know," Paula said. "And while she's at it, she's ruining all my good work." She often used this expression of the children, as if they were a length of Red Cross knitting. As the Major drank his coffee, he made marks in a notebook on the table. She sighed and, rising with the plates in her hands, said, "We'll leave it for now, because of the picnic. But tomorrow you and I must have a long talk. About everything."

"Of course," the Major said. "We'll talk about everything — the little Goulds, too. And you might try, just this once, to be nice to Mrs. Baring."

"I'll try," said Paula, "but I can't promise." There were tears in her eyes, of annoyance at having to be nice to Colonel Baring's wife.

Madame Pégurin, in the interim, descended from the shuttered gloom of her room and went out to the garden, trailing wings of gray chiffon, and followed by the children and Louise, who were bearing iced tea, a folding chair, a parasol, a hassock, and a blanket. Under the brim of her hat her hair was drawn into tangerine-colored scallops. She sat down on the chair and put her feet on the hassock. On the grass at her feet, Margaret and Ellen lay prone, propped on their elbows. John sat beside them, eating something. The little Goulds, identical in striped jerseys, stood apart, holding a ball and bat.

"And how is your mother?" Madame Pégurin asked Joey and Henry. "Does she still have so very much trouble with the vegetables?"

"I don't know," Henry said innocently. "Where we live now, the maid does everything."

"Ah, of course," Madame Pégurin said, settling back in her chair. Her voice was warm and reserved — royalty at a bazaar. Between her and the two girls passed a long look of feminine understanding.

In the kitchen, attacking the sandwiches, Paula Marshall wondered what, if anything, Mrs. Baring would say to Madame Pégurin, for the Barings had been snubbed by her so severely that, thinking of it, Paula was instantly cheered. The Barings had wanted to live with Madame Pégurin. They had been impressed by the tidy garden, the house crowded with the salvage of something better, the portrait of Monsieur Pégurin, who had been, they understood, if not an ambassador, something just as nice. But they had offended Madame Pégurin, first by giving her a Christmas present, a subscription to the *Reader's Digest* in French, and then by calling one afternoon without an invitation. Mrs. Baring had darted about the drawing room like a fish, remarking, in the sort of voice reserved for the whims of the elderly, "*My* mother collects milk glass." And the Colonel had confided to Madame Pégurin that his wife spoke excellent French and would, if pressed, say a few words in that language—a confidence that was for Madame Pégurin the depth of the afternoon. "I wouldn't think of taking into my house anyone but the General," she was reported to have said. "Or someone on his immediate staff." The Barings had exchanged paralyzed looks, and then the Colonel, rising to it, had said that he would see, and the following week he had sent Sergeant Gould, who was the General's driver, and his wife, and the terrible children. The Barings had never mentioned the incident, but they often, with little smiles and movements of their eyebrows, implied that by remaining in a cramped room at the Hotel Bristol and avoiding Madame Pégurin's big house they had narrowly escaped a season in Hell.

Now they were all going to the picnic, that symbol of unity, Sergeant Gould driving the General and Madame Pégurin, the Barings following with the mayor of Virolun, and the Marshalls and the little Goulds somewhere behind.

The Major came into the kitchen, carrying his notebook, and Paula said to him, "It will be queer, this thing today."

"Queer?" he said absently. "I don't see why. Look," he said. "I may have to make a speech. I put everyone on the agenda but myself, but I may be asked." He frowned at his notes. "I could start with 'We are gathered together.' Or is that stuffy?"

"I don't know," Paula said. With care, and also with a certain suggestion of martyrdom, she rolled bread around watercress. "Actually, I think it's a quote."

"It could be." The Major looked depressed. He ate an egg sandwich from Paula's hamper. The basket lunch had been his idea; every family was bringing one. The Major had declared the basket lunch to be typically American, although he had never in his life attended such a function. "You should see them all in the garden," he said, cheering up. "Madame Pégurin and the kids. What a picture! The photographer should have been there. He's never around when you want him."

Describing this scene, which he had watched from the dining-room windows, the Major was careful to leave out any phrases that might annoy his wife, omitting with regret the filtered sunlight, the golden summer garden, and the blue shade of the parasol. It had pleased him to observe, although he did not repeat this either, that even a stranger could have detected which children were the little Goulds and which the little Marshalls. "I closed the dining-room shutters," he added. "The sun seems to have moved around." He had become protective of Madame Pégurin's house, extending his care to the carpets.

"That's fine," Paula said. In a few minutes, the cars would arrive to carry them all away, and she had a sudden prophetic vision of the day ahead. She saw the tiny cavalcade of motorcars creeping, within the speed limit, through the main street and stopping at the 1914 war memorial so that General Wirtworth could place a wreath. She foresaw the failure of the Coca-Cola to arrive at the picnic grounds, and the breakdown of the movie projector. On the periphery, scowling and eating nothing, would be the members of the Virolun Football Club, which had been forced to postpone a match with the St. Etienne Devils because of the picnic. The Major would be everywhere at once, driving his sergeant before him like a hen. Then the baseball, with the mothers of Virolun taking good care to keep their pinafored children away from the wayward ball and the terrible waving bat. Her imagination sought the photographer, found him on a

picnic table, one sandaled foot next to a plate of dough-
nuts, as he recorded Mrs. Baring fetching a cushion for
General Wirtworth and Madame Pégurin receiving from
the little Goulds a cucumber sandwich.

Paula closed the picnic hamper and looked at her husband with compassion. She suddenly felt terribly sorry
for him, because of all that was in store for him this day,
and because the picnic was not likely to clarify his status,
as he so earnestly hoped. There would be fresh misunder-
standings and further scandals. She laid her hand over
his. "I'm sorry," she said. "I should have been listening
more carefully. Read me your speech, and start with 'We
are gathered together.' I think it's quite appropriate and
very lovely."

"Do you?" said the Major. His eyes hung on her face,
trusting. "But then suppose I have to give it in French?
How the hell do you say 'gathered together' in French?"

"You won't have to give it in French," Paula said, in
just such a voice as she used to her children when they
had a fever or nightmares. "Because, you see, the mayor
will speak in French, and that's quite enough."

"That's right," said the Major. "I can say, in French,
'Our good French friends will excuse this little talk in
English.' "

"That's right," Paula said.

Reassured, the Major thrust his notes in his pocket and
strode from the kitchen to the garden, where, squaring his
shoulders, he rallied his forces for the coming battle.

The Deceptions
of Marie-Blanche

Marie-Blanche wrote from Canada a few days ago to
say that she was engaged again. Her letter was, for one
betrothed, uncommonly cynical. "This one seems all right,"
it said, "but I'm not buying my trousseau or anything else
until the last minute. This one is a widower. He has a little
bakery, and behind it *un joli logement*. He has kept the
hair of his first wife. Little plaster doves standing in a circle
hold the hair in their beaks so that it forms *un cordon*. In
the middle are paper roses, and over it all is a glass cover.
It stands on the dining-room table. *C'est un homme de
sentiment*."

For the sake of Marie-Blanche, I hope that he is a man of
sentiment. I also hope that he isn't paying for anyone's
music lessons and that he doesn't own a horse and that he
isn't too attached to one of his own cousins. The reminder
of her engagement is, for me, only a reminder of her deceptions. When I lived with Marie-Blanche and her mother in
Montreal during the war, I saw the rise and fall of three
love affairs in a very short time. Marie-Blanche is decep-

tion-prone the way some people keep bumping their heads or spraining their ankles. For nearly twenty-five years her married sister and her cousins have been drawing on their reservoirs of eligible men, funneling them one after the other into the Dumards' front parlor. Marie-Blanche loves them all, without favor; but something always goes wrong.

The parting scene is always very beautiful. Usually she cries, and so does her mother, Madame Dumard, who is never far away. "You're too good for me," the departing suitor says, misty-voiced. He presses her hand and calls her a saint or a little white flower. Sometimes he asks for a keepsake and Marie-Blanche cuts off a lock of her hair and gives it to him. This is a nuisance for her. It breaks the symmetry of her headdress, and a neighboring curl must be divided, like the fission of an amoeba, to replace the missing one.

There are thirty-one curls on Marie-Blanche's head, and the number is no accident. Many years ago, when she saw Shirley Temple in the cinema for the first time, she wrote to a French-language newspaper that ran a questions column and asked for specific instructions on how to make Shirley Temple curls. Shirley Temple has long outgrown these little corkscrews, but Marie-Blanche is faithful forever. When I knew her, the curls bounced over her ears and on her forehead. Sometimes she held them in check with two enamel hairpins shaped like pansies. When her hair, which was a light fluffy yellow, had been washed, the curls would swell to the size of Polish sausages and the effect was truly striking. Between the curls, her face peeped out, alert and inquisitive. Her eyes were blue and innocent, and her cheeks were like a Baroque baby's. She was inordinately proud of the size and shape of her mouth, which was so small that she frequently called attention to it by eating blueberries one at a time.

I have seen a picture of Marie-Blanche taken when she was nineteen, before Shirley Temple was born. Most of her hair then was hidden under a deep cloche hat, but the trusting, anticipatory expression is still the same. "That was the happiest year of my life," Marie-Blanche would often say, putting the picture in a tin box that also contained handkerchiefs and a rosary. "It was the year of my first love and my first deception." The first deceiver was an Irish boy called Georgie O'Ryan. The Dumard family pronounce it Georgie Rhine, with a stress on every other syllable so that the final effect is nearly that of a yodel. Georgie Rhine courted Marie-Blanche for nearly six months, at the end of which he left, bearing a lock of her hair and assuring her that any man would be lucky to have her. A few months later he married an Irish girl from his own parish. Marie-Blanche never knew why, but Madame Dumard had an explanation that she provided for all the friends and relations indiscreet enough to ask. *"Il avait un grand défaut,"* she would say. "So great that we never speak of it." This statement, Machiavellian in its cunning, removed from Marie-Blanche all suspicion of having been rejected and implied, indeed, that she had been mercifully saved from something too grave to mention.

Actually, Georgie may have been discouraged, as were subsequent suitors, by the courting protocol laid down by Madame Dumard. Marie-Blanche's admirers, once the first minuet of introduction was over, were expected to call one evening a week. The evening was Friday and the hour was half past seven. By that time, the supper dishes were put away and Marie-Blanche and her mother dressed and ready. The suitor was received in the parlor, a small, icy room at the end of their long flat. The walls of the room were papered in brown with a creeping pattern of flowers. An imitation fireplace filled most of one wall, and over it hung a colored picture of the San Francisco earthquake. There were also pictures of saints, rendered cross-eyed by a faulty printing process, of Swiss mountains, of the Pope, and of Queen Elizabeth as a baby, all cut from magazines.

Marie-Blanche's suitor would sit on one of the plum-covered upholstered chairs. At his side was a small table covered with a white doily and on the doily was a small brass ash tray, the only one in the house. It bore the trademark of a brand of good Canadian beer. Across the room, side by side on the sofa, sat Marie-Blanche and her mother. Their hands were folded in their laps and their ankles were crossed. Madame Dumard wore black: she had many cousins, and she was in perpetual mourning for one or more of them. Her ears were pierced and through them drawn the thin gold earrings that had been hung there in childhood to ward off eye infections. Marie-Blanche, her hair a triumphant monument to Shirley Temple, wore crepe in some electric shade.

Every light in the room was turned on, from the hanging chandelier with its cluster of orange lampshades to the modern bridge lamp that looked like a traffic signal in the world of the future. Behind the sofa, a curtain tied back with ball fringe revealed an extra bedroom. This room was never used, but because of its exposed position it contained the family's most elegant furniture: a high, polished imitation-oak bedstead, a pink satin chair on which no one sat, a Pierrot doll, and a fluffy dressing table with a three-way mirror. The bedroom opened onto a small balcony, and here the three — Madame Dumard, Marie-Blanche, and the suitor — would sit when the weather was fine.

There was nothing more entertaining than to sit on the balcony and watch the cars and bicycles going by. Up and down the street ran rows of red brick flats with winding outside staircases on which the children of the neighborhood played and from which they frequently fell. They were hearty children, nourished on jam, bread and mayonnaise, and a sickly imitation cola drink on which they had been weaned as infants. There was not a tree on the street, not a bird, not a blade of grass. The Dumards felt sorry for people who had to live in the country, and sometimes, when they visited relatives who lived on farms, they were bored and unhappy and hurried back to Montreal.

Next door to the Dumards, in a low two-story building, lived a large family in whose rickety garage was conducted what Marie-Blanche called "*un beau grand* crap game." On summer evenings it was pleasant to see the big cars pull up at the curb, their well-fed occupants stopping to pat the neighbors' little children on the head before they proceeded inside. It was Marie-Blanche who first pointed out to me that successful gamblers wear black knit ties while *les petits bon-à-riens* wear the hand-painted ones. On this street a French-Canadian parish merged with a Jewish district, full of kosher meat markets and dingy shops. In her peripatetic career as a salesgirl, Marie-Blanche had often worked for Jews and as a result she spoke a singular kind of English, with a French-Canadian accent and a Yiddish lilt.

She also used many Yiddish words, believing them to be English, and some of her accounts of clashes and tiny bargains between clerk and customer were exceedingly funny.

However, none of this was ever related to her suitor, which was probably a pity. Conversation during the courting evenings was polite and circumspect, never ruffled by anything so coarse as humor. The suitor was expected to express many sentiments of a noble nature about one's mother, earning money, and marriage. During this preliminary, or prologue stage of the drama he was said to be "frequenting" Marie-Blanche. If the courtship went well the verb was used reflexively and they were said to be frequenting each other.

After a few months, if the noble young man had not dropped out of the race, he was permitted to call on an additional evening, every Tuesday. "That's enough for the first year," Madame Dumard would say. She liked to describe her own courtship, which had taken place in the years 1894 and 1895, and how her husband had held her hand for the first time as they were leaving the church after the wedding. Georgie Rhine had been the first to sound the knell that what would pass as courting in Madame Dumard's day served only to dishearten Marie-Blanche's admirers. But whenever Marie-Blanche tried to point this out, her mother would remind her of what a good marriage her sister, Agnès, had made, omitting the lucky accident of history that had rushed Agnès to the altar.

Agnès had been married very quickly one day in 1940 when it was announced on the radio that young men not married by a certain date in June would be considered bachelors thereafter for the purposes of military service. To the Dumards, the war came and went like a distant, murmuring stream, but they were alive to such irritants as rationing and military service. Agnès was married at once in a borrowed dress. They had great difficulty finding a ring; all the jewelry shops in the area were sold out. I lived with the Dumards for a period of several months that included Pearl Harbor, the fall of Hong Kong and Singapore, and the blunder of Dieppe, but I do not recall that the war was ever discussed except as a perplexing nuisance conducted for the pleasure and profit of muddle-headed Anglo-Saxons.

That winter, Marie-Blanche was being frequented by a suitor called Wilfrid. Wilfrid's attendance was then in its second year and Marie-Blanche, who had never until now received so much encouragement, had assembled a trousseau of pillowcases and towels embroidered with bowknots. He was a big, blond hulk of a man, with manicured hands and a boneless handshake. His conversation was filled with meaningless curlicues that Madame Dumard considered real *politesse*. Every Friday he brought Marie-Blanche a corsage of tinted carnations, tortured onto wire stems and embalmed in prickly greenery. For Madame there was a box of chocolates, each piece wrapped in colored tinfoil. On the cover of the box was a young person, dressed as Columbine, looking at the moon. Wilfrid talked a great deal about his own mother, who had died, and as he spoke tears coursed down his round cheeks, and there were answering tears in Madame's eyes and sympathetic sounds from Marie-Blanche. After they had cried for a while they put away their handkerchiefs and moved solemnly into the dining room, where they drank scalding tea and ate éclairs and creamy pastries called *religieuses* because their shape resembles little nuns.

Wilfrid did not appear disturbed by the courting rules of the house. He sat in perfect ease and happiness two nights a week and talked about his dead mother. He had once begun preparation for holy orders but had decided in time he lacked the true vocation; however, he had acquired (or had been born with) many characteristics of an urban priest in a sound, prosperous parish, where the parishioners want to hear good things said about private property. He pressed the tips of his fingers together when he talked, and he pursed his mouth and closed his eyes when he listened. He moved quietly and slowly, and it took him ten minutes to say "Good morning," or "How do you do?" so beautifully did he phrase the message.

Madame Dumard was enchanted with him. She permitted him to take Marie-Blanche to the cinema, where they were chaperoned by a young friend of Wilfrid's called Jean-Jacques. Jean-Jacques was a sweet, nervous young man with the smile of a pious child. He was a singer by profession, and sang on the radio many songs about love, joy, or frustration in Paris. He sounded exactly like Tino Rossi. When he sang he tilted his head and turned his eyes to Heaven, as if he were posing for a picture on the occasion of his First Communion. Madame Dumard liked him almost as well as Wilfrid and he often sang, just for her, her two favorite songs, *"Hirondelle"* and *"J'ai Deux Amours."*

One Sunday, as Marie-Blanche was leaving church after eleven o'clock Mass, she was surprised to see Jean-Jacques waiting for her on the steps with what she later described as an agitated air. He begged her to accompany him to a drug store, where they could talk. He guided her into a booth and ordered ice cream for them both. When it came, a tear formed in his eye and fell in the dish.

"I'm very fond of Wilfrid," he said. It is difficult to report this conversation, because Marie-Blanche's histrionic talents later got in the way of her giving a straight account. But she held firm on a few of Jean-Jacques' declarations.

"Wilfrid pays for my singing lessons," he said next. He stirred his ice cream to soup while Marie-Blanche privately decided she would soon put a stop to *that* once she and Wilfrid were married.

"When Wilfrid marries, I will be alone in the world," said Jean-Jacques. "He is my only friend."

"Have you no *maman?*" said Marie-Blanche. She was beginning to think that Jean-Jacques asked a great deal in the name of friendship.

Jean-Jacques shook his head. "Wilfrid often speaks of getting married," he said. "And then, he's so fond of your mother. This time, I think he's serious." He lifted his heavy-lashed eyes and looked straight across the table. She later described his expression as sinister, but it was probably only stagily tragic and third-rate tragedy at that. "Why can't we go on just as we are?" he said. "All going to the cinema together once a week, and Wilfrid calling on your mother? We would be so happy and have such fun."

Marie-Blanche remarked that it didn't seem like much fun to her, at which Jean-Jacques pronounced: "If you marry Wilfrid you will be unhappy all your life." He paid for the ice cream and departed, leaving Marie-Blanche to run home with the exciting news.

The family spent an agreeable though tiring day trying to decide what Jean-Jacques meant. Marie-Blanche thought it meant another wife, but Madame Dumard was all for some congenital ailment, like having fits. On Tuesday, when Wilfrid came to call, they told him what had happened, chattering like a pair of squirrels. Wilfrid turned red, then he looked blank, then he sat down and remained so silent and depressed for the rest of the evening that Marie-Blanche assured him she would never, never mention the distressing incident again. Her promise was just, for that was the last time she saw him. He wrote a poetic letter in decorated handwriting. He said Jean-Jacques' singing lessons were so expensive he felt he couldn't support a wife. He called Marie-Blanche his never-to-be-forgotten little white flower.

None of the Dumards, nor any of their friends, knew what to make of it. Their parish priest, whom they consulted, solicited a small sum for prayers of gratitude that Marie-Blanche had been spared, which confused them more than ever. They began to read something criminal and vicious into the behavior of these immature and silly men. Although I was often asked for one, I never contributed a solution because I much preferred Madame Dumard's summing up. She often told the story to callers, from beginning to end, concluding with these words: "*Il avait un grand défaut,* but we don't know what it was and so we never speak of it."

Later they heard that Wilfrid was engaged again and moving in a more elevated society: she was the daughter of a city councilor. Wilfrid and the fiancée and Jean-Jacques were frequently seen at the cinema together, and the Dumards, when they were told of this, indulgently decided that it was just Wilfrid's way.

It was hard for Marie-Blanche to get used to the ordinary

cut of man after someone so *raffiné*, but a few weeks later, in the spring, a cousin introduced her to a new cavalier and she began to perk up. The new one was called Télèsphore Ouimette, and he was a tailor. Madame Dumard, still brokenhearted over Wilfrid's defection, looked upon him with immediate dislike. He had a head of rich, black, glossy waves that he combed every few minutes, lovingly pushing the ridges into shape. When he came to call, he would stop in the hall and comb his hair in the mirror with a swan painted on it. Then, in the parlor, he would peer from time to time into the beveled looking glass that was covered with etched grapes. The haircombings punctuated the bantering wit that was his mating cry to Marie-Blanche.

Madame Dumard disliked him so much that she could not sit in the same room. She would rock fiercely by the kitchen stove, observing him (for the sake of decorum) down the hall through the two opened doors, muttering to herself. Télèsphore called her Mémère, as if she were a country grandmother, and this infuriated her almost more than anything else he might have done. After Wilfrid's splendid French,.Télèsphore's ripe local accent fell harshly on her ears, and she often pretended not to know what he was saying. Of this he seemed unaware. He would saunter into the kitchen and comb his hair in the only mirror he could find, which was part of the stove. The stove was glossy and black. It supported a panel of creamy tiles decorated with pink roses, and over the tiles was the warming oven, whose curving nickel-plated front, which Madame Dumard kept at a fevered state of polish, formed an excellent looking glass. Here Télèsphore would comb and comb, unmindful of the bread she was toasting on top of the stove.

Being a tailor was evidently profitable, for he was the only one of Marie-Blanche's suitors who owned a car. It was a Ford convertible of dusky red, and sometimes, on warm spring nights, Marie-Blanche was permitted to drive with him. The problem of a duenna was difficult at this period. Agnès was launched on the second of her many pregnancies, and Madame Dumard would as soon have been caught in a downtown bar as a red convertible. One day she asked me, rather shyly, if I would chaperon the two on their Friday night sorties. Marie-Blanche was, biologically at least, old enough to be my mother, and Télèsphore was already launched on a fattish middle-age; but no one seemed to find my presence silly or incongruous, and even Télèsphore seemed to take it for granted that I would come along.

The order of the evening was that we drove at a pace that was almost a standstill through the streets of the quarter, so that Marie-Blanche could be seen and admired by one and all. Then we drove west along Sherbrooke Street, picking up speed, out to the west-end suburbs, where he would weave in and out of innumerable chintzy crescents, drives, and circles, while Marie-Blanche stared solemnly at the attitudes of suburbia on a spring night. This was evidently an accepted form of outing, like going to the zoo; and it was clear that the customs of suburban dwellers were as foreign to her as the life of the penguin. After the monotonous colonial houses and imitation Tudor had been fully appreciated, he drove a short distance out of the city to a curb-service restaurant and bought us potato chips and a soft drink. Then we drove home.

During the drives, their conversation floated back to me on the warm spring air. It was as innocent as that of the

Babes in the Woods. Rendered in English it amounted, in effect, to two lines: "You don't really like me," and "Oh, you don't mean that." Back at the house, I always tried to hurry up the stairs so that they could be alone for at least a second. Their courtship was, to say the least of it, blameless, although he sometimes would give her a pat on her soundly armored behind as he helped her into the car. Télèsphore tailored all his own clothes, of course, and I particularly remember a brown suit with stripes in a lighter tone, and a long green jacket with magnificent shoulders. Marie-Blanche began to recover from Wilfrid's *grande déception*, and what with the potato chips and drives through the suburbs and the little pats, she became quite cheerful and began to put on weight.

Early in the summer, Télèsphore began missing Fridays; and one night he took Marie-Blanche's hand in his and said he was not the marrying kind. When she replied tearfully that *no* man was the marrying kind, but that she would wait if he thought he ever could be, he said she was a saint and better off without him. A few weeks later, having obtained a hurried dispensation to do so, he married his third cousin. Marie-Blanche attended the wedding, her head high. She wore a new hat decorated with blue and pink velvet *choux*. There was no need to mention a *grand défaut*; the condition of the bride, inadequately concealed under tucks, drapes, and flowing panels of white, spoke of it eloquently. I was surprised at Marie-Blanche's lack of restraint in discussing the wedding; she was indignant, but not really shocked. It was simply another drama, like the story of Wilfrid, an example of the inexplicable ways of men. I also realized, gradually, that she had only the haziest notion of how the situation had come about; her information was pieced together from romantic magazine stories, the prudishly censored confidences of her married sister, and the unprudish stories of salesmen in the shops where she worked. Madame Dumard, of course, would rather have died on the spot than utter one enlightening word to an unmarried daughter; and even had she chosen to do so, at Marie-Blanche's age it would have seemed rather silly.

After Télèsphore came many smaller deceptions, men who frequented for a few Fridays and fell away. It is difficult to remember the minor suitors who emerged that year, as distinct from those who have happened since. There had been men named for flowers, for saints, and for martyred heroes. There have been men whose names were a euphonious stringing together of syllables, meaning nothing, and impossible on the Anglo-Saxon tongue. There were suitors who drove buses and streetcars, who sold aspirin and bandaids, who dealt in false teeth and in shoes. She would, of course, have married any one of them, had he not disappeared after his fellows, unequivocally labeled with a *grand défaut*; however, like most women she aspired to a marriage above her station. She looked upward (in vain) to the plateau on which dwelt dentists, notaries and radio announcers. There were still more euphoric heights, peopled with doctors and lawyers and civil engineers — in the Dumard's circle one still said *"Madame Docteur Tremblay"* or *"Madame l'Avocat Arsenault."* But Marie-Blanche knew better than to sour her disposition by dreaming of that.

Once, and only once, was she courted by someone socially beneath herself, and that was at the end of the terrible year that began with Wilfrid and Télèsphore. In the autumn, disillusioned into a devil-may-care attitude, she permitted herself to be frequented by a farmer. Sylvestre Dancereau fell in love with Marie-Blanche one Sunday afternoon when, as she was visiting cousins thirty miles outside the city, he saw her posing for a snapshot. She was wearing white eyelet and had ribbons in her hair. Marie-Blanche usually poses by wetting her lips and parting them in a curly half-smile. Sometimes she rests her head on one hand or, again, looks beyond the camera as if she had just been surprised by a rainbow. Sylvestre, who lived nearby and had come over for some sociable purpose, spoke of his feelings almost at once. Everyone was pleased and astonished; he was nearly forty, and had never in his life courted anyone. Marie-Blanche's cousins broke their necks bringing the two together and the Dumards accepted the new suppliant with a tolerant air. The superiority of city over country people was too established to require pointing out; they would wait and see.

Early in October Sylvestre began calling in town. He arrived a little later than the accustomed hour — he had a complicated schedule that involved changing buses twice — and he left at nine to avoid missing any link in his chain of transport. The Dumards were relieved. His visits were a terrible strain. He was a thin, gangling man who dressed as all farmers do when they come to the city. He sat with one hand on each of his knees and unless someone spoke to him directly he hung his head and looked at the carpet. He was shy and miserable and terrified of committing a social blunder. He even left the parlor when he had to blow his nose. And, although they spread out for him their usual tea and pastry, he could not bring himself to eat in their presence. Sometimes he drank a little tea, with the spoon firmly held between two fingers so that it would not hit him in the eye.

In November, he asked Marie-Blanche's cousins to ask her if she would marry him, and she wrote a gracious note of acceptance. The cousins, now awhirl with intrigue and message-bearing, were asked to point out to Sylvestre that she would not, of course, be expected to live on the farm. Sylvestre would have to come into town and get a job. The cousins could see the point: a girl with Marie-Blanche's knowledge of English, her intimacy with the business world and all aspects of city life, including the mores of crap shooters, could not be expected to cook over an iron range or pump her own water in the country. Sylvestre was made to see this; his father and his brother could easily carry on.

Marie-Blanche's brother-in-law, who was a milkman, was commissioned to find Sylvestre a job. He exerted his influence for several weeks and finally turned up a job for Sylvestre in the bottling department. The plant was out of town and work began at seven in the morning, but everyone agreed that Sylvestre was accustomed to early rising. His starting salary was twenty-two dollars and fifty cents a week. Sylvestre put off the move as long as possible. He muttered excuses that were connected with the farm and frequently said there was someone he didn't like to leave. Marie-Blanche knew there was no woman in his life other than herself and guessed that he meant his mother. She approved of this, for it was often repeated in the Dumard's circle that men who loved their mothers made excellent husbands.

On New Year's Day, the most festive day of their calendar, Sylvestre was required to desert his home and spend the day with his fiancée's assembled family. He was to present Marie-Blanche with a ring (he had already given her, for Christmas, a heart-shaped locket with an imitation pearl at its center) and their engagement would be acknowledged before the eyes of all. Marie-Blanche wept the morning of New Year's Day because, the previous year, it had been Wilfrid who had sat at her Aunt Elzema's table, nibbling turkey with delicate bites, modestly refusing a glass of wine with an upturned hand. When Madame Dumard reproached her for weeping, she dried her eyes and said somberly, *"Dieu me comprend."* Then they went off together down the snowy street, two little cocoons of wool, overshoes, veils and something black with furry accretions wrapped over it all.

I had spent the day somewhere else and arrived back about an hour before the Dumards. They entered the flat in silence, shaking the snow from their coats without a word. Still wearing their hats and overshoes they proceeded to the kitchen, that lap of comfort, without a word. Madame Dumard shook the fire down and put some wood on it and put the kettle on for tea. I wandered in and sat down and we looked at each other. "Le Sylvestre," said Marie-Blanche at last, as if she were pronouncing the name of a brother drowned at sea. "Wait till I tell you. Some guy."

"Parle donc français," said her mother sharply. She was in a terrible mood. Marie-Blanche sighed and removed her hat. The imprisoned curls expanded. She placed the hat on the kitchen table and Madame Dumard said at once: "Haven't we had enough bad luck for one day?" She brushed the hat onto a chair. She looked at me and drew a long breath. "Try to imagine the scene," she said, and both women settled back for a good dramatic account.

There had been thirty-five people at Aunt Elzema's, but good humor had prevailed and they had eaten in shifts. It had been *un diner* extra, with seven kinds of dessert, including a huge *bûche*, a cake shaped like a log with little sugar rosebuds all over it. And wine. "For the men, of course," Madame said hastily.

"And Sylvestre?" It was one of those accounts that requires a shove from time to time.

"Sylvestre. *Ah, ça.*" First of all, there had been his table manners. There had been a little side dish of green peas that he had tried to eat with a fork instead of the teaspoon so clearly provided for the purpose. He had picked up his dainty glass of tomato juice and said audibly: *"Qu'est-ce que c'est donc, cette affaire, donc, donc,"* the additions of *"doncs"* being the cadence of his unfortunate country speech. Unlike Wilfrid, he had not, smilingly, demurred when offered wine. He drained not one glass but many and then, flushed with alcohol and love, had risen on his trembling legs and made a little speech. He was coming into the city, he said, for the sake of the one he loved; and here he had leered in the direction of his betrothed. But on this festive day, he went on, he wanted to show them a few snapshots, to show what this move meant to him. He had drawn out his wallet; Marie-Blanche had looked modestly at the tablecloth, remembering the autumn day, the eyelet frock and the hair ribbons. But Sylvestre produced a handful of pictures, and they were not of Marie-Blanche. They were of a horse.

"Victorine," said Sylvestre. Victorine was so clever she could almost talk. She understood everything one said. Grace, beauty, fidelity, intelligence; tribute after tribute fell from his lips. Many of the photos included Sylvestre, of course. There was Sylvestre in a cowboy suit, waving his hat in a dashing manner; Sylvestre offering Victorine a lump of sugar; Sylvestre negligently rolling a cigarette with the bridle lying slack. He told them his chaps and gauntlets were hand-made by Indians out west.

"I thought 'e'd never shut up about the damned 'orse," Marie-Blanche told me, in English.

The pictures had gone round the table silently, and then producing increasing hilarity. One of the cousins began to sing "Joe, le Cowboy," and from there they went on to "Le Cowboy des Western Plains." "Le Cowboy Canadian," and finally united in many rolicking choruses of "Dans Les Plains du Fa-ar West." Sylvestre led the singing while Marie-Blanche and her mother sat, mortified but stony-faced. Marie-Blanche held the pictures in her hand. There was not one of her. Sylvestre was so happy and excited that he forgot all about the ring. It was still in his pocket when the Dumards left, swept out on the sympathetic clucking of their female relatives. The males were still singing. "It's a terrible thing to marry a drunk," one of her aunts remarked.

Marie-Blanche spoke only once to Sylvestre, a memorable parting line. She returned to him his packet of snapshots before the eyes of all and, addressing him in her perfect English, said: "To heach 'is own, Monsieur Dancereau."

"Ah, well," Madame Dumard sighed, beginning to make the tea. "It's just as well we know now what he is. *Il a un grand défaut . . .*" She would have said more, but Marie-Blanche slammed her hand down on the table with exasperation.

"*Défaut* be damned," she said. "He's just like the rest of them, nothing but a big schlemiel."

Wing's Chips

OFTEN, since I grew up, I have tried to remember the name of the French-Canadian town where I lived for a summer with my father when I was a little girl of seven or eight. Sometimes, passing through a town, I have thought I recognized it, but some detail is always wrong, or at least fails to fit the picture in my memory. It was a town like many others in the St. Lawrence Valley — old, but with a curious atmosphere of harshness, as if the whole area were still frontier and had not been settled and cultivated for three hundred years. There were rows of temporary-looking frame and stucco houses, a post office in somebody's living room, a Chinese fish-and-chip store, and, on the lawn of the imposing Catholic church, a statue of Jesus, arms extended, crowned with a wreath of electric lights. Running straight through the center of town was a narrow river; a few leaky rowboats were tied up along its banks, and on Sunday afternoons hot, church-dressed young men would go to work on them with rusty bailing tins. The girls who clustered giggling on shore and watched them wore pastel stockings, lacy summer hats, and voile dresses that dipped down in back and were decorated low on one hip with sprays of artificial lilac. For additional Sunday divertisse-ment, there was the cinema, in an old barn near the railway station. The pictures had no sound track; airs from "My Maryland" and "The Student Prince" were played on a piano and there was the occasional toot of the suburban train from Montreal while on the screen ladies with untidy hair and men in riding boots engaged in agitated, soundless conversation, opening and closing their mouths like fish.

Though I have forgotten the name of this town, I do remember with remarkable clarity the house my father took for that summer. It was white clapboard, and surrounded by shade trees and an untended garden, in which only sun-flowers and a few perennials survived. It had been rented furnished and bore the imprint of Quebec rural taste, run-ning largely to ball fringes and sea-shell-encrusted religious art. My father, who was a painter, used one room as a studio — or, rather, storage place, since he worked mostly out-of-doors — slept in another, and ignored the remaining seven, which was probably just as well, though order of a sort was kept by a fierce-looking local girl called Pauline, who had a pronounced mustache and was so ill-tempered that her nickname was *P'tit-Loup* — Little Wolf.

Pauline cooked abominably, cleaned according to her mood, and asked me questions. My father had told her that my mother was in a nursing home in Montreal, but Pauline wanted to know more. How ill was my mother? Very ill? Dying? Was it true that my parents were sep-arated? Was my father *really* my father? *"Drôle de père,"* said Pauline. She was perplexed by his painting, his animals (that summer his menagerie included two German shepherds, a parrot, and a marmoset, which later bit the finger of a man teasing it and had to be given away to Montreal's ratty little zoo, where it moped itself to death), and his total indifference to the way the house was run. Why didn't he work, like other men, said Pauline.

I could understand her bewilderment, for the question of my father's working was beginning to worry me for the first time. All of the French-Canadian fathers in the town worked. They delivered milk, they farmed, they owned rival hardware stores, they drew up one another's wills. Nor were they the only busy ones. Across the river, in a faithful reproduction of a suburb of Glasgow or Manchester, lived a small colony of English-speaking summer residents from Montreal. Their children were called Al, Lily, Winnie, or Mac, and they were distinguished by their popping blue eyes, their excessive devotion to the Royal Family, and their contempt for anything even vaguely queer or Gallic. Like the French-Canadians, the fathers of Lily and Winnie and the others worked. Every one of them had a job. When they were not taking the train to Montreal to attend to their jobs, they were crouched in their gardens, caps on their heads, tying up tomato plants or painting stones to make gay multicolored borders for the nasturtium beds. Saturday night, they trooped into the town bar-and-grill and drank as much Molson's ale as could be poured into the stomach before closing time. Then, awash with ale and nostalgia, they sang about the maid in the clogs and shawl, and something else that went, "Let's all go down to the Strand, and 'ave a ba-na-ar-na!"

My father, I believed, was wrong in not establishing some

immediate liaison with this group. Like them, he was English — a real cabbage, said Pauline when she learned that he had been in Canada only eight or nine years. Indeed, one of his very few topics of conversation with me was the England of his boyhood, before the First World War. It sounded green, sunny, and silent — a sort of vast lawn rising and falling beside the sea; the sun was smaller and higher than the sun in Canada, looking something like a coin; the trees were leafy and round, and looked like cushions. This was probably not at all what he said, but it was the image I retained — a landscape flickering and flooded with light, like the old silents at the cinema. The parents of Lily and Winnie had, presumably, also come out of this landscape, yet it was a bond my father appeared to ignore. It seemed to me that he was unaware of how much we had lost caste, and what grievous social errors we had committed, by being too much identified with the French. He had chosen a house on the wrong side of the river. Instead of avoiding the French language, or noisily making fun of it, he spoke it whenever he was dealing with anyone who could not understand English. He did not attend the English church, and he looked just as sloppy on Sundays as he did the rest of the week.

"You people Carthlic?" one of the fathers from over the river asked me once, as if that would explain a lot.

Mercifully, I was able to say no. I knew we were not Catholic because at the Pensionnat Saint-Louis de Gonzague, in Montreal, which I attended, I had passed the age at which children usually took the First Communion. For a year and more, my classmates had been attending morning chapel in white veils, while I still wore a plain, stiff, pre-

Communion black veil that smelled of convent parlors, and marked me as one outside the limits of grace.

"Then why's your dad always around the frogs?" asked the English father.

Drôle de père indeed. I had to agree with Pauline. He was not like any father I had met or read about. He was not Elsie's Mr. Dinsmore, stern but swayed by tears. Nor did he in the least resemble Mr. Bobbsey, of the Bobbsey Twins books, or Mr. Bunker, of the Six Little Bunkers. I was never scolded, or rebuked, or reminded to brush my teeth or say my prayers. My father was perfectly content to live his own summer and let me live mine, which did not please me in the least. If, at meals, I failed to drink my milk, it was I who had to mention this omission. When I came home from swimming with my hair wet, it was I who had to remind him that, because of some ear trouble that was a hangover of scarlet fever, I was supposed to wear a bathing cap. When Lon Chaney in *The Hunchback of Notre Dame* finally arrived at the cinema, he did not say a word about my not going, even though Lily and Winnie and many of the French-Canadian children were not allowed to attend, and boasted about the restriction.

Oddly, he did have one or two notions about the correct upbringing of children, which were, to me, just as exasperating as his omissions. Somewhere in the back of his mind lingered a recollection that all little girls were taught French and music. I don't know where the little girls of the England of his childhood were sent to learn their French — presumably to France — but I was placed, one month after my fourth birthday, in the Pensionnat, where for two years I had the petted privilege of being the youngest boarder in the history of the school. My piano lessons had also begun at four, but lasted only a short time, for, as the nun in charge of music explained, I could not remember or sit still, and my hand was too small to span an octave. Music had then been dropped as one of my accomplishments until that summer, when, persuaded by someone who obviously had my welfare at heart, my father dispatched me twice a week to study piano with a Madame Tessier, the convent-educated wife of a farmer, whose parlor was furnished entirely with wicker and over whose household hung a faint smell of dung, owing to the proximity of the outbuildings and the intense humidity of summer weather in the St. Lawrence Valley. Together, Madame Tessier and I sweated it out, plodding away against my lack of talent, my absence of interest, and my strong but unspoken desire to be somewhere else.

"Cette enfant ne fera jamais rien," I once heard her say in despair.

We had been at it four or five weeks before she discovered at least part of the trouble; it was simply that there was no piano at home, so I never practiced. After every lesson, she had marked with care the scales I was to master, yet, week after week, I produced only those jerky, hesitant sounds that are such agony for music teachers and the people in the next room.

"You might as well tell your father there's no use carrying on unless you have a piano," she said.

I was only too happy, and told him that afternoon, at lunch.

"You mean you want me to get you a *piano?*" he said, looking around the dining room as if I had insisted it be installed, then and there, between the window and the mirrored china cabinet. How unreasonable I was!

"But you make me take the lessons," I said. How unreasonable *he* was!

A friend of my father's said to me, years later, "He never had the faintest idea what to do with you." But it was equally true that I never had the faintest idea what to do with him. We did not, of course, get a piano, and Madame Tessier's view was that because my father had no employment to speak of (she called him a *flâneur*), we simply couldn't afford one — the depth of shame in a town where even the milkman's daughters could play duets.

No one took my father's painting seriously as a daily round of work, least of all I. At one point during that summer, my father agreed to do a pastel portrait of the daughter of a Madame Gravelle, who lived in Montreal. (This was in the late twenties, when pastel drawings of children hung in every other sitting room.) The daughter, Liliane, who was my age or younger, was to be shown in her First Communion dress and veil. Madame Gravelle and Liliane drove out from Montreal, and while Liliane posed with docility, her mother hung about helpfully commenting. Here my father was neglecting to show in detail the pattern of the lace veil; there he had the wrong shade of blue for Liliane's eyes; again, it was the matter of Liliane's diamond cross. The cross, which hung from her neck, contained four diamonds on the horizontal segment and six on the vertical, and this treasure he had reduced to two unimpressive strokes.

My father suggested that Madame Gravelle might be just as happy with a tinted photograph. No, said Madame

Gravelle, she would not. Well, then, he suggested, how about a miniature? He knew of a miniaturist who worked from photographs, eliminating sittings, and whose fee was about four times his own. Madame Gravelle bore Liliane, her cross, and her veil back to Montreal, and my father went back to painting around the countryside and going out with his dogs.

His failure weighed heavily on me, particularly after someone, possibly Pauline, told me that he was forever painting people who didn't pay him a cent for doing it. He painted Pauline, mustache and all; he painted some of the French-Canadian children who came to play in our garden, and from whom I was learning a savory French vocabulary not taught at Pensionnat Saint-Louis de Gonzague; he very often sketched the little Wing children, whose family owned the village fish-and-chip store.

The Wing children were solemn little Chinese, close in age and so tangled in lineage that it was impossible to sort them out as sisters, brothers, and cousins. Some of the adult Wings — brothers, and cousins — ran the fish-and-chip shop, and were said to own many similar establishments throughout Quebec and to be (although no one would have guessed it to see them) by far the richest people in the area. The interior of their store smelled wonderfully of frying grease and vinegar, and the walls were a mosaic of brightly painted tin signs advertising Player's Mild, Orange Crush, Sweet Marie chocolate bars, and ginger ale. The smaller Wings, in the winter months, attended Anglican boarding schools in the west, at a discreet distance from the source of income. Their English was excellent and their French-Canadian idiom without flaw. Those nearest my age were Florence, Marjorie, Ronald, and Hugh. The older set of brothers and cousins — those of my father's generation — had abrupt, utilitarian names: Tommy, Jimmy, George. The still older people — most of whom seldom came out from the rooms behind the shop — used their Chinese names. There was even a great-grandmother, who sat, shrunken and silent, by the great iron range where the chips swam in a bath of boiling fat.

As the Wings had no garden, and were not permitted to play by the river, lest they fall in and drown, it was most often at my house that we played. If my father was out, we would stand at the door of his studio and peer in at the fascinating disorder.

"What does he do?" Florence or Marjorie would say. "What does your father do?"

"He paints!" Pauline would cry from the kitchen. She might, herself, consider him loony, but the privilege was hers. She worked there, not a pack of Chinese.

It was late in the summer, in August, when, one afternoon, Florence and Marjorie and Ronald and Hugh came up from the gate escorting, like a convoy, one of the older Wings. They looked anxious and important. "Is your father here?" said the grown-up Wing.

I ran to fetch my father, who had just started out for a walk. When we returned, Pauline and the older Wing, who turned out to be Jimmy, were arguing in French, she at the top of her voice, he almost inaudibly.

"The kids talk about you a lot," said Jimmy Wing to my father. "They said you were a painter. We're enlarging the store, and we want a new sign."

"A sign?"

"I told you!" shrieked Pauline from the dining-room door, to which she had retreated. *"Ce n'est pas un peintre comme ça."*

"Un peintre, c'est un peintre," said Jimmy Wing, imperturbable.

My father looked at the little Wings, who were all looking up at him, and said, "Exactly. *Un peintre, c'est un peintre.* What sort of sign would you like?"

The Wings didn't know; they all began to talk at once. Something artistic, said Jimmy Wing, with the lettering fat and thin, imitation Chinese. Did my father know what he meant? Oh, yes. My father knew exactly.

"Just 'Wing's Chips'?" my father asked. "Or would you like it in French — 'Les Chips de Wing'?"

"Oh, *English*," said all the Wings, almost together. My father said later that the Chinese were terrible snobs.

He painted the sign the next Sunday afternoon, not in the studio but out in the back garden, sitting on the wide kitchen steps. He lacquered it black, and painted — in red-and-gold characters, fat and thin — "Wing's Chips," and under this he put the name of the town and two curly little letters, "P.Q.," for "Province of Quebec."

Tommy and Jimmy Wing and all the little ones came to fetch the sign the next day. The two men looked at it for a long time, while the little ones looked anxiously at them to see if they liked it. Finally, Jimmy Wing said, "It's the most beautiful thing I ever saw."

The two men bore it away, the little Wings trailing behind, and hung it on a horizontal pole over the street in front of their shop, where it rocked in the hot, damp breeze from the river. I was hysterically proud of the sign and, for quite the first time, of my father. Everyone stopped before the shop and examined it. The French-Canadians admitted that it was *pas mal, pas mal du tout,* while the English adults said approvingly that he must have been paid a fine penny for it. I could not bring down our new stature by admitting that he had painted it as a favor, and that it was only after Jimmy and Tommy had insisted that he had said they could, if they liked, pay for the gold paint, since he had had to go to Montreal for it. Nor did I tell anyone how the Wings, burdened with gratitude, kept bringing us chips and ice cream.

"Oh, yes, he was paid an awful lot," I assured them all.

Every day, I went to look at the sign, and I hung around the shop in case anyone wanted to ask me questions about it. There it was, "Wing's Chips," proof that my father was an ordinary workingman just like anybody else, and I pointed it out to as many people as I could, both English and French, until the summer ended and we went away.

The Legacy

LATE IN THE AFTERNOON after Mrs. Boldescu's funeral, her four children returned to the shop on St. Eulalie Street, in Montreal, where they had lived when they were growing up. Victor, the youngest, drove quickly ahead, leaving, like an unfriendly country, the trampled grass of the cemetery and the sorrowing marble angels. Several blocks behind came Marina and the two older boys, Carol and Georgie, side by side in the long black car that had been hired for the day. Emptied of flowers, it still enclosed a sickly smell of lilies and of Carol's violet horseshoe, that had borne on a taffeta ribbon the words "Good Luck to You, Mama."

These three sat in silence, collapsed against the prickling plush of the cushions. Marina was thankful that Victor had driven up from Bloomfield, New Jersey, in his own three-year-old Buick. It would have been too much at this moment to have shared the drive with his American wife, Peggy Ann, hearing her voice carried out on the hot city air as she exclaimed over the slummy landscape and congratulated her husband on his plucky triumph over environment. Glancing at Carol and Georgie, Marina decided they might not have cared. Their triumph had been of a different nature. They stared out of the car at brick façades, seemingly neither moved nor offended by the stunning ugliness of the streets that had held their childhood. Sometimes one of them sighed, the comfortable respiration of one who has wept.

Remembering the funeral, Marina bent her head and traced a seam of her black linen suit where the dye had taken badly. Her brothers had cried with such abandon that they had commended themselves foreve⁻ to Father Patenaude and every neighborhood woman at church. "Those bad pennies," Marina had heard Father Patenaude say. "Bad pennies they were, but they loved their mother. They did all of this, you know."

By "all of this," he meant the first-class funeral, the giant wreaths, the large plot they had purchased in perpetuum, to which their father's coffin, until now at rest in a less imposing cemetery, had been removed. There was space in the new plot for them all, including Victor's wife, who would, Marina thought, be grateful to know that thanks to her brothers-in-law's foresight her bones need not be turned out, for lack of burial space, until the Day of Judgment. A smaller tract, spattered with the delicate shadow of a weeping willow, had been set aside for Victor s children. He was the only one of her brothers who had married, and his as-yet-unconceived offspring were doomed to early extinction if one considered the space reserved for their remains. Marina could only imagine the vision of small crosses, sleeping babies, and praying cherubs that had been painted for Carol and Georgie. At the same time, she wondered what Victor felt about his brothers' prescience. His expression at the funeral had been one of controlled alarm, perhaps because of his wife, whose fidgetings and whisperings had disturbed even the rolling tide of Carol's and Georgie's grief. These two had stared hard at Peggy Ann on the edge of the grave, and Georgie had remarked that nothing worthy of life or death was likely to come out of that blond, skinny drink of water — which Marina took to be a reference to the babies' plot.

The way they had been grouped at the funeral — Marina unwillingly pressed between her weeping brothers, Victor a little apart — had seemed to her prophetic. The strain of her mother's long illness had made her superstitious. Visiting her mother at the hospital toward the end, she had seen an omen in every cloud, a message in a maple leaf that, on a treeless street, unexpectedly fell at her feet. Sometimes she felt that all of them had combined to kill their mother — Victor by behaving too well, the others by behaving badly, herself through the old-maidish asperity that had lately begun to creep through her conversation like an ink-stain. She had even blamed Father Patenaude, remembering, in her mother's last moments, the cold comfort her mother had brought home from the confession box. Watching the final office of death, Marina waited for him to speak the words of reassurance her mother wanted; but nothing came, and Mrs. Boldescu was permitted to die without once being told that the mores of St. Eulalie Street and not her own inadequacies had permitted Victor's escape into a Protestant marriage, and Georgie's and Carol's being led away again and again by the police.

Marina had quarreled with Father Patenaude, right then

and there in the hospital, where all the nurses could hear. The priest's thin face had been pink with annoyance, and the embarrassment of Carol and Georgie caused them, later on, to press upon him a quite unnecessary check. His sins of omission — they had possibly been caused, she now realized, through nothing sterner than lack of imagination — were for God and not Marina to judge, Father Patenaude said.

Mrs. Boldescu had only by courtesy been attached to his flock. She belonged by birth and breeding to the Greek Catholic Church, that easy resting place between Byzantium and Rome. The Father was French-Canadian, with the peasant distrust of all his race for the exotic. Perhaps, Marina thought, he had detected her mother's contempt for the pretty, pallid Western saints, each with his crown of electric lights. In the soaring exaltation of her self-reproach, Father Patenaude must have sensed the richness of past devotions, seen the bearded priest, the masculine saints, the gold walls glittering behind the spears of candlelight, the hanging ruby lamp swaying in the thick incense-laden air. Victor's marriage had probably offended him most. Even Georgie and Carol, for all their cosmic indifference to the affairs of their sister and brother, had been offended.

However Mrs. Boldescu might deplore the deviation of her youngest son, she trusted his good business sense. It was to Victor that the shop had been left. Now, driving back to it for the final conference, Marina could not have said if Carol and Georgie minded. Their feelings toward each other as children had been so perfunctory that jealousy, then, would have struck any one of them as much too familiar to be comfortable. Of course, Carol and Georgie might have changed; meeting over their mother's bed, after a separation of years, they had had no time to sift their memories, even had they chosen to do anything so out of character. Their greeting had been in the matter-of-fact tones of consanguinity, and Marina had retired at once to a flower-banked corner of the hospital room, so that her brothers might have scope and space for their emotions.

The two had scarcely glanced at her again. Pale and tired, graced with only the ghost of a racial bloom they had long disavowed and now failed to recognize, Marina appeared to satisfy their image of a sister. To her, however, the first few moments had been webbed in strangeness, and she had watched her brothers as if they came from an alien land. They knelt by the bed, barred with the shadow of the hospital shade, their glossy, brilliantined heads bowed on clasped hands. Disliking their rings, their neckties, their easy tears, she remembered what had formed them, and saw behind her brothers a tunnel of moldering corridors, the gray and stifling walls of reformatories named for saints. Summoning this image, like a repeated apology, she was able to pardon the violet horseshoe, the scene of distracted remorse on the brink of the grave. Their strangeness vanished; boredom took its place. She remembered at last what her brothers were like — not the somber criminal of sociological texts, denied roller skates at a crucial age; still less the hero-villain of films; but simply men whose moments of megalomaniacal audacity were less depressing than their lack of common sense and taste. It was for their pleasure, she thought, that people manufactured ash trays shaped like little outhouses, that curly-haired little girls in sailor suits were taught to tap-dance, and night-club singers gave voice to "Mother Machree" and "Eli, Eli."

Still, she thought, neither of them would have married into apostasy like Victor, nor flustered poor Father Patenaude by listening to his sermons as if analyzing them for truth and intellectual content, as she herself did every week. The Father was horrified that the shop had been left to Victor instead of to them. "It might have been their redemption," Marina had heard him say after the funeral, as she threaded her way out between the elaborate graves. "And they were so good to her; they loved their mother."

Certainly, their periodic descents on St. Eulalie Street had been more impressive than Victor's monthly check and letter, or Marina's faithful presence at Sunday dinner. Carol and Georgie, awash in the warm sea of Mother's Day, had left in their wake a refrigerator for the shop that could hold fifteen cases of beer, a radio inlaid with wood in a waterfall pattern, a silver brush and mirror with Old English initials, a shrine containing a Madonna with blue glass eyes, a pearl-and-diamond pin shaped like a daisy, a Persian lamb coat with summer storage prepaid for ten years, two porcelain lamps of shepherd and shepherdess persuasion, and finally the gift that for some reason appealed most strongly to Carol and Georgie — a sherry decanter and ten tiny glasses, each of which sounded a note of gratifying purity when struck with a knife.

The coat, the pin, the shrine, and the brush and mirror had been left to Marina, who, luckily, bore the same initials. Carol and Georgie, awarded similar tokens, had been warm in their assurances that neither of them wanted the shop. No one, they said, was more suited to shopkeeping than Victor — a remark that offended Victor's wife into speechlessness for half an hour.

She and Victor were standing on the sidewalk in front

of the shop when the hired car drew up to the curb. Peggy Ann, when she saw them, made exaggerated gestures of melting away in the sun, and then incomprehensible ones of laying her head on a pillow, which drew an unflattering remark from Georgie.

"Home," Carol said, evidently without sarcasm, looking up and down the shadeless chasm of brick, here and there enlived by Pepsi-Cola signs. A few children, sticky with popsicles, examined the New Jersey license of Victor's Buick and then the shining splendor of the rented limousine. Not recognizing it, they turned back to the Buick and then suddenly scattered into the street, where Georgie had thrown a handful of quarters. Some of the children, Marina's pupils at a parochial school named for Saint Valerie the Martyr, glanced at her shyly.

"They look scared of you," Georgie said. "What do you do, beat them?"

"I'd like to," Marina said.

"I'm sure she doesn't mean that," Peggy Ann said, smiling.

A wide ribbon of crepe hung on the shop door, and green shades were pulled at door and window, bearing in shadow the semicircle of words on the glass, "Rumania Fancy Groceries," and then in smaller letters, "Mrs. Maria Boldescu."

"How many times did I get up on a ladder and wash that window!" Georgie said, as if the memory were enchanting.

"Victor, too?" said Peggy Ann. "I'll bet he was an old lazy."

No one replied, and Victor fitted the key into the padlock while Carol, restless, hummed and executed a little dance step. The smell of the shut-up store moved out to

meet them. Carol, with a look of concern, went at once to
the cash register, but Marina had forestalled him. "I took
it all out when Mama took sick," she said.

"Good idea," said Georgie, approving.

"You were awfully clever to think of everything," Peggy
Ann said. "Although it seems to me that, with crepe on the
door and everything, no one would break in." She stopped,
as if she had uttered an indelicate thought, and went on
rapidly, "Oh, Victor, do look! What a sweet little store.
Look at all the salami and my goodness, all the beer! Cases
and cases!"

"We bought Mama the beer license," Carol said. He
walked around, rattling change in his pocket.

"She must have been pleased," said Peggy Ann. "Victor,
look at all the things — all the tins of soup, and the spa-
ghetti."

Marina, parting the blue chintz curtains at the end of
the counter, moved into the kitchen behind the shop. She
lifted her hand and, without glancing up, caught the string
of an overhead light. Two doors, varnished to simulate oak,
led off to the bedrooms — the one she had shared with her
mother, until, at twenty-three, she had overcome her
mother's objections to her having a place of her own, and
the other room in which had slept, singly or together, the
three boys. The kitchen window looked out on a fenced-in
yard where Mrs. Boldescu had tried to grow vegetables and
a few flowers, finally managing a tough and spiky grass.
Marina opened the window and pushed back the shutters,
admitting a shifting layer of soot. Weeds grew as high as
the sill, and wild rhubarb, uncontrolled in this summer of
illness, flourished along the fence. A breath of city air

entered the room, and an old calendar bearing a picture of the shrine at St. Anne de Beaupré suddenly flapped on its pin. She straightened it, and then, from some remembered prudence, turned out the light.

Carol, who had come in behind her, glanced at the calendar and then at her. Then he said, "Now that we're alone, tell me just one thing. Was that a nice funeral or wasn't it?"

"It was charming," she said. "It was nice that you and Georgie were both free for it at once."

Carol laughed; evidently he expected this sour, womanly reprimand, and now that their mother was dead he would expect it still more from Marina. "You ought to get married," he said.

"Thanks. The boys I grew up with were all so charming." She sat down, tipping her chair against the wall in a way her mother had disliked. She and Carol were alone as they had seldom been in childhood, able now to take stock of each other. Twenty, fifteen years before they had avoided each other like uncongenial castaways, each pursuing some elusive path that led away from St. Eulalie Street. Considering the way they had lived, crowded as peas in a pod, their privacy, she now thought, must have been a powerful act of will. In the darkening room, she saw herself ironing her middy blouse, the only one she owned, a book propped insecurely on the ironing board. Georgie and Carol came and went like cats, and Victor shouted outside in a game of kick-the-can. Again, she did her homework under the overhead light while Georgie and Carol, shut in their room for punishment, climbed out the window and were fetched home by the police. At last, her memory alighted on one shining summer with both the older boys "away" (this was the only word Mrs. Boldescu had ever used) and Marina, afloat with happiness, saying to every customer in the shop, "I'm going to France; have you heard? I'm going to France."

"I'm *talking* to you," said Carol. "Don't judge all the boys you knew by me. Look at old Victor."

"The pride of the street," said Marina, remembering that summer.

"*Was* he?" said Peggy Ann. She stood in the doorway, holding back the curtains with either hand. "I never get a thing out of him, about the store, or his childhood, or anything. Victor, do look at this room! It's just like a farmhouse kitchen! And the adorable shrine . . . Did your mother bring it from Rumania?"

"I bought that," said Carol. He looked at it, troubled. "Does it look foreign or something?" he said to Marina. "It came from Boston."

"I would have said Rumania," said Peggy Ann. She sat down and smiled at the coal-and-wood stove.

"Well," Victor said, smiling at them all. "Well, the old place." He dropped his cigarette on the floor and stepped on it.

"It's all yours now," Georgie said. He sat down at the round table under the light, Carol beside him. Victor, after glancing about uncertainly, sat opposite, so that they appeared to face him like inquisitors. "Yours," Georgie repeated with finality.

"I wouldn't say that," Victor said, unnecessarily straightening his necktie. "I mean to say, I think Mama meant me to have it in trust, for the rest of you. My idea was — "

"We ought to have a drink," Georgie said. He looked at Marina, who was sitting a little apart, as if to confound the prophecy of the graveyard that they would someday all lie together. "Would it be all right, today I mean?"

"You're old enough to know if you want a drink," Marina said. She had no intention of becoming the new matriarch of the family; but the others still waited, uncertain, and she finally found in a cupboard a bottle and the glasses that were her brothers' special pride. "Mama's brandy," she said. "Let's drink to Victor, the heir."

"No," said Victor, "honestly, now, I keep trying to tell you. I'm not exactly the heir in the way you mean." He was still talking as the others picked up their glasses and drank. Marina filled the glasses again and then sat away from the table, tipping her chair against the wall. The kitchen was cool after the flat glare of the cemetery and the stuffiness of the drive home. Sounds filtered through the shop from the street; a cat dropped from the fence and sniffed the wild rhubarb plants. The calendar, its shrine surrounded by a painted garland of leaves, stared at her from the opposite wall.

Her brothers talked on, Victor with some sustained and baffling delicacy retreating from the idea of his inheritance. Opening her eyes, Marina saw the calendar again and remembered the summer — the calendar bore its date — when she had looked at the room and thought, Soon I'll never have to see any of this again unless I want to.

". . . would care to live here again," Peggy Ann's high voice cut into a silence. Carol refilled the glasses, and the conversation rose. Peggy Ann leaned toward Marina and repeated, "I was saying, we think we should keep the store and all, but I don't think Victor would care to live here again."

"I can't imagine why not," Marina said, looking thoughtfully at the torn linoleum. "Mama thought it was Heaven. Where she grew up, they all lived in one room, along with a goat."

"I know," Peggy Ann said, distracted. "It would make a difference in your point of view, wouldn't it? But you know, Victor left so young."

"You might say that all of my brothers left young, one way or another," said Marina. "You might even say I was the patsy." She handed her glass to Carol, who filled it, frowning a little; he did not like women to drink. "You might even say," Marina went on, "that it was Victor's fault."

"I don't see how it could be *Victor's* fault," Peggy Ann said. "He was so different from the rest, don't you think?" She folded her hands and regarded them primly. "I mean to say, he's a C.P.A. now, and awfully well thought of. And we own our own home."

"A triumph of education," said Marina. "The boy who went to college." She finished her brandy and extended the glass, this time to Georgie.

"*You're* educated," said Peggy Ann graciously. "Victor's awfully proud of you. He tells everyone how you teach in the very same school you went to! It must be wonderful for those children, having someone from the same — who understands the sort of home background. I mean it must help you a lot, too, to have come from the same — " She sighed and looked about the room for succor. "You must have liked your school," she said at last. "Victor hated his. Somebody beat him with a snow shovel or something."

"I loved mine," Marina said. She looked into the depths

of her glass. *"Loved* it. I had a medal every week that said on it 'Perfection.' Just the same, I was ungrateful. I used to say to myself, Well, all told, I don't give a goddamn if I never see these dark green walls again. . . . But then, as you say, the home background helps a lot. I look at my pupils, and I see nine little Carols for every little Victor. I don't see myself anywhere, though, so I guess there's nothing much between the Victors and the Carols."

"Yes, I see what you mean," said Peggy Ann. She slid back her white organdie cuff and glanced at her watch. "The boys do talk on, don't they? Of course, they haven't seen each other for so long . . . There's something we wanted to talk to you about, but I guess Victor's just never going to get around to it." She smiled at Marina, wide-eyed, and went on. "We wondered if you wouldn't want to have this little apartment for your own."

"My own?"

"To live in," Peggy Ann said. "We thought it was such a good idea. You'd be right near your school, and you wouldn't have to pay any rent — only the heat and gas. If there *is* heat or gas," she said uncertainly, glancing around. "It was Victor's idea. He thinks the store belongs to the family and you should all get something out of it. Victor says you really deserve something, because you always took such good care of your mother, and you made so many sacrifices and everything."

"Live here?" said Marina. She straightened her chair suddenly and put down her glass. "Courtesy of Victor?" She looked across the table at her brother, and then, rising, unhooked the calendar from its pin. "Victor — " she said, cutting through a remark of Carol's — "dear, sweet little Victor. Now that you're proprietor of Rumania Fancy

Groceries, there's a keepsake I want you to take home. You might like to frame it." She placed the calendar carefully before him on the table.

"I was just coming to that," said Carol. "I was just going to say — "

"Well, I said it," said Marina, "so shut up."

"What a memory," Georgie said. "God — women and elephants!" He pulled the calendar toward him and read aloud, "Nineteen thirty-seven."

"The year I did not go to France," said Marina. "The year I had the scholarship to Grenoble."

"I remember," Victor said, smiling a little but glancing uneasily at his wife.

"You should," his sister said. "You damn well should remember."

"Victor, what *is* it?" said Peggy Ann. "You know, we should start back before dark." She looked appealingly at Marina standing over the table.

Turning the calendar over, Georgie read, "Sergeant-detectives Callahan and Vronsky, and two phone numbers. You ought to know them by heart, Vic."

"Not exactly," Victor said. He shook his head, amused and rueful. "I'd rather just forget it."

"We haven't," Carol said. He pushed the calendar back toward his brother, staring at him.

"It's a long time ago now," Victor said, relaxing in his chair as if the effort of leaving were hopeless. "You sort of started it all, as I remember."

"*I* started it," said Marina. She moved around the table to stand between Carol and Georgie, the better to face Victor. "I had the scholarship in France and Mama had the money to send me."

"What has that —" Carol began, annoyed, glancing up at her.

"Women," Georgie said. "They always have to be first in the act. It was Carol started it."

"Your brother-in-law, Carol," said Marina to Peggy Ann. "was arrested for some schoolboy prank one Sunday morning as the Boldescu family returned from church. Brother Georgie was 'away,' and after Carol's departure, amid the tears of his sister and mother —"

"Peggy Ann doesn't want to hear this," Victor said.

" — a gun was discovered on a shelf in the shop, between two tins of chocolate empire biscuits," said Marina. "Which our mother took and with a rich Rumanian curse —"

"That part's a lie," said Georgie, shouting.

" — flung as far as she could out the kitchen window. I guess her arm wasn't too good, because it fell in the snow by the fence."

"She never swore in her life," said Georgie. "That's a lousy thing to say the day of her funeral." His voice went hoarse, brandy having failed to restore the ravages of weeping.

"Since when do you drink so much, too?" Carol asked her. "I'd like Mama to see you." Virtuously, he pushed her empty glass out of her reach.

"In the spring," said Marina, "after the snow melted some, little brother Victor wandered out in the yard —"

"I was a kid," Victor told his wife, who wore a faint, puzzled smile, as if the end of this could only be a wonderful joke.

"A stripling," Marina said. "Full of admiration for the pranks of his older brothers."

"Tell the story or shut up," said Carol.

"Found the little gun," said Marina, "all wet and rusty. Was it, Vic? I've forgotten that part. Anyway he took it to school and after making sure that every boy in class had admired it —"

"The dumb little bastard," said Carol, looking moodily at the floor.

" — took it to a pawnshop that can be seen from the front door here, and, instead of pawning it, poked it into the stomach of a Mr. Levinson. It was noon —"

"Twelve o'clock noon," said Carol. "Jesus."

"I don't believe this," said Peggy Ann. Her eyebrows drew together, fumbling in her handbag, she found a handkerchief with a rolled tiny black border. "I don't believe it."

"As I said, it was noon," said Marina. She clutched the back of Carol's chair, looking straight at Victor. "Little children were passing by. Mr. Levinson called out to them — small girls in convent dresses, I think they were. Victor must have been nervous, because he took one look at the little girls and cut for home, running down the street waving the gun like a flag."

"It isn't true," said Peggy Ann, mopping her eyes. "Anyway, if he ever did do anything wrong, he had plenty of example. I name no names."

"Don't cry," Victor told her. "Marina's acting crazy. You heard what Carol said; she's an old maid. She always took sides against me, even though I never gave Mama half the trouble —"

"We know," Georgie said, smiling. "Mama knew it. That's why she left you the store. See?" He tapped Victor affectionately on the arm, and Victor jumped.

"I never took sides," Marina said. "I never knew any of

you were even alive." She brushed lint from her dyed suit and glanced across at Peggy Ann's fragile and costly black summer frock. "Do I finish this story, or not?"

"Tell it, tell it," said Georgie. "You don't have to make it a speech. Callahan and Vronsky came and told Mama for six hundred there'd be no charge. So Mama paid it, so that's the end."

"They looked at Mama's bankbook," Marina said. "Vronsky had a girl my age at home, he said, just eighteen, so that meant he had to pat my behind. Mama had just the six, so they said that would do."

"Six," Georgie said. The injustice of the sum appeared to overwhelm him anew. "For a first offense. They would have settled for one-fifty each in those days."

"You weren't around to advise us," Marina said. "The nice thing was that we had it to give. As I said before, that was the year I didn't go any place."

"For Christ's sake stop harping on that," Victor said. "Sure, Mama did it for me. Why wouldn't she want to keep me out of trouble? Any mother would've done it."

"Any," said Peggy Ann, looking around the table. "Any mother."

"You keep your snotty face out of this," Carol said. He stood up, shouting. "Do you know what she had to do to get six hundred, how many bottles of milk and pounds of butter and cans of soup she had to sell?" He leaned over the table, tipping a glass of brandy. It dripped on Peggy Ann's dress, and she began once more to cry.

Marina sat down, exhausted. "It was Victor's insurance policy," she said. "We looked at it that way. They wrote their names on the back of the calendar. They told Mama if he ever got in trouble again she should call them."

"It was the only thing I ever did," Victor told his wife, who pushed away his consoling hand. "The only thing in my whole life."

"Then we paid the money for nothing," said Marina. "It was your immunity. You should have kept on doing things, just for the hell of it. That's why Mama kept the calendar: insurance for Heaven on the front and on the back for this earth. She told Father Patenaude about it afterward, but he never saw the joke."

"Never mind all that," said Carol, impatient. "Let's get this the hell over with. You got the store, Vic; now we want to know what you're going to do about this," and he pointed again to the calendar.

"What can I do?" Victor said. "What do you want me to do, turn myself in?" Gaining confidence, he pushed back his chair. "It's crazy to even talk about it. We came back here to talk about the store. I thought that was settled."

"Well, it isn't," said Georgie. "Mama left it to you, but there's a couple of guys who owe you six. You ought to collect it."

"Collect it?" Victor said. He looked at Marina. "Are you in this, too? You want me to go out and beat up a couple of middle-aged cops, old men? Make a lot of trouble? And for what? You know we'd never get that money back."

"For Mama," Carol said, sitting down.

"I never heard anything so crazy," Peggy Ann said. "Why should Victor get mixed up in all these old things?"

"If Mama had wanted it, she'd have said so in her lifetime," Victor said.

"She left you the shop," Georgie said, "and the calendar along with it."

"How about it?" Victor asked Marina once more. "Did you plan this together, to show me up in front of my wife? Or are you so jealous because Mama left it to me? Do you think I ought to make a lot of trouble for Mama's sake?"

"For mine," Marina said, twisting her fingers. She did not look up.

"She's crazy," Georgie said. "Listen," he told her, "you'd better get married or something. Or something."

"Honestly, Victor," said Peggy Ann. "It's too awful."

"I know." He stood up. "Look," he said, "this damn place is no good to me. I only wanted it to keep it in the family for Mama's sake. But I give up. Wherever she is, she sees me now, and she knows I'm acting for the best."

"You better not talk about where she is," Carol said, glancing at the ceiling. "Unless you do something before you die," and he glanced at Peggy Ann.

"The hell with this," Victor said. He drew the key to the shop from his pocket and placed it quietly on the table. "We can't work anything out. You're all so jealous and — "

"And awful," said Peggy Ann. "Just awful."

"Melodramatic," Victor said firmly. "As for Marina, she gets crazier every time I see her, crazier by the year. If she was so damn crazy to study in France, she could have taken a job and saved some money. She blames me because I got out and she never had the guts. You could have gone next year, or the next," he told her.

"There was the war," she said, still looking away.

"So I started the war," Victor said. "I sent Mama money every month. I never gave her trouble, only that once. The hell with it; I'm going. Come on," he told his wife, who stumbled after him between the curtains, adjusting her hat.

"I'm sorry I met you under such circumstances," she paused to say to Marina. "I imagine at heart you're a very fine person."

"Come on," Victor said, and in a moment the front door slammed behind them.

Peggy Ann had left her handkerchief on the table. Carol looked at it and grunted. "He deserves her," he remarked.

Marina looked around the room, now nearly dark. Carol pulled the light cord, and the sickly ring of yellow swayed back and forth on the walls. Marina clutched the edge of· her chair, in a sudden impulse to run after Victor and away; but Carol, who had picked up the key, now held it out to her.

"It's yours now," he said. "Yours, and in the family." He was smiling, and Georgie, a little behind him, smiling, too.

"What for?" Marina said. She put her hands behind her. "What am I supposed to do with it?"

"Keep it," Carol said. "Run the business. With the beer license its a nice little business now. If you want to fix up this place behind it, we'll kick in."

"We figured it out," Georgie said. "Mama would have wanted it. Victor's a rat. He doesn't deserve it. Look at what he wouldn't do for Mama. He's only a rat. But what about you? You can't teach forever, and it doesn't look like you're going to get married. So we set the thing up for you."

"For *me*?" Marina said. "For *me*?" Carol took her hand and pressed the key into it.

"If you're still so crazy to go to France," he said, indulgent at the thought of her feminine whim, "you could make enough in a year to close it up for a month next summer, maybe. Anyway, it's a hell of a lot more than you'll make as a teacher."

He started to say something else, but Marina flung out her arm, almost striking him as she threw the key away. "For me?" she cried again. "I'm to live here?" She looked around as if to find, once more, the path away from St. Eulalie Street, the shifting and treacherous path that described a circle, and if her brothers, after the first movement, had not held her fast, she would have wrecked the room, thrown her chair out the window, pulled the shrine from the wall, the plates from their shelves, wrenched the curtains from the nails that held them, and smashed every one of the ten tiny glasses that were her brothers' pride.

One Morning
in June

By half past ten, a vaporish heat had gathered on the road above the Mediterranean, and the two picknickers, Barbara Ainslie and Mike Cahill, walked as slowly as they could. Scuffing their shoes, they held themselves deliberately apart. It was the first time they had been alone. Barbara's aunt, with whom she was staying in Menton, had begun speaking to Mike on the beach — she thought him a nice young boy — and it was she who had planned the picnic, packing them off for what she termed a good romp, quite unaware that her words had paralyzed at once the tremulous movement of friendship between them.

So far, they had scarcely spoken at all, passing in silence — in the autobus — between the shining arc of the beach and the vacant hotels that faced it. The hotels, white and pillared like Grecian ruins, were named for Albert and Victoria and the Empire. Shelled from the sea during the war, they exposed, to the rain and the road, cube-shaped rooms and depressing papered walls that had held the sleep of a thousand English spinsters when the pound was still a thing of moment. At sixteen, Barbara was neutral to decay but far too shy in the presence of Mike to stare at anything that so much as suggested a bedroom. She had looked instead at the lunch basket on her lap, at her bitten nails, at the shadow of her canvas hat, as if they held the seed of conversation. When they were delivered from the bus at last and had watched it reeling, in its own white dust, on to Monte Carlo, they turned together and climbed the scrambling path to Cap Martin.

"What will we talk about?" Barbara had asked her aunt, earlier that morning. "What will I say?"

Barbara's aunt could see no problem here, and she was as startled as if a puppy tumbling in a cushioned box had posed the same question.

"Why, what do young people have to say anywhere?" she had asked. "Tell him about your school, if you like, or your winter in Paris." Having provided that winter, she did not see why its value should be diminished in June, or, indeed, why it should not remain a conversational jewel for the rest of Barbara's life.

"I suppose so," Barbara had said, determined not to mention it at all. She was in France not as a coming-out present or because she had not smoked until she was eighteen but ignominiously, because she had failed her end-of-term examinations for the second year running. She had been enrolled in one of the best day schools in New York, a fact that she was frequently reminded of and that somehow doubled her imperfection. Her mother had consulted a number of people — an analyst she met at a party, two intimate women friends, the doctor who had delivered Barbara but had noticed nothing unusual about her at the time —

and finally, when the subject was beginning to bore her, she
had dispatched Barbara to Paris, to the distressed but duti-
ful sister of Barbara's late father. Barbara was conscious,
every moment of the day, that she was to get something
from her year in France, and return to America brilliant,
poised, and educated. Accordingly, she visited all the mu-
seums and copied on slips of paper the legends of monu-
ments. Her diary held glimpses of flint tools, angular modern tapestries, cave drawings, the Gioconda ("quite small"),
and the Venus de Milo ("quite big"); of a monument
"that came by ship from Africa and was erected to the
cheers of a throng"; and of a hotel where Napoleon had
stayed as a young man, "but which we did not really see
because it had been pulled down." These mementos of
Paris she buttressed with snapshots in which ghostly buildings floated on the surface of the Seine, and the steps of the
Sacré-Coeur, transparent, encumbered the grass at Ver-
sailles. The snapshots she mounted and shielded with tissue
in an album called "Souvenirs de France."

She was proud of the year, and of the fact that she had
shivered in unheated picture galleries and not spent her
time drinking milk shakes in the American Embassy restaurant; still, she felt her year no match for Mike's. When her
aunt, testing, asked him where he lived in Paris, he had
replied, "Oh, St. Germain," and Barbara had been ill with
envy, unaware that he stayed at a recommended *pension*,
the owner of which sent fortnightly reports to his mother.

Glancing now at Mike shyly, as they walked along the
upper road, Barbara caught from the corner of her eye the
movement of her own earrings, Moroccan hoops she had
bought, in the merciful absence of her aunt, from an Arab

on the beach. With his sweaty fez and his impertinent speech, the Arab had seemed to Barbara the breathing incarnation of oil, greed, and problems. She had read a great deal in the winter, and she could have told anyone that Africa seethed, Asia teemed, and that something must be done at once about the Germans, the Russians, the Chinese, and the Spanish or Heaven only knew what would happen. She had also been cautioned that these difficulties were the heritage of youth, and this she acknowledged, picturing the youth as athletic, open-shirted, vaguely foreign in appearance, and marching in columns of eight.

"Straight over there is the Middle East," she said to Mike, placing him without question in those purposeful ranks. She pointed in the direction of Corsica, and went on, "All the Arabs! What are we going to do about the Arabs?"

Mike shrugged.

"And the Indians," Barbara said. "There are too many of them for the food in the world. And the Russians. What are we going to do about the Russians?"

"I don't know," Mike said. "Actually, I never think about it."

"I suppose you don't," she said. "You have your work to do."

He glanced at her sharply, but there was no need to look twice. He had already observed her to be without guile, a fact that confused and upset him. Her good manners, as well, made him self-conscious. Once, when she mentioned her school, he had not mentioned his own New York high school and then, annoyed with himself, had introduced it with belligerence. He might have saved himself the trouble; she had never heard of it and did not know that it was a public school. He blamed his uneasiness, unfairly, on the fact that she had money and he had not. It had not occurred to him, inexperienced as he was, placing her with the thinnest of clues, that she might not be rich.

Mike was older than Barbara, although not by a great deal. He had come to France because the words "art" and "Paris" were unbreakably joined in his family's imagination, the legend of Trilby's Bohemia persisting long after the truth of it had died. When his high school art teacher, a young woman whose mobiles had been praised, pronounced that his was a talent not to be buried under the study of medicine or law, his family had decided that a year in Paris would show whether or not his natural bent was toward painting. It was rather like exposing someone to a case of measles and watching for spots to break out.

In Paris, Mike had spent the first three weeks standing in the wrong queue at the Beaux-Arts, and when no one seemed able to direct him to the right one, he had given up the Beaux-Arts entirely and joined a class instructed by an English painter called Chitterly, whose poster advertisement he had seen in a café. It was Mr. Chitterley's custom to turn his young charges loose on the city and then, once a week or so, comment on their work in a borrowed studio on the Quai d'Anjou. Mike painted with sober patience the bridges of the Seine, the rain-soaked lawns of the Tuileries, and a head-on view of Notre Dame. His paintings were large (Mr. Chitterley was nearsighted), askew (as he had been taught in the public schools of New York), and empty of people (he had never been taught to draw, and it was not his nature to take chances).

"Very *interesting*," said Mr. Chitterley of Mike's work.

Squinting a little, he would add, "Ah! I *see* what you were trying to do here!"

"You do?" Mike wished he would be more specific, for he sometimes recognized that his pictures were flat, empty, and the color of cement. At first, he had blamed the season, for the Paris winter had been sunless; later on, he saw that its gray contained every shade in a beam of light, but this effect he was unable to reproduce. Unnerved by the pressure of time, he watched his work all winter, searching for the clue that would set him on a course. Prodded in the direction of art, he now believed in it, enjoying, above all, the solitude, the sense of separateness, the assembling of parts into something reasonable. He might have been equally happy at a quiet table, gathering into something ticking and ordered the scattered wheels of a watch, but this had not been suggested, and he had most certainly never given it a thought. At last, when the season had rained itself to an end (and his family innocently were prepared to have him exhibit his winter's harvest in some garret of the Left Bank and send home the critics' clippings), he approached Mr. Chitterley and asked what he ought to do next.

"Why, go to the country," said Mr. Chitterley, who was packing for a holiday with the owner of the Quai d'Anjou studio. "Go south. Don't stop in a hotel but live on the land, in a tent, and paint, paint, paint, paint, paint!"

"I can't afford it," Mike said. "I mean I can't afford to buy the tent and stuff. But I can stay over here until August, if you think there's any point. I mean is it wasting time for me to paint, paint, paint?"

Mr. Chitterley shot him an offended look and then a

scornful one, which said, How like an American! The only
measuring rods, time and money. Aloud, he suggested
Menton. He had stayed there as a child, and he remembered it as a paradise of lemon ice and sunshine. Mike, for
want of a better thought, or even a contrastive one, took
the train there a day later.

Menton was considerably less than paradise. Shelled,
battered, and shabby, it was a town gone to seed, in which
old English ladies, propelling themselves with difficulty
along the Promenade George V, nodded warmly to each
other (they had become comrades during the hard years of
war, when they were interned together in the best hotels,
farther up the coast) and ignored the new influx of their
countrymen — embarrassed members of the lower middle
classes, who refused to undress in the face of heat and
nakedness and who huddled miserably on the beach in hot
city clothing, knotted handkerchiefs on their heads to shield
them from the sun.

"Not the sort of English one likes," Barbara's aunt had
said sadly to Mike, who was painting beside her on the
beach. "If you had seen Menton before the war! I had a
little villa, up behind that hotel. It was shelled by the
Americans. Not that it wasn't necessary," she added, recall-
ing her origins. "Still — And they built a fortification not
far away. I went up to look at it. It was full of rusted wire,
and nothing in it but a dead cat."

"The French built it," Barbara said. "The *pension* man
told me."

"It doesn't matter, dear," her aunt said. "Before the war,
and even when it started, there was nothing there at all. It
was so different." She dropped her knitting and looked

about, as if just the three of them were fit to remember what
Menton had been. It was the young people's first bond of
sympathy, and Barbara tried not to giggle; before the war
was a time she didn't remember at all. "In those days, you
knew where you were *at*," her aunt said, summing up the
thirties. She picked up her knitting, and Mike went on with
his painting of sea, sky, and tilted sailboat. Away from Mr.
Chitterley and the teacher who had excelled in mobiles, he
found that he worked with the speed and method of Barbara's aunt producing a pair of Argyle socks. Menton, for all
its drawbacks, was considerably easier to paint than Paris,
and he rendered with fidelity the blue of the sea, the pink
and white of the crumbling villas, and the red of the geraniums. One of his recent pictures, flushed and accurate as a
Technicolor still, he had given to Barbara, who had written
a touched and eager letter of thanks, and then had torn the
letter up.

Mike had brought his painting things along on the picnic,
for, as Barbara's aunt had observed with approbation, he
didn't waste an hour of his day. Barbara carried the picnic
basket, which had been packed by the cook at Pension Bit
o' Heather and contained twice as much bread as one would
want. Around her shoulders was an unnecessary sweater
that she had snatched up in a moment of compulsive
modesty just before leaving her room. She carried her
camera, slung on a strap, and she felt that she and Mike
formed, together, a picture of art, pleasure, and industry
which, unhappily, there was no one to remark but a fat man
taking his dog for a run; the man gave them scarcely a
glance.

Rounding a bend between dwarfed ornamental orange

trees, they saw the big hotel Barbara's aunt had told them about. From its open windows came the hum of vacuum cleaners and the sound of a hiccuping tango streaked with static. The gardens spread out before them, with marked and orderly paths and beds of brilliant flowers. Barbara's aunt had assured them that this place was ideal for a picnic lunch, and that no one would disturb them. There was, on Cap Martin, a public picnic ground, which Barbara was not permitted to visit. "You wouldn't like it," her aunt had explained. "It is nothing but tents, and diapers, and hairy people in shorts. Whenever possible in France, one prefers private property." Still, the two were unconvinced, and after staring at the gardens and then at each other they turned and walked in the other direction, to a clearing around a small monument overlooking the bay.

They sat down on the grass in the shade and Mike unpacked his paints. Barbara watched him, working over in her mind phrases that, properly used, would give them a subject in common; none came, and she pulled grass and played with her wristwatch. "We're leaving tomorrow," she said at last.

"I know." After some peering and indecision he had decided to face the hotel gardens instead of the sea. "I may not stay much longer, either. I don't know."

Barbara, bound to her aunt's unyielding cycle of city, sea, and mountains, marveled at his freedom. She fancied him stepping out of his hotel one morning and suddenly asking himself, "Shall I go back to Paris now, or another day?" and taking off at once for Paris, or Rome, or Lisbon, or, having decided he had had enough of this, his parents' house.

"My father thinks I should go to Venice and Florence, now that I'm south." He spoke with neither enthusiasm nor resentment; had his father ordered him home, he would have set off with the same equable temper.

"Then you might go to Italy soon," Barbara said. He nodded. "I'm going home in September," she said. "My mother's coming for the summer, and we're going back together. I guess I'll go back to school. I have to do something — learn something, I mean."

"What for?"

"Well, it's just that I have to do *something*. It's different for you," she said, helplessly. "You have something to do. You've got — " She blushed, and went on, with resolution, "You've got this art to do."

Startled by her reminder of his vocation, he dropped his arm. He knew he would have to decide very soon whether to go on with painting or begin something else. If someone who knows would come along and tell me what to do this minute, he thought, I would do whatever he said.

Barbara, believing him in contact with some life of the spirit from which she was excluded, looked at him with admiration; and when he did not move for a moment longer, she focused her camera and took his picture, so that her album called "Souvenirs de France" would include this image of Mike looking rapt and destined, his eyes secretively shadowed, high above the sea.

"It's different for me," Barbara said, forgetting once more to wind her film. "I can't do anything. There's nothing I'm good at. I'm really dumb in school." She laid her camera in the shade. "Really dumb," she repeated, shaking her head at the thought. Confronted with ruled examination paper, the electric clock purring on the wall, she was lost — sometimes she was sick and had to leave the room; sometimes she just wrote nonsense. At school, they had tested her for aptitudes and found only that she liked to cook and had played with dolls until it was a scandal; her mother had had to give the dolls away. Anybody could cook and grow up to be a parent, the brisk, sallow student psychologist from N.Y.U. who had tested her implied, and he had then written something terrible — Barbara could only imagine the summing up of her inadequacies — that had been shown to all her teachers and to her mother.

"You should worry," Mike said. "You'll probably get married sometime, anyway, so what does it matter what you learn?"

The effect of this was to strike her into silence.

She drew her knees up and examined her dusty sandals; she pulled at her skirt so that it covered her legs, and drew her sweater close. Does he mean *to him*, she wondered. It had occurred to her many times in this lonely winter that only marriage would save her from disgrace, from growing up with no skills and no profession. Her own mother did nothing all day, but she was excused by having once been married. It was the image of her aunt that Barbara found distressing — her aunt filling her day with scurrying errands, writing letters of complaint (Bus conductors were ruder than before the war. Why did young girls shrink from domestic service? The streets of Paris were increasingly dirtier) to the "Letters" column of the Continental *Daily Mail*. But who would marry me, Barbara had thought. From her reading she knew that she would never meet men or be of interest to them until she could, suddenly and brilliantly, perform on the violin, become a member of Macy's Junior Executive Squad, or, at the very least, take shorthand at a hundred and twenty words a minute.

She peered up at Mike now, but he was looking only at his canvas, daubing in another patch of perfectly red geraniums. "For a while, they thought I could act," she said, offering him this semiprecious treasure. "I had a radio audition last year, when I was still fifteen. Really," she said quickly, as if he were about to round on her with complete disbelief. "My speech-class teacher was nice. When my mother came to school to see why I wasn't doing so well, she met all my teachers. This teacher, Mr. Peppner, told her — something. He's the only man teacher in the whole school." She frowned, wondering once again what Mr. Peppner in his polished dark blue suit had found to say to Mrs. Ainslie; probably she, moist-eyed and smelling expensive, had been so warm, so interested, that Mr. Peppner had had no idea he was being treated like a meritorious cook and had said something extravagant. A few days later, Barbara's mother had asked to dinner a bald young man in spectacles, who had stared hard at Barbara and said, gracefully, that her coloring was much too delicate for television but that he would make an appointment for her with someone else.

"It's not that my mother wanted me to work, or anything," Barbara explained to Mike, "but a friend of hers said it would give me poise and confidence. So I went to be tested. I had to read lines in a play. There was someone else being tested, a man, and then there was a girl, a real actress. She was only helping. My name in the play was Gillian. It was called 'The Faltering Years.'"

Mike had never heard of it.

"Well, neither did I, but they all seemed to know it," Barbara said. "I don't think it was one of the great plays of our time, or anything like that. Of our time," she repeated thoughtfully, having frequently read this phrase on the jackets of books. "Anyway, I had to be this Mayfair debutante. I was the girl friend of this man, but I was leaving him."

"For a rich lord?" Mike said, smiling.

"No," she said, seriously. "*He* was the lord, only poor. I was leaving him for a rich industrialist. I had to say, 'Peter, won't you try to understand?' Then he said something. I forget what. Then I had to say, 'It isn't you, Peter, and it isn't me. It's just.' The line ended that way, but like a question. That was my main part, or most of it. Then I went away, but I was sorry. They skipped all that. Then the man being tested had this big scene with the actress. She was the nurse to his sick mother, who wins his heart. I forget what *they* said."

"It sounds to me like she had the best part," said Mike.

"She was around thirty," Barbara said. "I think she was the director's girl friend. He took her to lunch afterwards. I saw them going out. Anyway, at the end I had to say to her, 'You love Peter very much, don't you?' And she had to say, 'Terribly.' Just the way she said that, the director told me, showed she was an actress. I guess he meant I wasn't. Anyway, they said I'd hear from them, but I never did."

"It's the craziest audition I ever heard of," Mike said.

He stopped working and turned to look at her. "You a Mayfair debutante, for God's sake. It wasn't a fair audition."

She looked up at him, troubled. "But they must know what they're doing, don't you think?" At this reminder of knowledge and authority, Mike agreed that they probably did. "Are you hungry?" she asked. She was tired of the conversation, of exposing her failures.

The sun was nearly overhead, and they moved under a parasol pine. "There's nothing to drink," Barbara said apologetically, "but she put in some oranges."

They ate their lunch in silence, like tired Alpinists resting on a ledge. Barbara screwed her eyes tight and tried to read the lettering on the monument; it was too hot to walk across the grass, out of their round island of shade. "It's to some queen," she said at last, and read out: " '*Elizabeth, impératrice d'Autriche et reine de la Hongrie.*' Well, I never heard of her, did you? Maybe she stayed at this hotel." Mike seemed to be falling asleep. "About Hungary, you know," she said, speaking rapidly. "One time, I went to a funny revue in Paris with my aunt. It was supposed to be in the war, and this lady was going to entertain the Russian Ambassador. She wanted to dress up her little dog in the Russian costume, in his honor, but she had only a Hungarian one. So she called all the embassies and said, 'Which side of the war is Hungary on?' and nobody knew. So then she finally called the Russian Ambassador and she said, 'I want to dress my little dog in your honor but I have only a Hungarian costume. Do you know which side the Hungarians are on?' And the Ambassador said, 'Yes, I do know, but I can't tell you until I've talked to Moscow.' "

Barbara looked anxiously at Mike. "Do you think that's funny?"

"Sure."

Neither of them had laughed.

"Do you remember the war?" he asked.

"A little." She got up as if she were suddenly uncomfortable, and walked to the edge of the grass, where the Cap fell away sharply to the sea.

"I remember quite a lot." said Mike. "My father was in Denver the whole time — I don't know why. We stayed home because they couldn't find us a place to live there. When he came home for leaves, we — my brother and I — wouldn't mind him, we were so used to our mother. When he'd tell us to do something, we'd ask her if it was all right." He smiled, remembering, "Was yours away?"

"Well, mine was killed," she said diffidently, as if by telling him this she made an unfair claim on his attention. "I was only five when he went away, so I don't remember much. He was killed later, when I was seven. It was right before my birthday, so I couldn't have a party." She presented, like griefs of equal value, these two facts. "People are always asking me — friends of my mother, I mean — do I remember him and what a wonderful sense of humor he had and all that. When I say no, I don't remember, they look at me and say — " Her voice went up to an incredulous screech: " 'But it can't be that long ago!' "

"Well, it is," Mike said, as if he were settling a quarrel. He stood up and moved beside her. Together, they looked down to the curving beach, where the sea broke lightly against the warm rocks, and the edge of the crumbling continent they had never seen whole. From above, they could see that beside each of the tumbled hotels a locked garden, secure against God knew what marauders, had gone wild; they could distinguish the film of weeds that brushed the top of the wall, the climbing roses that choked the palms. Above, out of their vision, was the fortification that had offended Barbara's aunt, and down on the beach was the aunt herself, a dot with a sunshade, knitting forever.

Say we might get married later, Barbara willed, closing her eyes against the quiet sea and the moldering life beside it. But Mike said nothing, thinking only of how dull a town Menton was, and wondering if it had been worth two weeks. He had been taught that time must be reckoned in value — and fiscal value, at that. At home, he would be required to account both for his allowance and for his days and weeks. "Did you get anything out of Menton?" his father would ask. "Was it worth it?"

"Oh, yes," he might tell them. "I worked a lot, and I met a rich girl."

His parents would be pleased. Not that they were vulgar or mercenary, but they considered it expedient for young artists to meet the well-born; they would accept, Mike was certain, the fact of his friendship with Barbara as a useful acquirement, justifying a fortnight of lounging about in the sun. When he thought of Barbara as a patroness, commissioning him, perhaps, for a portrait, he wanted to laugh: yet the seed of the thought — that the rich were of utility — remained, and to rid himself of it he asked her sharply if she had brought her bathing suit.

Stricken, looking about as if it might be lying on the grass, she said, "I didn't think — But we can go home and get it."

They gathered up their scattered belongings and walked back the way they had come. Barbara, in her misery, further chastened herself by holding a geranium leaf on her nose — she had visions of peeling and blisters — and she trotted beside Mike in silence.

"Do you write letters?" he said at last, for he had remembered that they both lived in New York, and he felt that if he could maintain the tenuous human claim of correspondence, possibly his acquaintance with Barbara might turn out to be of value; he could not have said how or in terms of what. And although he laughed at his parents, he was reluctant to loosen his hold on something that might justify him in their sight until he had at least sorted out his thoughts.

She stood stock-still in the path, the foolish green leaf on her nose, and said solemnly, "I will write to you every day as long as I live."

He glanced at her with the beginning of alarm, but he was spared from his thoughts by the sight of the autobus on the highway below. Clasping hands, they ran slipping and falling down the steep embankment, and arrived flushed, bewildered, exhausted, as if their romp had been youthful enough to satisfy even Barbara's aunt.

About Geneva

GRANNY was waiting at the door of the apartment. She looked small, lonely, and patient, and at the sight of her the children and their mother felt instantly guilty. Instead of driving straight home from the airport, they had stopped outside Nice for ice cream. They might have known how much those extra twenty minutes would mean to Granny. Colin, too young to know what he felt, or why, began instinctively to misbehave, dragging his feet, scratching the waxed parquet. Ursula bit her nails, taking refuge in a dream, while the children's mother, Granny's only daughter, felt compelled to cry in a high, cheery voice, "Well, Granny, here they are, safe and sound!"

"Darlings," said Granny, very low. "Home again." She stretched out her arms to Ursula, but then, seeing the taxi driver, who had carried the children's bags up the stairs, she drew back. After he had gone she repeated the gesture, turning this time to Colin, as if Ursula's cue had been irrevocably missed. Colin was wearing a beret. "Wherever did that come from?" Granny said. She pulled it off and stood still, stricken. "My darling little boy," she said, at last.

"What have they done to you? They have cut your hair. Your lovely golden hair. I cannot believe it. I don't want to believe it."

"It was high time," the children's mother said. She stood in the outer corridor, waiting for Granny's welcome to sub- side. "It was high time someone cut Colin's hair. The curls made such a baby of him. We should have seen that. Two women can't really bring up a boy."

Granny didn't look at all as if she agreed. "Who cut your hair?" she said, holding Colin.

"Barber," he said, struggling away.

"Less said the better," said Colin's mother. She came in at last, drew off her gloves, looked around, as if she, and not the children, had been away.

"He's not my child, of course," said Granny, releasing Colin. "If he were, I can just imagine the letter I should write. Of all the impudence! When you send a child off for a visit you expect at the very least to have him returned exactly as he left. And you," she said, extending to Ursula a plump, liver-spotted hand, "what changes am I to expect in you?"

"Oh, Granny, for Heaven's sake, it was only two weeks." She permitted her grandmother to kiss her, then went straight to the sitting room and hurled herself into a chair. The room was hung with dark engravings of cathedrals. There were flowers, red carnations, on the rickety painted tables, poked into stiff arrangements by a maid. It was the standard seasonal Nice *meublé*. Granny spent every winter in rented flats more or less like this one, and her daughter, since her divorce, shared them with her.

Granny followed Ursula into the room and sat down, erect, on an uncomfortable chair, while her daughter, trail-

ing behind, finally chose a footstool near the empty fireplace. She gave Granny a gentle, neutral look. Before starting out for the airport, earlier, she had repeated her warning:
There were to be no direct questions, no remarks. It was all
to appear as natural and normal as possible. What, indeed,
could be more natural for the children than a visit with
their father?

"What, indeed," said Granny in a voice rich with meaning.

It was only fair, said the children's mother. A belief in
fair play was so embedded in her nature that she could say
the words without coloring deeply. Besides, it was the first
time he had asked.

"And won't be the last," Granny said. "But, of course,
it is up to you."

Ursula lay rather than sat in her chair. Her face was
narrow and freckled: She resembled her mother who, at
thirty-four, had settled into a permanent, anxious-looking,
semi-youthfulness. Colin, blond and fat, rolled on the floor.
He pulled his mouth out at the corners, then pulled down
his eyes to show the hideous red underlids. He looked at
his grandmother and growled like a lion.

"Colin has come back sillier than ever," Granny said. He
lay prone, noisily snuffing the carpet. The others ignored
him.

"Did you go boating, Ursula?" said Granny, not counting
this as a direct question. "When I visited Geneva, as a girl,
we went boating on the lake." She went on about white
water birds, a parasol, a boat heaped with colored cushions.

"Oh, Granny, no," said Ursula. "There weren't even any
big boats, let alone little ones. It was cold."

"I hope the house, at least, was warm."

But evidently Ursula had failed to notice the temperature of her father's house. She slumped on her spine (a habit Granny had just nicely caused her to get over before the departure for Geneva) and then said, unexpectedly, "She's not a good manager."

Granny and her daughter exchanged a look, eyebrows up.

"Oh?" said Ursula's mother, pink. She forgot about the direct questions and said, "Why?"

"It's not terribly polite to speak that way of one's hostess," said Granny, unable to resist the reproof but threatening Ursula's revelation at the source. Her daughter looked at her, murderous.

"Well," said Ursula, slowly, "once the laundry didn't come back. It was her fault, he said. Our sheets had to be changed, he said. So she said Oh, all right. She took the sheets off Colin's bed and put them on my bed, and took the sheets off my bed and put them on Colin's. To make the change, she said."

"Dear God," said Granny.

"Colin's sheets were a mess. He had his supper in bed sometimes. They were just a mess.'

"Not true," said Colin.

"Another time . . . ," said Ursula, and stopped, as if Granny had been right, after all, about criticizing one's hostess.

"Gave us chocolate," came from Colin, his face muffled in carpet.

"Not every day, I trust," Granny said.

"For the plane."

"It might very well have made you both airsick," said Granny.

"Well," said Ursula, "it didn't." Her eyes went often to

the luggage in the hall. She squirmed upright, stood up, and sat down again. She rubbed her nose with the back of her hand.

"Ursula, do you want a handkerchief?" said Granny.

"No," said Ursula. "Only it so happens I'm writing a play. It's in the suitcase."

Granny and the children's mother looked at each other again. "I *am* pleased," Granny said, and her daughter nodded, agreeing, for, if impertinence and slumping on one's spine were unfortunate inherited tendencies, this was something else. It was only fair that Ursula's father should have bequeathed her *something* to compensate for the rest. "What is it about?" said Granny.

Ursula looked at her feet. After a short silence she said, "Russia. That's all I want to tell. It was her idea. She lived there once."

Quietly, controlled, the children's mother took a cigarette from the box on the table. Granny looked brave.

"Would you tell us the title, at least?" said Granny.

"No," said Ursula. But then, as if the desire to share the splendid thing she had created were too strong, she said, "I'll tell you one line, because they said it was the best thing they'd ever heard anywhere." She took a breath. Her audience was gratifyingly attentive, straining, nearly, with attention and control. "It goes like this," Ursula said. " 'The Grand Duke enters and sees Tatiana all in gold.' "

"Well?" said Granny.

"Well, what?" said Ursula. "That's it. That's the line." She looked at her mother and grandmother and said, "*They* liked it. They want me to send it to them, and everything else, too. She even told me the name Tatiana."

"It's lovely, dear," said Ursula's mother. She put the cigarette back in the box. "It sounds like a lovely play. Just when did she live in Russia?"

"I don't know. Ages ago. She's pretty old."

"Perhaps one day we shall see the play after all," said Granny. "Particularly if it is to be sent all over the Continent."

"You mean they might act in it?" said Ursula. Thinking of this, she felt sorry for herself. Ever since she had started "The Grand Duke" she could not think of her own person without being sorry. For no reason at all, now, her eyes filled with tears of self-pity. Drooping, she looked out at the darkening street, to the leafless trees and the stone façade of a public library.

But the children's mother, as if Granny's remark had for her an entirely different meaning, not nearly so generous, said, "I shall give you the writing desk from my bedroom, Ursula. It has a key."

"Where will you keep your things?" said Granny, protesting. She could not very well say that the desk was her own, not to be moved: Like everything else — the dark cathedrals, the shaky painted tables — it had come with the flat.

"I don't need a key," said the children's mother, lacing her fingers tightly around her knees. "I'm not writing a play, or anything else I want kept secret. Not any more."

"They used to take Colin for walks," said Ursula, yawning, only vaguely taking in the importance of the desk. "That was when I started to write this thing. Once they stayed out the whole afternoon. They never said where they'd been."

"I wonder," said her mother, thoughtful. She started to

say something to Ursula, something not quite a question, but the child was too preoccupied with herself. Everything about the trip, in the end, would crystallize around Tatiana and the Grand Duke. Already, Ursula was Tatiana. The children's mother looked at Ursula's long bare legs, her heavy shoes, her pleated skirt, and she thought, I must do something about her clothes, something to make her pretty.

"Colin, dear," said Granny in her special inner-meaning voice, "do you remember your walks?"

"No."

"I wonder why they wanted to take him alone," said Colin's mother. "It seems odd, all the same."

"Under seven," said Granny, cryptic. "Couldn't influence girl. Too old. Boy different. Give me first seven years, you can have rest."

"But it wasn't seven years. He hasn't been alive that long. It was only two weeks."

"Two very impressionable weeks," Granny said.

"I understand everything you're saying," Ursula said, "even when you talk that way. They spoke French when they didn't want us to hear, but we understood that, too."

"I fed the swans," Colin suddenly shouted.

There, he had told about Geneva. He sat up and kicked his heels on the carpet as if the noise would drown out the consequence of what he had revealed. As he said it, the image became static: a gray sky, a gray lake, and a swan wonderfully turning upside down with the black rubber feet showing above the water. His father was not in the picture at all; neither was *she*. But Geneva was fixed for the rest of his life: gray, lake, swan.

Having delivered his secret he had nothing more to tell.

He began to invent. "I was sick on the plane," he said, but Ursula at once said that this was a lie, and he lay down again, humiliated. At last, feeling sleepy, he began to cry.

"He never once cried in Geneva," Ursula said. But by the one simple act of creating Tatiana and the Grand Duke, she had removed herself from the ranks of reliable witnesses.

"How would you know?" said Granny bitterly. "You weren't always with him. If you had paid more attention, if you had taken care of your little brother, he wouldn't have come back to us with his hair cut."

"Never mind," said the children's mother. Rising, she helped Colin to his feet and led him away to bed.

She stood behind him as he cleaned his teeth. He looked male and self-assured with his newly cropped head, and she thought of her husband, and how odd it was that only a few hours before Colin had been with him. She touched the tender back of his neck. "Don't," he said. Frowning, concentrating, he hung up his toothbrush. "I told about Geneva."

"Yes, you did." He had fed swans. She saw sunshine, a blue lake, and the boats Granny had described, heaped with colored cushions. She saw her husband and someone else (probably in white, she thought, ridiculously bouffant, the origin of Tatiana) and Colin with his curls shorn, revealing ears surprisingly large. There was nothing to be had from Ursula — not, at least, until the Grand Duke had died down. But Colin seemed to carry the story of the visit with him, and she felt the faintest stirrings of envy, the resentfulness of the spectator, the loved one left behind.

"Were you really sick on the plane?" she said.

"Yes." said Colin.

"Were they lovely, the swans?"

But the question bore no relation to anything he had seen. He said nothing. He played with toothpaste, dawdling.

"Isn't that child in bed yet?" called Granny. "Does he want his supper?"

"No," said Colin.

"No." said his mother. "He was sick on the plane."

"I thought so," Granny said. "That, at least, is a fact."

They heard the voice of Ursula, protesting.

But how can they be trusted, the children's mother thought. Which of them can one believe? "Perhaps," she said to Colin, "one day, you can tell me more about Geneva?"

"Yes," he said perplexed.

But, really, she doubted it; nothing had come back from the trip but her own feelings of longing and envy, the longing and envy she felt at night, seeing, at a crossroad or over a bridge, the lighted windows of a train sweep by. Her children had nothing to tell her. Perhaps, as she had said, one day Colin would say something, produce the image of Geneva, tell her about the lake, the boats, the swans, and why her husband had left her. Perhaps he could tell her, but, really, she doubted it. And, already, so did he.

Señor Pinedo

Bᴇᴄᴀᴜsᴇ there was nothing to separate our rooms but the thinnest of plaster partitions, it sometimes seemed as if the Pinedos — Señor, Señora, and baby José María — and I were really living together. Every morning, we four were roused by the same alarm clock. At night, we all went to bed to the sound of Señora Pinedo's prayers. She prayed in a bored, sleepy voice, invoking a great many saints of the Spanish calendar, while her husband, a fussy Madrid civil servant, followed along with the responses.

"San Juan de la Cruz . . ." Señora Pinedo would say, between yawns. "San Agustín de Cantórbery . . . Santa Anatolia . . ."

"Pray for us!" her husband would command after every name.

After the prayers, I would hear them winding the clock and muffling door and window against harmful, wayward drafts of night air. Then, long after all the lights in the *pension* we lived in had been put out, and against a background of the restless, endless racket of the Madrid night, their voices would sound almost against my ear as they talked about money.

"I have only one dress for the summer, and it's too tight," the Señora would say, into the dark. "José María's doctor came right to the house today. I pretended I was out. 'I know she never goes out,' he said. By Monday, we have to pay the interest on the silver crucifix at the Monte de Piedad, or we lose it." The Monte de Piedad was the municipal pawnshop, a brisk, banklike place, into which occasionally vanished not only the crucifix but also José María's silver christening cup and Señora Pinedo's small radio.

"I know," Señor Pinedo would reply, with somewhat less authority than he used in his prayers. Or, "It can't be helped."

Sometimes the baby cried, interrupting the sad little catalogue of complaints. He would cry again in the morning, jolted by the alarm, and I would hear Señor Pinedo swearing to himself as he stumbled about the room getting dressed and preparing José María's early morning *biberón* of dark wheat flour and milk. Señora Pinedo never rose until much later; it was understood that, having given birth to José María a few months before, she had done nearly as much as could be expected of her. Hours after her husband had gone off to his Ministry desk and his filing trays, she would inch her way out of bed, groaning a little, and, after examining her face for signs of age (she was twenty-three), complete her toilette by drawing on a flowered cotton wrapper that at night hung on a gilded wall candle bracket, long fallen away from its original use.

"Is it a nice day?" she would call, knocking on the wall.

Our windows faced the same direction, but she liked to be reassured. "Shall I go out? What would you do in my place?" It took several minutes of talking back and forth before the problem could be settled. If the day seemed to lack promise, she turned on the radio and went back to bed. Otherwise, she dragged a chair out to the courtyard balcony that belonged to both our rooms and sat in the sun, plucking her eyebrows and screaming companionably at the neighbors. Since it was well known that crying developed the lungs, José María was usually left indoors, where he howled and whimpered in a crib trimmed with shabby ribbons. His cries, the sound of the radio, and Señor Pinedo's remarks all came through the wall as if it had been a sieve.

The Pinedos and I did, in a sense, share a room, for the partition divided what had once been the drawing room of a stately third-floor flat. The wall was designed with scrupulous fairness; I had more space and an extra window, while the Pinedos had the pink marble fireplace, the candle brackets, and some odd lengths of green velvet drapery gone limp with age. Each side had a door leading out to the balcony, and one semicircle of plaster roses on the ceiling, marking the place where a chandelier had hung.

Like many *pensions* in Madrid, the flat had once housed a rich middle-class family. The remnants of the family, Señorita Elvira Gómez and her brother, lived in two cramped rooms off the entrance hall. The rest of the house was stuffed with their possessions — cases of tropical birds, fat brocaded footstools, wardrobes with jutting, treacherous feet. Draperies and muslin blinds maintained the regulation *pension* twilight. In the Pinedos' room, the atmos-

phere was particularly dense, for to the mountain of fur-
nishings provided for their comfort they had added all
the odds and ends of a larger household. Chairs, tables,
and chimneypiece were piled with plates and glasses that
were never used, with trinkets and paperweights shaped
like charging bulls or Walt Disney gnomes. In one corner
stood a rusty camping stove, a relic of Señor Pinedo's
hearty, marching youth. The stove was now used for heat-
ing José María's bottles.

Added to this visual confusion was the noise. The baby
wept tirelessly, but most of the heavy sounds came from
the radio, which emitted an unbroken stream of jazz, flam-
enco, roaring *fútbol* games, the national anthem, Spanish
operetta with odd, muddled overtones of Viennese, and,
repeatedly, a singing commercial for headache tablets.
The commercial was a particular favorite with Señora Pinedo. *"Okal!"* she would sing whenever it came on the air.
"Okal! Okal es un producto superior!" There were three
verses and three choruses, and she sang them all the way
through. Sometimes it was too much for Señor Pinedo,
and I would hear him pitting his voice against the uproar
of his room in a despairing quaver of *"Silencio!"* He was
a thin, worried-looking man, who bore an almost comic re-
semblance to Salvador Dali. Nevertheless, he was a Spanish husband and father, and his word, by tradition, was law.
"Silencio!" he commanded.

"Viva a tableta Okal!" sang his wife.

I had arrived at the *pension* on a spring morning, for a
few weeks' stay. Señorita Elvira warned me about the noise
next door, without for a moment proposing that anything
might be done about it. Like so many of the people I was

to encounter in Madrid, she lived with, and cherished, a galaxy of problems that seemed to trail about her person. The Pinedo radio was one. Another stemmed from the fact that she didn't report her lodgers to the police and pay the tax required for running a *pension*. No government inspector ever visited the house, nor, I discovered from the porter downstairs, had anyone so much as asked why so many people came and went from our floor. Still Señorita Elvira lived in a frenzy of nervous apprehension, shared, out of sympathy, by her tenants.

On my first day, she ushered me in with a rapid succession of warnings, as dolorous and pessimistic as the little booklets of possible mishaps that accompany the sale of English cars. First, if a government inspector asked me questions, I was to say nothing, nothing at all. Then (frantically adjusting her helmet of tortoise-shell hairpins), I was not to use the electric fan in the room, because of the shaky nature of the fuses; I was to sign a little book whenever I made a telephone call; I was not to hang clothes on the balcony railing, because of some incoherent reason that had to do with the neighbors; and, finally, I was not to overtip the maid, who, although she earned the sturdy sum of two hundred pesetas — or five dollars — a month, became so giddy at the sight of money there was no keeping her in the kitchen. All her tenants were distinguished, Señorita Elvira said — *muy, muy* distinguished — and the most distinguished of all was my neighbor, Señor Pinedo. No matter how noisy I might find my accommodations, I was to remember how distinguished he was, and be consoled.

Later in the morning, I met my distinguished neighbor's

wife. She was sunning herself on the balcony in nightgown
and wrapper, her bare feet propped flat against the warm
railing. Her hair was tied back with a grubby ribbon, and
on the upper and lower lids of her eyes, which were lovely,
she had carefully applied make-up, in the Arab manner.

"I heard the old one," she said, evidently meaning Señorita Elvira. "Do you like music? Then you won't mind
the radio. Will you be here long? Did you bring many
bags? Do you like children? Do children where you come
from cry at night?"

"I don't think so," I said. "Not after a certain age." It
seemed to me a strange sort of introductory conversation.
The courtyard, formed by adjoining apartment blocks, was
so narrow that women on balconies across the way could
hear, and were listening with interest.

"Some babies are forced not to cry," said Señora Pinedo.
"Many are drugged, to make them sleep. *Qué horror!*"

An assenting murmur went around the court. Suddenly
maternal, Señora Pinedo went indoors and fetched José
María. For the next few minutes — until it bored her —
she entertained him by shaking a ring of bells in his face,
so that he shrieked with annoyance.

The courtyard, crisscrossed with lines of washing that
dripped onto the cobbles below, seemed to be where the
most active life of the apartment houses took place. Children played under the constant rain from the laundry,
and the balconies were crowded with women sewing, preparing vegetables, and even cooking on portable charcoal
stoves. The air was cloudy with frying olive oil. In spite of
the sun, everyone, and particularly the children, seemed to
me inordinately pale — perhaps because they had not yet

shaken off the effects of the tiring Castilian winter. Against a wall that made a right angle with ours hung a huge iron block attached to a cable. At irregular intervals it rose and descended, narrowly scraping between the balconies. I asked Señora Pinedo about it finally, and she explained that it was the weight that counterbalanced the elevator in the building around the corner. Sometimes the little boys playing in the courtyard would sit on the block, holding on to the cable from which it was suspended, and ride up as far as the second-floor balconies, where they would scramble off; frequently the elevator would stall before they had travelled any distance. From our third-floor balcony, the children below looked frail and small. I asked Señora Pinedo if the block wasn't dangerous.

"It is, without doubt," she said, but with a great dark-rimmed glance of astonishment; it was clear that this thought had never before entered her head. "But then," she added, as if primly repeating a lesson, "in Spain we do things our own way."

Only after meeting Señor Pinedo could I imagine where she had picked up this petulant and, in that context, meaningless phrase. He arrived at two o'clock for his long lunch-and-siesta break. Señora Pinedo and I were still on the balcony, and José Maria had, miraculously, fallen asleep on his mother's lap. Señor Pinedo carried out one of Señorita Elvira's billowing chairs and sat down, looking stiff and formal. He wore a sober, badly cut suit and a large, cheap signet ring, on which was emblazoned the crossed arrows of the Falange. He told me, as if it were important this be made very clear, that he and his wife were living in such crowded quarters only temporarily. They were used to much finer things. I had the impression that they were between apartments.

"Yes, we've been here four and a half years," said Señora Pinedo, cheerfully destroying the impression. "We were married and came right here. My trousseau linen is in a big box under the bed."

"But you are not to suppose from this that there is a housing problem in Spain," said Señor Pinedo. "On the contrary, our urban building program is one of the most advanced in Europe. We are ahead of England. We are ahead of France."

"Then why don't we have a nice little house?" his wife interrupted dreamily. "Or an apartment? I would like a salon, a dining room, three bedrooms, a balcony for flowers, and a terrace for the laundry. In my uncle's house, in San Sebastián, the maids have their own bathroom."

"If you are interested," said Señor Pinedo to me, "I could bring you some interesting figures from the Ministry of Housing."

"The maids have their own bathtub," said Señora Pinedo, bouncing José Mariá. "How many people in Madrid can say the same? Twice every month, they have their own hot water."

"I will bring you the housing figures this evening," Señor Pinedo promised. He rose, hurried his wife indoors before she could tell me anything more about the maids in San Sebastián, and bowed in the most ceremonious manner, as if we would not be meeting a few moments later in the dining room.

That evening, he did indeed bring home from his office a thick booklet that bore the imprint of the Ministry of Housing. It contained pictures of a workers' housing project in Seville, and showed smiling factory hands moving into their new quarters. The next day, there was something else — a chart illustrating the drop in infant mortality. And after that came a steady flow of pamphlets and graphs, covering milk production, the exporting of olive oil, the number of miles of railroad track constructed per year, the improved lot of agricultural workers. With a triumphant smile, as if to say, "Aha! *Here's* something you didn't know!" Señor Pinedo would present me with some new document, open it, and show me photographs of a soup kitchen for nursing mothers or of tubercular children at a summer camp.

The Pinedos and I were not, of course, the only tenants of Señorita Elvira's flat. Apart from the tourists, the honeymooning couples from the province, and the commercial travelers, there was a permanent core of lodgers, some of whom, although young, appeared to have lived there for years. These included a bank clerk, a student from Zaragoza, a civil engineer, a bullfighters' impresario, and a former university instructor of Spanish literature, who, having taken quite the wrong stand during the Civil War — he had been neutral — now dispensed hand lotion and aspirin in a drugstore on the Calle del Carmen. There was also the inevitable Englishwoman, one of the queer Mad Megs who seem to have been born and bred for *pension* life. This one, on hearing me speak English in the dining room, looked at me with undisguised loathing, picked up knife, fork, plate, and wineglass, and removed herself to the far corner of the room; the maid followed with the Englishwoman's own private assortment of mineral water, digestive pills, Keen's mustard, and English chop sauce.

All these people, with the exception of the Englishwoman, seemed to need as much instruction as I did in the good works performed by the state. Every new bulletin published by the Ministry of Propaganda was fetched home by Señor Pinedo and circulated through the dining room, passing from hand to hand. All conversation would stop, and Señor Pinedo wöuld eagerly search the readers' faces, waiting for someone to exclaim over, say, the splendid tidings that a new luxury train had been put into operation between Madrid and the south. Usually, however, the only remark would come from the impresario, a fat, noisy man who smoked cigars and wandered about the halls in his underwear. Sometimes he entertained one of his simple-minded clients in our dining room; on these occasions, Señorita Elvira, clinging gamely to her boast that everyone was *muy, muy* distinguished, kept the conversation at her table at a rattling pitch in order to drown out the noise matador and impresario managed to make with their food and wine.

"How much did this thing cost?" the impresario would ask rudely, holding Señor Pinedo's pamphlet at arm's length and squinting at it. "Who made the money on it? What's it good for?"

"Money?" Señor Pinedo would cry, seriously upset. "Good for?" Often, after such an exchange, he was unable to get on with his meal, and sat hurt and perplexed, staring at his plate in a rising clatter of dishes and talk.

Sometimes his arguments took on a curious note of pleading, as if he believed that these people, with their genteel pretensions, their gritty urban poverty that showed itself in their clothes, their bad-tasting cigarettes, their obvious avoidance of such luxuries as baths and haircuts, should understand him best. "Am I rich?" he would ask. "Did I make black-market money? Do I have a big house, or an American car? I don't love myself, I love Spain. I've sacrificed everything for Spain. I was wounded at seventeen. Seventeen! And I was a volunteer. No one recruited me."

Hearing this declaration for the twentieth time, the tenants in the dining hall would stare, polite. It was all undoubtedly interesting, their faces suggested; it was even important, perhaps, that Señor Pinedo, who had not made a dishonest céntimo, sat among them. In another year, at another period of life, they might have been willing to reply; however, at the moment, although their opinions were not dead, they had faded, like the sepia etching of the Chief of State that had hung in the entrance hall for more than thirteen years and now blended quietly with the wallpaper.

In Señor Pinedo's room, between the portraits of film stars tacked up by his wife, hung another likeness, this one of José Antonio Primo de Rivera, the founder of the Falange, who was shot by the Republicans during the Civil War.

"He was murdered," Señor Pinedo said to me one day when I was visiting the Pinedos in their room. "Murdered by the Reds." He looked at the dead leader's face, at the pose, with its defiant swagger, the arms folded over the famous blue shirt. "Was there ever a man like that in your country?" Under the picture, on a shelf, he kept an old, poorly printed edition of José Antonio's speeches and a framed copy of the Call to Arms, issued on the greatest day of Señor Pinedo's life. Both these precious things he gave me to read, handling the book with care and reverence. "Everything is here," he assured me. "When you have read these, you will understand the true meaning of the movement, not just foreign lies and propaganda."

Everything was there, and I read the brave phrases of revolution that had appealed to Señor Pinedo at seventeen. I read of a New Spain, mighty, Spartan, and feared abroad. I read of the need for austerity and sacrifice. I read the promise of land reform, the denunciation of capitalism, and, finally, the Call to Arms. It promised "one great nation for all, and not for a group of privileged."

I returnêd the book and the framed declaration to Señor Pinedo, who said mysteriously, "Now you know," as if we shared a great secret.

That spring, there was an unseasonable heat wave in Madrid; by the time Easter approached, it was as warm as a northern June. The week before Palm Sunday, the plane trees along the Calle de Alcalá were in delicate leaf, and on the watered lawns of the Ministry of War roses drooped on thin tall stalks, like the flowers in Persian art. Outside the Ministry gates, sentries paced and wheeled, sweating heroically in their winter greatcoats.

The table in the entrance hall of the *pension* was heaped with palms, some of them as tall as little trees. Señorita Elvira planned to have the entire lot blessed and then affixed to the balconies on both sides of the house; she believed them effective against a number of dangers, including lightning. The Chief of State, dusted and refreshed after a spring-cleaning, hung over the palms, gazing directly at a plaster Santa Rita, who was making a parochial visit. She stood in a small house that looked like a sentry box, to which was tacked a note explaining that her visit brought good fortune to all and that a minimum fee of two pesetas was required in exchange. It seemed little enough in return for good fortune, but Señor Pinedo, who sometimes affected a kind of petulant anticlericalism, would have no part of the pink-faced little doll, and said that he was not planning to go to church on Palm Sunday — an annoucement that appeared to shock no one at all.

On Saturday night, four of us accidentally came home at the same time and were let into the building and then into the pension by the night porter. Señor Pinedo had been to the cinema. The stills outside the theatre had promised a rich glimpse of American living, but in line with some imbecility of plot (the hero was unable to love a girl with money) all the characters had to pretend to be poor until the last reel. They wore shabby clothes, and walked instead of riding in cars. Describing the movie, Señor Pinedo sounded angry and depressed. He smelled faintly of the disinfectant with which Madrid cinemas are sprayed.

"If I belonged to the Office of Censorship," he said, "I would have had the film banned." Catching sight of Santa Rita, he added, "And no one can make me go to church."

Later, from my side of the partition, I heard him describing the film, scene by scene, to his wife, who said "*Sí, claro*" sleepily, but with interest, from time to time. Then they said their prayers. The last voice in the room that night came from the radio. "*Viva Franco!*" it said, signing off. "*Arriba España!*"

It seemed to me not long afterward that I heard the baby crying. It was an unusual cry — he sounded frightened — and, dragged abruptly awake, I sat up and saw that it was daylight. If it was José Maria, he was outside. That was where the cry had come from. Señor Pinedo was out of bed. I heard him mutter angrily as he scraped a chair aside and went out to the balcony. It wasn't the baby, after all, for Señora Pinedo was talking to him indoors, saying, "It's nothing, only noise." There was a rush of voices from the courtyard and, in our own flat, the sound of people running in the corridor and calling excitedly. I pulled on a dressing gown and went outside.

Señor Pinedo, wearing a raincoat, was leaning over the edge of the balcony. In the well of the court, a little boy lay on his back, surrounded by so many people that one could not see the cobblestones. The spectators seemed to have arrived, as they do at Madrid street accidents, from nowhere, panting from running, pale with the fear that something had been missed. On the wall at right angles to ours there was a mark that, for a moment, I thought was paint. Then I realized that it must be blood.

"It was the elevator," Señor Pinedo said to me, waving his hand toward the big iron block that now hung, motionless, just below the level of the second-floor balconies. "I knew someone would be hurt," he said with a kind of gloomy triumph. "The boys never left it alone."

The little boy, whose name was Jaime Gámez, and who lived in the apartment directly across from our windows, had been sitting astride the block, grasping the cable, and when the elevator moved, he had been caught between the block and the wall.

"One arm and one leg absolutely crushed," someone announced from the courtyard, calling the message around importantly. The boy's father arrived. He had to fight through the crowd in the court. Taking off his coat, he wrapped Jaime in it, lifted him up, and carried him away. Jaime's face looked white and frightened. Apparently he had not yet begun to experience the pain of his injuries, and was simply stunned and shocked.

By now, heads had appeared at the windows on all sides of the court, and the balconies were filled with people dressed for church or still in dressing gowns. The courtyard suddenly resembled the arena of a bull ring. There was the same harsh division of light and shadow, as if a line had been drawn, high on the opposite wall. The faces within the area of sun were white and expressionless, with that curious Oriental blankness that sometimes envelops the whole arena during moments of greatest emotion.

Some of the crowd of strangers down below sauntered away. The elevator began to function again, and the huge weight creaked slowly up the side of the house. Across the court, Jaime's family could be heard crying and calling inside their flat. After a few moments, the boy's mother, as if she were too distracted to stay indoors, or as if she had to divert her attention to inconsequential things, rushed out on her balcony and called to someone in the apartment above ours. On a chair in the sun was Jaime's white sailor suit, which he was to have worn to church. It had long trousers and a navy-blue collar. It had been washed and ironed, and left to dry out thoroughly in the sun. On a stool beside it was his hat, a round sailor hat with "España" in letters of gold on the blue band.

"Look at his suit, all ready!" cried Jaime's mother, as if one tragedy were not enough. "And his palms!" She disappeared into the dark apartment, and ran out again to the hard light of the morning carrying the palms Jaime was to have taken to church for the blessing. They were wonderfully twisted and braided into a rococo shape, and dangling and shining all over them were gilt and silver baubles that glinted in the sun.

"Terribly bad luck," said Señor Pinedo. I stared at him, surprised at this most Anglo-Saxon understatement. "If the palms had been blessed earlier," he went on, "this might not have happened, but, of course, they couldn't have known. Not that I have beliefs like an old woman." He gazed at the palms in an earnest way, looking like Salvador Dali. "Doña Elvira believes they keep off lightning. I wouldn't go so far. But I still think . . ." His voice dropped, as if he were not certain, or not deeply interested in, what he did think.

Someone called the mother. She went inside, crying, carrying the palms and the sailor suit. A few of the people around the courtyard had drifted indoors, but most of them seemed reluctant to leave the arena, where — one never knew — something else of interest might take place. They looked down through the tangle of clotheslines to the damp stones of the court, talking in loud, matter-of-fact voices about the accident. They spoke of hospitalization, of amputation — for the rumor that Jaime's hand was to be amputated had started even before I came out — and of limping and crutches and pain and expense.

"The poor parents," someone said. A one-armed child would be a terrible burden, and useless. Everyone agreed, just as, on my first day, they had all agreed with Señora Pinedo that it was bad to drug one's children.

Señor Pinedo, beside me, drew in his breath. "Useless?" he said loudly. "A useless child? Why, the father can claim compensation for him — a lifetime pension."

"From the angels?" someone shouted up.

"From the building owners, first," Señor Pinedo said, trying to see who had spoken. "But also from our government. Haven't any of you thought of that?"

"No," said several voices together, and everyone laughed.

"Of couse he'll have a pension!" Señor Pinedo shouted. He looked around at them all and said, "Wasn't it promised? Weren't such things promised?" People hung out of windows on the upper floors, trying to see him under the overhang of the balcony. "I guarantee it!" Señor Pinedo said. He leaned over the railing and closed his fist like an orator, a leader. The railing shook.

"Be careful," I said, unheard.

He brought his fist down on the railing, which must have hurt. "I guarantee it," he said. "I work in the office of pensions."

"Ah!" That made sense. Influence was something they all understood. "He must be related to little Jaime," I heard someone say, sounding disappointed. "Still, that's not a bad thing, a pension for life." They discussed it energetically, citing cases of deserving victims who had never received a single céntimo. Señor Pinedo looked around at them all. For the first time since I had known him, he was smiling happily. Finally, when it seemed quite clear that nothing more was to happen, the chatter died down, and even the most persistent observers, with a last look at the blood, the cobbles, and the shuttered windows of Jaime's flat, went indoors.

Señor Pinedo and I were the last to leave the court. We parted, and through the partition I heard him telling his wife that he had much to do that week, a social project connected with the hurt child. In his happiness, he sounded almost childlike himself, convinced, as he must convince others, of the truth and good faith of the movement to which he had devoted his life and in which he must continue to believe.

Later, I heard him repeating the same thing to the *pension* tenants as they passed his door on the way to church. There was no reply. It was the silence of the dining room when the bulletins were being read, and as I could not see his listeners' faces, I could not have said whether the silence was owing to respect, delight, apathy, or a sudden fury of some other emotion so great that only silence could contain it.

A Day Like
Any Other

JANE AND ERNESTINE were at breakfast in the hotel dining room when the fog finally lifted. It had clung to the windows for weeks, ever since the start of the autumn rains, reducing a promised view of mountains to a watery blur. Now, unexpectedly, the fog rose; it went up all in one piece, like a curtain, and when it had cleared away, the children saw that the mountains outside were covered with snow. Because of their father's health, they had always, until this year, wintered in warm climates. They abandoned their slopped glasses of milk and stared at slopes that were rough with trees, black and white like the glossy postcards their mother bought to send to aunts in America. Down below, on a flat green plain, were villages no bigger than the children's cereal plates. Some of the villages were in Germany and some were over in France — their governess, Frau Stengel, had explained about the frontier, with many a glum allusion — but from here the toy houses and steeples looked all alike; there was no hedge, no fence, no mysterious cleft in the earth to set them apart, although, staring hard, one *could* see something, a winding line, as thin as a hair. That was the Rhine.

"Look," said Jane, to the back of her mother's newspaper. She said it encouragingly, preparing Mrs. Kennedy for shock. It did not enter her head that her mother knew what snow was like. To the two little girls winter meant walks in parks where every pebble had a correct place underfoot and geraniums grew in rows, like soldiers marching. The sea was always there, but too cold to bathe in. Overhead, and outside their window at night, palms rustled bleakly, like unswept leaves.

"Look," Jane repeated, but Mrs. Kennedy, who read the local paper every day in order to improve her German, didn't hear. "You can see everything," said Jane, giving her mother up. "Mountains."

"Hitler's mountains," said Ernestine, repeating a phrase that Frau Stengel had used. The girls had no idea who Hitler was, but they had seen his photograph — Frau Stengel kept it pressed between two film magazines on her bookshelf — and she frequently spoke of his death, which she appeared to have felt keenly. The children, because of this, assumed that Hitler and Frau Stengel must have been related. "Poor Hitler, Frau Stengel's dead cousin," Ernestine sang, inventing a tune, making whirlpools in her porridge with a spoon. Some of the people at nearby tables in the dining room turned to smile mistily at the children. What angels the Kennedy girls were, the hotel guests often remarked — so pretty and polite, and always saying the most intelligent things! "Frau Stengel says there wouldn't have been a war that time, only all these other people were so greedy," and "Only one little, little piece of Africa, Frau Stengel says. Frau Stengel says . . ." Someone had started the rumor that Jane and Ernestine were not Mrs. Kennedy's daughters at all but had been adopted here in Germany. How else was one to account for their blond hair? Mrs. Kennedy was quite dark, and old enough to be, if not their grandmother (although some of the women in the hotel were willing to push it that far), at least a sort of elderly adoptive aunt. Mrs. Kennedy, looking up in time to catch the looks of tender good will beamed toward her daughters, would think, How fond they are of children! But then Jane and Ernestine are particularly attractive. She had no notion of the hotel gossip concerning their origins and would have been deeply offended if she had been told about it, for Jane and Ernestine were not German and not adopted. They had come along quite naturally, if disconcertingly, less than a year apart, just at a time when Mrs. Kennedy had begun to regard all children as a remote, alarming race. The second surprise had come when they had turned out to be more than commonly pretty. "Like little dolls," Frau Stengel had said on first seeing them. "Just like dolls."

"I have been told that they resemble little Renoirs," Mrs. Kennedy had replied, with just a trace of correction.

Their charm, after all, was not entirely the work of nature; one's character was just as important as one's face, and the girls, thanks to their mother's vigilance on their behalf, were as unblemished, as removed from the world and its coarsening effects, as their guileless faces suggested. Unlike their little compatriots, whom they sometimes met on their travels, and from whom they were quickly led away, they had never, Mrs. Kennedy was able to assure herself, heard a thought expressed that was cheapening or less than kind. They wore, in all seasons, clothing that matched the atmosphere created for their own special world — ribboned straw hats, fluffy little sweaters, starched frocks trimmed with rows and rows of *broderie anglaise*, made to order wherever a favorable exchange prevailed — and the result was that, with their long, brushed tresses, they did indeed resemble dolls, or even, in a rosy light, little Renoirs.

What marriages they would make! Mrs. Kennedy, without complaining of her own, nevertheless hoped her girls would accomplish something with just a little more glitter — a double wedding in a cathedral, for instance. Chartres would be nice, though damp. Observing the children now, over the breakfast table, she saw the picture again — perfumed, cloudy, with a pair of faceless but utterly suitable bridegrooms hovering in the background. Mr. Kennedy, who did not believe in churches and thought they should all be turned into lending libraries, would simply have to put aside his scruples for the occasion. Mrs. Kennedy, mentally, had it out with him. "Very well," he replied, vanquished. "I certainly owe you this much consideration after the splendid way you've brought them up." He led them into the cathedral, one on each arm. After a tuneful but, to spare Mr. Kennedy, nondenominational ceremony, the two couples emerged under the crossed swords of a guard of honor. "The girls are charming, and they owe it all to their mother," someone was heard to remark in the crowd. Returning to the breakfast table, Mrs. Kennedy heard Jane saying, "Just this one movie, and I'll never ask again."

"One *what!*"

"This movie," said Jane. "The one I was just telling about, *Das Herz Einer Mutti*. Frau Stengel could take us this afternoon, she says. She already went twice. She cried like anything."

"Frau Stengel should know better than to suggest such a thing," said Mrs. Kennedy, looking crossly at her brides. "There's milk all over your mouth, and Ernestine's hands are filthy. Do you want to make my life a trial?"

"No," said Jane. She opened a picture book she had brought to the table and began to read aloud in German, in a high, stumbling recitative. One silky tress of hair lay on the buttered side of a piece of bread. She wiped her mouth on the fluffy sleeve of her pale blue sweater.

"Well, really, sometimes I just — " Mrs. Kennedy began, but Jane was reading, and Ernestine singing, and she said, annoyed, "What is that book, if you please?"

"Nothing," said Jane. It was a book Frau Stengel had given them, the comic adventures of Hansi, a baboon. Hansi was always in mischief, bursting in where grown-up people were taking baths, and that kind of thing, but the most enchanting thing about him, from the children's point of view, was his heart-shaped scarlet behind, on which the artist had dwelt with loving exactitude.

Mrs. Kennedy drew the book toward her. She glanced quickly through the pages, then put it down by her coffee cup. She said nothing.

"Is it cruel?" said Jane nervously. She tried again: "Is it too cruel, or something?"

"It is worse than cruel," said Mrs. Kennedy, when at last she could speak. "It is vulgar. I forbid you to read it."

"We already have."

"Then don't read it again. If Frau Stengel gave it to you, give it back this morning."

"It has our names written in it," said Jane.

Momentarily halted, Mrs. Kennedy looked out at the view. Absorbed with her own problem — the children, the book, whether or not she had handled it well — she failed to notice that the fog had lifted, and felt just as hemmed in and baffled as usual. If only one could consult one's husband, she thought. But Mr. Kennedy, who lay at this very moment in a nursing home half a mile distant, waiting for his wife to come and read to him, could not be counted on for advice. He cherished an obscure stomach complaint and a touchy liver that had withstood, triumphantly, the best attention of twenty doctors. It was because of Mr. Kennedy's stomach that the family moved about so much, guided by a new treatment in London, an excellent liver man on the Riviera, or the bracing climate of the Italian lakes. A weaker man, Mrs. Kennedy sometimes thought, might have given up and pretended he was better, but her husband, besides having an uncommon lot of patience, had been ailing just long enough to be faddish; this year it was a nursing home on the rim of the Black Forest that had taken his fancy, and here they all were, shivering in the unaccustomed damp, dosed with a bracing vitamin tonic sent over from America and guaranteed to replace the southern sun.

Mr. Kennedy seldom saw his daughters. The rules of the private clinics he frequented were all in his favor. In any case, he seldom asked to see the girls, for he felt that they were not at an interesting age. Wistfully, his wife sometimes wondered when their interesting age would begin — when they were old enough to be sent away to school, perhaps, or, better still, safely disposed of in the handsome marriages that gave her so much concern.

Reminded now of Mr. Kennedy and the day ahead, she looked around the dining room, wondering if anyone would like to come along to the nursing home for a little visit. She stared coldly past the young American couple who sat before the next window; they were the only other foreigners in the hotel, and Mrs. Kennedy had swept them off to the hospital one morning before they knew what was happening. The visit had not been a success. Cheered by a new audience, Mr. Kennedy had talked about his views — views so bold that they still left his wife quite breathless after fourteen years of marriage. Were people fit to govern themselves, for instance? Mr. Kennedy could not be sure. Look at France. And what of the ants? Was not their civilization, with its emphasis on industry and thrift, superior to ours? Mr. Kennedy thought that it was. And then there was God — or was there? Mr. Kennedy had talked about God at some length that morning, and the young couple had listened, looking puzzled, until, at last, the young woman said, "Yes, well, I see. Agnostic. How sweet."

"Sweet!" said Mr. Kennedy, outraged.

Sweet? thought his wife. Why, they were treating Mr. Kennedy as if he were funny and old-fashioned, somebody to be humored. If they could have heard some of the things he had said to the bishop that time, they might have more respect! She had given the young man a terrible look, and he had begun to speak valiantly of books, but it was too late. Mr. Kennedy was offended, and he interrupted sulkily to snap, "Well, no one had to revive Kipling for *me*," and the visit broke up right after that.

Really, no one would do for Mr. Kennedy, thought his

wife — but she thought it without a jot of censure, for she greatly admired her husband and was ready to show it in a number of practical ways; not only did she ungrudgingly provide the income that permitted his medical excursions but she sat by his bedside nearly every day of the year discussing his digestion and reading aloud the novels of Upton Sinclair, of which he was exceedingly fond.

Sighing, now, she brought her gaze back from the window and the unsuitable hotel guests. "You might as well go to lessons," she said to the girls. "But remember, no movies."

They got down from their chairs. Each of them implanted on Mrs. Kennedy's cheek a kiss that smelled damply of milk. How grubby they looked, their mother thought, even though the day had scarcely begun. Who would believe, seeing them now, that they had been dressed not an hour before in frocks still warm from the iron? Ernestine had caught her dress on something, so that the hem drooped to one side. Their hair . . . But Mrs. Kennedy, exhausted, decided not to think about their hair.

"You look so odd sometimes," she said. "You look all untidy and forlorn, like children without mothers to care for them, like little refugees. Although," she added, conscientious, "there is nothing the matter with being a refugee."

"Like Frau Stengel," said Jane, straining to be away.

"Frau Stengel? What on earth has she been telling you about refugees?"

"That you should never trust a Czech," said Jane.

Mrs. Kennedy could not follow this and did not try. "Haven't you a message for your father?" she said, holding

Jane by the wrist. "It would be nice if you showed just a little concern." They stood, fidgeting. "Shall I tell him you hope he feels much better?"

"Yes."

"And that you hope to see him soon?"

"Yes. Yes."

"He will be pleased," their mother said, but, released, they were already across the room.

Frau Stengel was, on the whole, an unsatisfactory substitute for a mother's watchful care, and it was only because Mrs. Kennedy had been unable to make a better arrangement that Frau Stengel had become the governess of Jane and Ernestine. A mournful *Volksdeutsch* refugee from Prague, she looked well over her age, which was thirty-nine. She lived — with her husband — in the same hotel as the Kennedy family, and she had once been a schoolteacher, both distinct advantages. The girls were too young for boarding school, and the German day school nearby, while picturesque, had a crucifix over the door, which meant, Mrs. Kennedy was certain, that someone would try to convert her daughters. Of course, a good firm note to the principal might help: "The children's father would be most distressed . . ." But no, the risk was too great, and in any case it had been agreed that the children's religious instruction would be put off until Mr. Kennedy had made up his mind about God. Frau Stengel, if fat, and rather commonplace, and given to tearful lapses that showed a want of inner discipline, was not likely to interfere with Mr. Kennedy's convictions. She admired the children just as they were, applauding with each murmur of praise their mother's painstaking efforts to see that they kept their bloom. "So sweet," she would say. "So *herzig*, the little sweaters."

The children were much too pretty to be taxed with lessons; Frau Stengel gave them film magazines to look at and supervised them contentedly, rocking and filing her nails. She lived a cozy, molelike existence in her room on the attic floor of the hotel, surrounded by crocheted mats, stony satin cushions, and pictures of kittens cut from magazines. Her radio, which was never still, filled the room with soupy operetta melodies, many of which reminded Frau Stengel of happier days and made her cry.

Everyone had been so cruel, so unkind, she would tell the children, drying her eyes. Frau Stengel and her husband had lived in Prague, where Herr Stengel, who now worked at some inferior job in a nearby town, had been splendidly situated until the end of the war, and then the Czechs sent them packing. They had left everything behind — all the tablecloths, the little coffee spoons!

Although the children were bored by the rain and not being allowed to go out, they enjoyed their days with Frau Stengel. Every day was just like the one before, which was a comfort; the mist and the rain hung on the windows, Frau Stengel's favorite music curled around the room like a warm bit of the fog itself, they ate chocolate biscuits purchased from the glass case in the dining room, and Frau Stengel, always good-tempered, always the same, told them stories. She told about Hitler, and the war, and about little children she knew who had been killed in bombardments or separated forever from their parents. The two little girls would listen, stolidly going on with their coloring or cutting out. They liked her stories, mostly because, like the room and the atmosphere, the stories never varied; they could have repeated many of them by heart, and they knew exactly at what point in each Frau Stengel would begin to cry. The girls had never seen anyone weep so much and so often.

"We like you, Frau Stengel," Jane had said once, meaning that they would rather be shut up here in Frau Stengel's pleasantly overheated room than be downstairs alone in their bedroom or in the bleak, empty dining room. Frau Stengel had looked at them and after a warm, delicious moment had wiped her eyes. After that, Jane had tried it again, and with the same incredulity with which she and Ernestine had learned that if you pushed the button the elevator would arrive, every time, they had discovered that either one of them could bring on the great, sad tears that were, almost, the most entertaining part of their lessons. "We like you," and off Frau Stengel would go while the two children watched, enchanted. Later, they learned that any mention of their father had nearly the same effect. They had no clear idea of the nature of their father's illness, or why it was sad; once they had been told that, because of his liver, he sometimes turned yellow, but this interesting evolution they had never witnessed.

"He's yellow today," Jane would sometimes venture.

"Ah, so!" Frau Stengel would reply, her eyes getting bigger and bigger. Sometimes, after thinking it over, she wept, but not always.

For the past few days, however, Frau Stengel had been less diverting; she had melted less easily. Also, she had spoken of the joyous future when she and Herr Stengel would emigrate to Australia and open a little shop.

"To sell what?" said Ernestine, threatened with change.

"Tea and coffee," said their governess dreamily.

In Australia, Frau Stengel had been told, half the people were black and savage, but one was far from trouble. She could not see the vision of the shop clearly, and spoke of coffee jars painted with hearts, a tufted chair where tired clients could rest. It was important, these days, that she fix her mind on rosy vistas, for her doctor had declared, and her horoscope had confirmed, that she was pregnant; she hinted of something to the Kennedy children, some revolution in her life, some reason their mother would have to find another governess before spring. But winter, the children knew, went on forever.

This morning, when Jane and Ernestine knocked on her door, Frau Stengel was sitting by her window in a glow of sunshine reflected from the snow on the mountains. "Come in," she said, and smiled at them. What pathetic little orphans they were, so sad, and so fond of her. If it had not been for their affection for her, frequently and flatteringly expressed, Frau Stengel would have given them up days ago; they reminded her, vaguely, of unhappy things. She had told them so many stories about the past that just looking at the two little girls made her think of it all over again — dolorous thoughts, certain to affect the character and appearance of the unborn.

"Mother doesn't want us to go to the movies with you," began Jane. She looked, expectant, but Frau Stengel said placidly, "Well, never do anything your mother wouldn't like." This was to be another of her new cheerful days; disappointed, the children settled down to lessons. Ernestine colored the pictures in a movie magazine with crayons, and Jane made a bracelet of some coral rosebuds from an old necklace her mother had given her.

"It's nice here today," said Jane. "We like it here."

"The sun is shining. You should go out," said Frau Stengel, yawning, quite as if she had not heard. "Don't forget the little rubbers."

"Will you come?"

"Oh, no," Frau Stengel said in a tantalizing, mysterious way. "It is important for me to rest."

"For us, too," said Ernestine jealously. "We have to rest. Everybody rests. Our father rests all the time. He has to, too."

"Because he's so sick," said Jane.

"He's dead," said Ernestine. She gave Gregory Peck round blue eyes.

Frau Stengel looked up sharply. "Who is dead?" she said. "You must not use such a word in here, now."

The children stared, surprised. Death had been spoken of so frequently in this room, on the same level as chocolate biscuits and coral rosebud bracelets.

"*He's* dead," said Ernestine. "He died this morning."

Frau Stengel stopped rocking. "Your father is *dead?*"

"Yes, he is," said Ernestine. "He died, and we're supposed to stay here with you, and that's all."

Their governess looked, bewildered, from one to the other; they sat, the image of innocence, side by side at her table, their hair caught up with blue ribbons.

"Why don't we go out now?" said Jane. The room was warm. She put her head down on the table and chewed the ends of her hair. "Come on," she said, bored, and gave Ernestine a prod with her foot.

"In a minute," her sister said indistinctly. She bent over the portrait she was coloring, pressing on the end of the crayon until it was flat. Waxy colored streaks were glued to the palm of her hand. She wiped her hand on the skirt of her starched blue frock. "All right, now," she said, and got down from her chair.

"Where are you going, please?" said Frau Stengel, breathing at them through tense, widened nostrils. "Didn't your mother send a message for me? When did it happen?"

"What?" said Jane. "Can't we go out? You said we could, before."

"It isn't true, about your father," said Frau Stengel. "You made it up. Your father is not dead."

"Oh, no," said Jane, anxious to make the morning ordinary again. "She only said it, like, for a joke."

"A joke? You come here and frighten me in my condition for a *joke*?" Frau Stengel could not deliver sitting down the rest of the terrible things she had to say. She pulled herself out of the rocking chair and looked down at the perplexed little girls. She seemed to them enormously fat and tall, like the statues in Italian parks. Fascinated, they stared back. "What you have done is very wicked," said Frau Stengel. "Very wicked. I won't tell your mother, but I shall never forget it. In any case, God heard you, and God will punish you. If your father should die now, it would certainly be your fault."

This was not the first time the children had heard of God. Mrs. Kennedy might plan to defer her explanations to a later date, in line with Mr. Kennedy's eventual decision, but the simple women she employed to keep an eye on Jane and Ernestine (Frau Stengel was the sixth to be

elevated to the title of governess) had no such moral ob-
stacles. For them, God was the catch-all answer to most
of life's perplexities. "Who makes this rain?" Jane had
once asked Frau Stengel.

"God," she had replied cozily.

"So that we can't play outside?"

"He makes the sun," Frau Stengel said, anxious to give
credit.

"Well, then — " Jane began, but Frau Stengel, sensing
a paradox, went on to something else.

Until now, however, God had not been suggested as a
threat. The children stayed where they were, at the table,
and looked wide-eyed at their governess.

Frau Stengel began to feel foolish; it is one thing to
begin a scene, she was discovering, and another to sustain
it. "Go to your room downstairs," she said. "You had
better stay there, and not come out. I can't teach girls who
tell lies."

This, clearly, was a dismissal, not only from her room
but from her company, possibly forever. Never before
had they been abandoned in the middle of the day. Was
this the end of winter?

"Is he dead?" cried Ernestine, in terror at what had become of the day.

"Goodbye, Frau Stengel," said Jane, with a ritual curtsy;
this was how she had been trained to take her leave, and
although she often forgot it, the formula now returned to
sustain her. She gathered up the coral beads — after all,
they belonged to her — but Ernestine rushed out, pushing
in her hurry to be away. "Busy little feet," said an old
gentleman a moment later, laboriously pulling himself up

with the aid of the banisters, as first Ernestine and then Jane clattered by.

They burst into their room, and Jane closed the door. "Anyway, it was you that said it," she said at once.

Ernestine did not reply. She climbed up on her high bed and sat with her fat legs dangling over the edge. She stared at the opposite wall, her mouth slightly open. She could think of no way to avert the punishment about to descend on their heads, nor could she grasp the idea of a punishment more serious than being deprived of dessert.

"It was you, anyway," Jane repeated. "If anything happens, I'll tell. I think I could tell anyway."

"I'll tell, too," said Ernestine.

"You haven't anything to tell."

"I'll tell everything," said Ernestine in a sudden fury. "I'll tell you chewed gum. I'll tell you wet the bed and we had to put the sheets out the window. I'll tell everything."

The room was silent. Jane leaned over to the window between their beds, where the unaccustomed sun had roused a fat, slumbering fly. It shook its wings and buzzed loudly. Jane put her finger on its back; it vibrated and felt funny. "Look, Ern," she said.

Ernestine squirmed over on the bed; their heads touched, their breath misted the window. The fly moved and left staggering tracks.

"We could go out," said Jane. "Frau Stengel even said it." They went, forgetting their rubbers.

Mrs. Kennedy came home at half past six, no less and no more exhausted than usual. It had not been a lively day or a memorably pleasant one but a day like any other, in the pattern she was now accustomed to and might even have missed. She had read aloud until lunch, which the clinic kitchen sent up on a tray — veal, potatoes, shredded lettuce, and sago pudding with jelly — and she had noted with dismay that Mr. Kennedy's meal included a bottle of hock, fetched in under the apron of a guilty-looking nurse. How silly to tempt him in this way when he wanted so much to get well, she thought. After lunch, the reading went on, Mrs. Kennedy stopping now and then to sustain her voice with a sip of vichy water. They were rereading an old Lanny Budd novel, but Mrs. Kennedy could not have said what it was about. She had acquired the knack of thinking of other things while she read aloud. She read in a high, uninflected voice, planning the debut of Jane and Ernestine with a famous ballet company. Mr. Kennedy listened, contentedly polishing off his bottle of wine. Sometimes he interrupted. "Juan-les-Pins," he remarked as the name came up in the text.

"We were there." This was the chief charm of the novels, that they kept mentioning places Mr. Kennedy had visited. "Aix-les-Bains," he remarked a little later. Possibly he was not paying close attention, for Lanny Budd was now having it out with Göring in Berlin. Mr. Kennedy's tone of voice suggested that something quite singular had taken place in Aix-les-Bains, when as a matter of fact Mrs. Kennedy had spent a quiet summer with the two little girls in a second-class pension while Mr. Kennedy took the mud-bath cure.

Mr. Kennedy rang for his nurse and, when she came, told her to send in the doctor. The reading continued; Jane and Ernestine found ballet careers too strenuous, and in any case the publicity was cheapening. For the fortieth time, they married. Jane married a very dashing young officer, and Ernestine the president of a university. A few minutes later, the doctor came in; another new doctor, Mrs. Kennedy noted. But it was only by constantly changing his doctor and reviewing his entire medical history from the beginning that Mr. Kennedy obtained the attention his condition required. This doctor was cheerful and brisk. "We'll have him out of here in no time," he assured Mrs. Kennedy, smiling.

"Oh, *grand*," she said faintly.

"Are you sure?" her husband asked the doctor. "There are two or three things that haven't been checked and attended to."

"Oh?" said the doctor. At that moment, he saw the empty wine bottle and picked it up. Mrs. Kennedy, who dreaded scenes, closed her eyes. "You waste my time," she heard the doctor say. The door closed behind him. She opened her eyes. These awful rows, she thought. They were all alike — all the nurses, all the clinics, all the doctors. Mr. Kennedy, fortunately, did not seem unduly disturbed.

"You might see if you can order me one of those books of crossword puzzles," he remarked as his wife gathered up her things to leave.

"Shall I give your love to Jane and Ernestine?" she said. But Mr. Kennedy, worn out with his day, seemed to be falling asleep.

Back at the hotel, Jane and Ernestine were waiting in the upper hall. They clung to Mrs. Kennedy, as if her presence had reminded them of something. Touched, Mrs.

Kennedy said nothing about the mud on their shoes but instead praised their rosy faces. They hung about, close to her, while she rested on the chaise longue in her room before dinner. "How I should love to trade my days for yours," she said suddenly, thinking not only of their magic future but of these days that were, for them, a joyous and repeated holiday.

"Didn't you have fun today?" said Jane, leaning on her mother's feet.

"Fun! Well, not what you chicks would call fun."

They descended to dinner together; the children held on to her hands, one on each side. They showed, for once, a nice sensibility, she thought. Perhaps they were arriving at that special age a mother dreams of, the age of gratitude and awareness. In the dining room, propped against the mustard jar, was an envelope with scrolls and curlicues under the name "Kennedy." Inside was a note from Frau Stengel explaining that, because she was expecting a child and needed all her strength for the occasion, she could no longer give Jane and Ernestine their lessons. So delicately and circuitously did she explain her situation that Mrs. Kennedy was left with the impression that Frau Stengel was expecting the visit of a former pupil. She thought it a strange way of letting her know. I wonder what she means by "harmony of spirit," she thought. The child must be a terror. She was not at all anxious to persuade Frau Stengel to change her mind; the incident of the book at breakfast, the mention of movies, the mud on the children's shoes all suggested it was time for someone new.

"Is it bad news?" said Jane.

Mrs. Kennedy was touched. "You mustn't feel things

so," she said kindly. "No, it is only that Frau Stengel won't be your governess any more. She is expecting" — she glanced at the letter again and, suddenly getting the drift of it, folded it quickly and went on — "a little boy or girl for a visit."

"Our age?"

"I don't know," said Mrs. Kennedy vaguely. Would this be a good occasion, she wondered, to begin telling them about . . . about . . . But no, not in a hotel dining room, not over a plate of alphabet soup. "I suppose I could stay home for a few days, until we find someone, and we could do lessons together. Would you like that?" They looked at her without replying. "We could do educational things, like nature walks," she said. "Why, what ever is the matter? Are you so unhappy about Frau Stengel?"

"Is he dead?" said Jane.

"Who?"

"Our father," said Jane in a quavering voice that carried to every table and on to the kitchen.

"Good heavens!" Mrs. Kennedy glanced quickly around the dining room; everyone had heard. Damp clouds of sympathy were forming around the table. "As a matter of fact, he is much better," she said loudly and briskly. "Perhaps, to be reassured, you ought to see him. Would you like that?"

"Oh, yes."

She was perplexed but gratified. "Father didn't want you to see him when he was so ill," she explained. "He wanted you to remember him as he was."

"In case he died?"

"I think we'll go upstairs," said Mrs. Kennedy, pushing

back her chair. They followed her across the room and up the staircase without protest. She had never seen them looking so odd. "You seem all pinched," she said, examining them by the light between their beds. "And a few minutes ago you seemed so rosy! Where are my little Renoir faces? I'm getting you liver tablets tomorrow. You'd better go to bed."

It was early, but they made no objection. "Are you really going to be home tomorrow?" said Jane.

"Well, yes. I can't think of anything else to do, for the moment."

"He's dead," said Jane positively.

"Really," said their mother, exasperated. "If you don't stop this at once, I don't know what I'll do. It's morbid."

"Will you read to us?" said Ernestine, shoeless and in her petticoat.

"Read?" Mrs. Kennedy said. "No, I couldn't." With quick, tugging motions, she began to braid their hair for the night. "I don't even want to speak. I want to rest my voice."

"Then could you just sit here?" said Jane. "Could we have the light?"

"Why?" said Mrs. Kennedy, snapping elastic on the end of a braid. "Have you been having bad dreams?"

"I don't know," said Jane, standing uncertainly by her bed.

"Healthy children don't dream," her mother said, confident that this was so. "You have no reason whatever to dream." She rose and put the hairbrush away. "Into bed, now, both of you."

They crept wretchedly into their separate beds. Mrs.

Kennedy kissed each of them and opened the window. She was at the door, her hand on the light switch, when Jane said, "Can God punish you for something?"

Mrs. Kennedy dropped her hand. She had been, she found with annoyance, about to say vaguely, "Well, that all depends." She said instead, "I don't know."

It was worse than anything the children had bargained for. "If *she* doesn't know — " said Ernestine. It was not clear whom she was addressing. " — then who does?"

"Nobody, really," said Mrs. Kennedy. They had certainly chosen a singular approach to the subject, and an odd time to speak of it, she thought, but curiosity of this sort should always be dealt with as it came up. "Many people think they know, one way or the other, but it is impossible for a thinking person — Father will tell you about it," she finished. "We'll arrange a visit very soon."

"If you don't *know,*" said Jane from her pillow, "then we don't know what can happen." She lay back and pulled the bedsheet up to her eyes. Mrs. Kennedy put out the light, promising again an interesting talk with their father, who would explain all over again how he didn't know, either, and why.

Just before going to bed, shortly after ten o'clock, Mrs. Kennedy softly re-entered the children's room. She carried a large dish of applesauce, two spoons, and two buttered rolls for the girls to discover in the morning. The room was totally dark, and stuffy; someone — one of the children — had closed the window and drawn the heavy double curtains straight across. Groping in the dark to their bedside table, she put down her burden of food, and then, as quietly as she could, pulled the draperies to one side. Moonlight filled the squares of the window. The breeze that came in when she unlatched the window smelled of snow. In the bright, cold, clear night, the lights from the villages down below blinked and wavered like stars. It was not often that Mrs. Kennedy had time to enjoy or contemplate something not directly dependent on herself or fated by one of her or her husband's decisions. For nearly a full minute, she stood perfectly still and admired the night. Then she remembered one of the reasons she had come into the room, and bent over to draw the covers up over her daughters.

Ernestine had got into bed with Jane, which was odd; they lay facing the same direction, like two question marks. With one hand Ernestine limply clutched at her sister's braids. Both children had wormed down into the middle of the bed, well below the pillow, under a tent of blankets; it was a wonder they hadn't smothered.

Mrs. Kennedy drew back the blankets and gently pulled Ernestine away. Without waking, but muttering something, Ernestine got up and walked to her own bed. The hair at her temples was wet, and she generated the nearly feverish warmth of sleeping children. Sleeping, she put her thumb in her mouth. Mrs. Kennedy turned to Jane and pulled her carefully up to the pillow. "I left my book outside," said Jane urgently and distinctly. Straightening up, Mrs. Kennedy gave the covers a final pat. She looked down at her little girls, frowning; they seemed at this moment not like little Renoirs, not like little dolls, but like rather ordinary children who for some reason of their own had shut and muffled the window and then crept into one bed, the better to hide. She was tempted to wake Jane, or

Ernestine, and ask what it was all about, this solicitude for Mr. Kennedy, this irrelevant talk of God. Perhaps Frau Stengel, in some blundering way, had mentioned her pregnancy. Despairing, Mrs. Kennedy wished she could gather her children up, one under each arm, and carry them off to a higher mountain, an emptier hotel, where nothing and no one could interfere, or fill their minds with the kind of thought she feared and detested. Their *minds*. Was she really, all alone, without Mr. Kennedy to help her, expected to cope with their minds as well as everything else?

But I am exaggerating, she thought, looking out at the peaceful night. They haven't so much as begun to think, about anything. Without innocence, after all, there was no beauty, and no one could deny the beauty of Jane and Ernestine. She did not look at them again as they lay, damp and vulnerable, in their beds, but, instantly solaced with the future and what it contained for them, she saw them once again drifting away on a sea of admiration, the surface unmarred, the interior uncorrupted by thought or any one of the hundred indecisions that were the lot of less favored human beings. Meanwhile, of course, they had still to grow up — but after all what was there between this night and the magic time to come but a link of days, the limpid days of children? For, she thought, smiling in the dark, pleased at the image, were not their days like the lights one saw in the valley at night, starry, indistinguishable one from the other? She must tell that to Mr. Kennedy, she thought, drawing away from the window. He would be sure to agree.